INDECENT PURSUIT

Sheena sipped her beer and thought about Rod's father and brothers as Rod placed his hand on her naked knee. She would get to meet them, she decided. This was her chance to get in with a rich family and make something of her life. All she had to do was buy some decent clothes and try to speak properly and she'd be accepted by the family. Deborah could go to hell, she thought as her plan evolved in her mind. If Rod dumped Deborah and ... She was thinking too far ahead, she knew, as Rod's hand slipped up her skirt and his fingers pressed into the warm swell of her tight knickers.

'Naughty boy,' she whispered.

'Naughty girl,' he returned.

'You're making me wet.'

'You're making me hard.'

'You *are* a naughty boy.'

INDECENT
PURSUIT

Ray Gordon

This book is a work of fiction.
In real life, make sure you practise safe, sane and consensual sex.

Published by Nexus 2008

4 6 8 10 9 7 5 3

First published in Great Britain in 2008 by

Nexus
Virgin Books
Random House
Thames Wharf Studios
Rainville Road
London W6 9HA
www.rbooks.co.uk

Addresses for companies within The Random House Group Limited can be found at: www.randomhouse.co.uk/offices.htm

The Random House Group Limited Reg. No. 954009

Distributed in the USA by Macmillan, 175 Fifth Avenue, New York, NY 10010, USA

A CIP catalogue record for this book is available from the British Library

ISBN 9780352341969

The Random House Group Limited supports The Forest Stewardship Council [FSC], the leading international forest certification organisation. All our titles that are printed on Greenpeace approved FSC certified paper carry the FSC logo. Our paper procurement policy can be found at www.rbooks.co.uk/environment

Typeset by TW Typesetting, Plymouth, Devon
Printed and bound in Great Britain by
CPI Bookmarque Ltd, Croydon, CR0 4TD

Symbols key

 Corporal Punishment

 Female Domination

 Institution

 Medical

 Period Setting

 Restraint/Bondage

 Rubber/Leather

 Spanking

 Transvestism

 Underwear

Uniforms

One

Sheena was aware of the young man looking at her as she shifted in her chair. He was standing at the bar ordering a drink, his dark eyes glancing at her every now and then. Wearing tight trousers and an open-neck white shirt, he was in his late twenties with dark, swept-back hair and a suntanned face. She thought that he was pretty good-looking, but she was waiting for a girlfriend to arrive and she wasn't on the pull. Making out that she hadn't noticed him as he approached her, she took her glass of beer from the table.

'All alone?' he asked her.

'No,' she returned, sipping her beer. 'I'm with a friend.'

He chuckled and looked at the empty chairs around the table. 'An invisible friend?'

'She ain't here yet.'

'Oh, right. I'm Rod, pleased to meet you.' Sheena said nothing as he sat opposite her at the table. 'Do you have a name?'

'I might.'

'You're a very attractive girl, if you don't mind my saying so?'

'I know I am.' Gazing at him, she realised that he wasn't the usual scum that hung around in the back-street pub. He was well-spoken and polite, which made a nice change. 'I'm Sheena,' she finally said.

'That's a nice name.'

1

'I don't think so. Look, I'm waiting for a friend so . . .'

'I'll leave when she gets here.'

She frowned. 'What are you doing in this dump?' she asked him. 'You don't look the type to come to a scumhole like this.'

'I was just passing and decided to call in for a drink. I have to admit that it's not the sort of place I usually go to.'

'So, where do you usually go?'

'The Castle Club. It's a . . .'

'I know what it is,' she cut in. 'It's posh. People with money go there.'

'Yes, I suppose it is posh.' He looked her up and down and chuckled.

'What's so funny?'

'Nothing, I . . .'

'I know what you're thinking,' she said accusingly. 'You're thinking that I'm common, aren't you?'

'No, not at all.'

'Well, you should be thinking that because I *am* common. They wouldn't let shit like me in that club.'

'You shouldn't put yourself down, Sheena. You're a very attractive girl.'

'Yeah, right.'

'Would you like me to take you to the club one evening?'

'I've already told you, they wouldn't let shit like me in.'

'Allow me to prove you wrong. How about tomorrow evening?'

'I ain't got nothing to wear.'

Taking his wallet from his trouser pocket, he passed her fifty pounds. She didn't hesitate to grab the cash, but she knew that he was only after one thing. Reckoning that he was married and had come to the seedy pub looking for a slut, she grinned. She had no qualms about taking money from men in return for sex. As far as she was concerned, she was happy to be paid to drop her knickers. She was a common slut, she reflected, recalling

2

an old man who'd been in the pub the previous evening. He was in his sixties and had given her twenty pounds in return for a hand-job beneath the table. Fifty quid for a fuck? she mused, gazing at Rod as she thrust the cash into her handbag. Easy money.

'Buy yourself something,' he said, smiling at her. 'You'd look great in a black dress.'

'Why don't you stop playing games?' she asked him. 'I know what you want.'

'I want you to come to the club with me, Sheena. I'm not playing games.'

'Yeah, right.'

'I'm serious. I find you incredibly attractive and I'd like to spend an evening with you.'

'You wouldn't want to be seen with me in that club. People would laugh at you.'

'Why would they laugh?'

'Because I'm a common slut, that's why. I know that you're only after one thing so why not admit it?'

'I'll take you to the club now, if you want me to.'

'OK, let's go.'

After finishing her beer, she left the table and walked to the door. She was wearing a red miniskirt with black leather boots and a loose-fitting white blouse, and she knew that Rod wouldn't be seen dead with her in the Castle Club. Leaving the pub, she turned and hovered on the pavement as the pub door closed. Would he back out? she wondered. Watching the door, waiting for it to open, she brushed her long blonde hair away from her face and sighed. Her hair was a little greasy and dishevelled. Expecting to spend the evening in the pub with her friend, she hadn't bothered to wash it.

'Ready, then?' Rod asked her as he left the pub and joined her on the pavement.

'If you are,' she murmured.

'So, tell me about yourself,' he said as they walked the short distance to the club.

'There ain't much to tell. I'm eighteen years old, I live in a poxy bedsit, and I'm common.'

'I do wish you'd stop putting yourself down, Sheena,' he breathed. 'You're a lovely girl.'

'If you say so.'

Rod said good evening to the man on the door as he ushered Sheena into the club. Feeling acutely self-conscious as she walked up several steps and across the plush blue carpet to the bar, she was aware of eyes staring at her. There were only half a dozen people in the club, but they were well-dressed and Sheena felt incredibly out of place. She was the youngest female there, she observed. The others were in their late twenties and early thirties, and they obviously had money.

'Are you being a naughty boy, Rodney?' a woman said, giggling as she looked Sheena up and down.

'Not at all,' he replied. 'This is Sheena, a friend of mine. Sheena, this is Elizabeth.'

'I'm pleased to meet you,' the woman said. 'Your skirt is rather ... How can I put it? It's rather ...'

'That will do, Elizabeth,' Rod cut in. 'What would you like to drink, Sheena?'

'Lager,' she replied.

Elizabeth giggled. 'Lager?' she echoed. 'This isn't a common public house, dear.'

'I don't care what it is, I want lager.'

'Where on earth did you find her, Rodney?' Elizabeth asked, shaking her head.

'He didn't find me,' Sheena said. 'Me and Rod are friends.'

'It's Rod and *I*,' Elizabeth corrected her.

'Let's go and sit down,' Rod sighed, leading Sheena to a secluded table.

Sheena sat at the table and watched Rod walk back to the bar and order the drinks. She didn't fit in at all, she mused as Elizabeth said something to Rod and then burst out giggling. Rod glanced at Sheena, looking embarrassed as he forced a smile. This wasn't a good idea, Sheena thought, wishing she'd stayed at the pub and waited for her girlfriend to arrive. At least she'd made fifty pounds. Finally joining Sheena with the drinks, Rod sat opposite her and apologised for Elizabeth's behaviour.

'I knew this was a mistake,' Sheena declared.

'Take no notice of Elizabeth,' he said. 'She's like that with everyone she meets.'

'It's Rod and I,' she said, mimicking the woman. 'Stuck-up bitch.'

'Forget about her. Tell me more about yourself.'

'I told you, there ain't nothing to tell.'

'Do you work?'

'I did have a job but I got sacked for nicking money out of the till.' She gazed at Rod and frowned. 'Are you rich?'

'Well, I'm comfortable.'

'Where do you work?'

'I'm a director of the family business. My brothers and I . . .'

'It's not me and my brothers, then?'

He chuckled. 'You're learning, Sheena. Well done.'

'I like you,' she said. 'You talk posh, but I like you.'

'And I like you, Sheena. Is your place far from here?'

'Just up the road. It's a dump.'

'I'm sure it's not.'

'You trying to get me to take you back to my place, then?'

'No, no, not at all.'

'Where do you live? In a posh house, I reckon.'

'I live on the Golden Beach estate.'

'Blimey, that private place with the big houses?'

'Yes, that's right.'

Sheena sipped her beer, wondering what it would be like to live on the private estate. The houses were huge, with expensive cars parked in the drives, and the people were rich, she knew, recalling the times she'd cycled around the estate when she was younger. Her parents had split up and she'd hated living with her mother and had left home when she was sixteen. She'd hoped to have made something of herself but, in her heart, she'd always known that she was destined to be broke and common. The Golden Beach private estate was another world. Maybe Rod could drag her out of poverty and give her a chance? she pondered wistfully.

'Why were you in that scummy pub?' she asked him. 'Was you looking for a slut?'

'No, I . . . I was just passing and I fancied a drink.'

'Are you married?'

'No, I'm not,' he replied honestly.

'So, was you looking for a slut?'

'It's where you . . . Yes, I was looking for a girl,' he confessed. 'Not a slut, but . . .'

'Don't you have a girlfriend?'

'I do, but she's . . .' He chuckled. 'She's posh, Sheena.'

'You mean, she don't fuck?'

'Yes, I suppose I do mean that. Look, I didn't pick you up for sex. I like you, Sheena. I like you as a person.'

'You want to fuck me, you mean?'

'No, I . . .'

'Be honest, Rod.'

'Yes, of course I want to . . . I mean, you're extremely attractive and . . .'

'Is that what the fifty quid was for?'

'No, that was for a new dress. Look, I have a girlfriend and she's posh and she isn't into the things I like. To be honest, my father chose her.'

'He chose her? What do you mean?'

'It's not easy to explain, Sheena. My family are . . .'

'Posh?'

'Well, yes, they are. My father wants me to marry Deborah because she comes from a good family and he has business connections with her father.'

6

'What would your old man think of me?' she cut in with a giggle. 'A common teenage slut you picked up in a back-street pub.'

'I . . . I don't think . . .'

'Shall we have another drink?'

'Yes, all right.'

As he took the empty glasses and left the table, Sheena wondered whether she'd ever get to meet his family. Looking at her painted fingernails, the chipped red varnish, she knew that he'd never take her home to meet them. They lived in another world, she brooded sadly. They lived in a world of money and luxury which was a million light years away from Sheena's world. Thinking that it would be nice to meet Rod now and then, she smiled as he brought the drinks to the table and sat next to her.

'I could be your bit of rough on the side,' she said hopefully.

'Sheena, you're more than just a . . .'

'Take me to your place to meet your mum and dad.'

'My mother isn't with us,' he said softly.

'Take me back to meet your dad, then.'

'Sheena, I can't do that. I have Deborah and . . .'

'And she's posh and I'm not?'

'Yes – no. I mean . . .'

'I know what you mean, Rod. You said that she's not into the things you like. What things do you like?'

'Sex,' he replied with a chuckle. 'All types of sex.'

'Won't she suck your cock?'

'Er . . . She's not into oral sex.'

'I love cock-sucking,' she said, her blue eyes sparkling lustfully. 'And I love a tongue up my cunt.'

'Shush, keep your voice down.'

'Sorry, I was forgetting that this is a posh place. Does that Elizabeth woman suck cock?'

'I have no idea.'

'I'll bet she's never had a mouthful of spunk in her life.'

7

'Sheena, keep your voice down.'

'Sorry.'

'I like you, Sheena. You're my type of girl.'

'But I'm not your dad's type?'

'No, sadly, you're not. My father is old-fashioned and . . . Look, we could see each other once or twice a week. If you want to, that is?'

'OK.'

'We could meet in the pub and then . . .'

'Go back to my bedsit and fuck?'

'Well, yes, if you want to.'

'And you'll pay me?'

'I'll help you out with cash if you're short.'

'OK.'

Sheena sipped her beer and thought about Rod's father and brothers as he placed his hand on her naked knee. She would get to meet them, she decided. This was her chance to get in with a rich family and make something of her life. All she had to do was buy some decent clothes and try to speak properly and she'd be accepted by the family. Deborah could go to hell, she thought as her plan evolved in her mind. If Rod dumped Deborah and . . . She was thinking too far ahead, she knew as Rod's hand slipped up her skirt and his fingers pressed into the warm swell of her tight knickers.

'Naughty boy,' she whispered.

'Naughty girl,' he returned.

'You're making me wet.'

'You're making me hard.'

'You *are* a naughty boy.'

As he moved her knickers aside and slipped a finger into the very tight sheath of her young vagina, she closed her eyes and let out a rush of breath. He wasn't common or crude. Unlike the other men she'd been with, he hadn't sworn or been at all vulgar. She needed a man like Rod, she decided. The more she thought about getting in with his family, the more she was determined to succeed. If she put on a posh voice and wore decent clothes, she was sure that they'd accept her.

'You're so hot and tight,' Rod whispered.

'Tighter than Deborah?'

'Yes, much tighter.'

'Are you going to dump her, Rod?'

'Well, no. No, I can't do that.'

'Why not?'

'Because – because it's all arranged. We're getting married and . . .'

'When?'

'In two months.'

'How old is she?

'Twenty-five.'

'OK.'

As Rod slipped a second finger into her contracting vagina, she considered the wedding. *It's all arranged, two months . . .* She had plenty of time to put a stop to it, she thought as she made her plans. Once stuck-up Deborah discovered that Rod had been fucking a teenage slut, she'd storm off and leave the door wide open for Sheena. This was going to be easy, Sheena thought as her clitoris swelled and her sex milk flowed.

'Shit, I'm going to come,' she breathed.

'No, not here,' he whispered, retrieving his hand and looking around. 'Let's go back to your place.'

'OK.'

'Sheena,' he began as she knocked back her drink. 'Sheena, do you have other men?'

'No,' she lied, smiling at him. 'Why?'

'I just wondered.'

'I'm not a prostitute, Rod. You won't give Deborah any diseases.'

'No, I didn't mean . . .'

'Come on, let's go.'

Formulating her plan as she led Rod along the street to her bedsit, she made a mental note of the things she needed to discover. Where did Deborah live? Where did she work and where did she go in the evenings? Sheena was determined to get her foot in the door of the family home, and she knew that she was going to have to do her homework if she was to destroy Rod's relationship with the woman.

When they arrived at the scruffy Victorian house, she led Rod up to her first-floor bedsit and showed him in. He looked around, obviously wondering how anyone could live in such a small room. Sheena gazed at several pairs of dirty knickers on the floor by the sink, the dirty clothes piled on a chair. She should have cleaned up, she reflected, kicking a crumpled magazine aside. But she'd arranged to meet her friend and hadn't expected to have a man back that evening. Rod tried not to show his distaste as he gazed at the dirty plates piled in the sink, but his expression betrayed his thoughts. Sitting on the edge of the single bed, he smiled at her.

'This is great,' he said. 'You've made it really cosy.'

'It's a fucking slum,' she sighed, picking her knickers up and tossing them on to the chair. 'I'll bet your wardrobe is bigger than this room.'

'Well, I . . . This is lovely, Sheena. I mean it, it's really nice.'

'You do talk crap, Rod. It's a crummy bedsit in a derelict house in a slum area. The fucking council won't find me a decent place. If I got stuffed, like that slut downstairs, then they'd give me a flat.'

'Slut downstairs?'

'Angela, she's in the bedsit downstairs. She's pregnant and the council are moving her into a flat next week. She deliberately got stuffed so that she could get a bloody flat. She's not totally screwy, though. She made sure that she got stuffed by a married bloke with money so he'll have to pay her maintenance for the kid. And he gives her money to stop her running to his wife.'

'I hope that's not what you're planning?'

'Fuck that,' she said, giggling as she joined him on the bed. 'The last thing I want is a screaming brat. It would be funny, though.'

'What would?'

'If you stuffed me and I had your kid.'

'It would be hilarious, Sheena,' he returned sarcastically. 'I'm sure it would go down extremely well with my family.'

'Tell me about Deborah.'

'Well, she's . . . There's nothing to tell, really.'

'Where is she now?'

'She's at home. She lives with her parents.'

'Does she live in a big house?'

'Yes, she does. Look, let's not talk about her.'

'Has she got a posh second name?'

'Sheena, please . . .'

'Tell me, Rod. And then you can pull my wet knickers down and lick my cunt.'

'Her surname is Gibson-Brown.'

'Deborah Gibson-Brown. Oh, very posh. My name is Sheena Collins. Boring, isn't it?'

'Your name is lovely, but *you* are becoming boring.'

Reclining on the bed, Sheena raised her buttocks as Rod thrust his hands up her short skirt and slipped his thumbs between the elastic of her knickers and her shapely hips. He eased her knickers down her long legs and over her feet, then parted her slender thighs and pushed her skirt up over her stomach. His dark eyes wide, he gazed longingly at her puffy vaginal lips, clearly visible beneath a sparse fleece of blonde pubic hair.

Sheena stared at the cracks in the ceiling as he scrutinised the most private part of her teenage body. She had to better herself, she decided as Rod knelt on the floor between her feet. She had to get out of her bedsit and make something of her life. Rod leaned forward, planted a kiss on the gentle rise of her mons and breathed

11

in her girl-scent as she parted her legs wider. She knew that, if she pleased him, she'd be seeing him again.

'You taste like heaven,' he murmured, his tongue probing her moist open slit.

'That's a new one,' she said, giggling. 'What does heaven taste like?'

'Like a beautiful girl of eighteen named Sheena Collins.'

'Suck my clit and bring me off,' she sighed as he parted the fleshy cushions of her outer lips and gazed at her wet inner folds. 'Give me a good licking-out and suck my clit and make me come.'

Wasting no time, Rod flicked the pink protrusion of her erect clitoris with the tip of his tongue and slipped a finger into her drenched vaginal duct as she writhed on her bed and gasped. Sheena let out a rush of breath as her clitoris responded to his caressing tongue and her juices of arousal flowed from her tightening vaginal sheath. Her outer labia swelling, her inner lips unfurling, she parted her thighs wide and arched her back as Rod attended to her most intimate feminine needs.

Rod obviously thought that their relationship could go nowhere, but Sheena was making her plans. Deborah Gibson-Brown, she mused, wondering where her rival lived. She suddenly recalled seeing the name Gibson-Brown on a large office building in town, and wondered whether there was a connection. It would be easy enough to find out, she reflected as Rod repeatedly swept his tongue over the sensitive tip of her hard clitoris.

'Do you like my cunt?' she asked him unashamedly.

'Very much,' he breathed. 'I like it when you say that word.'

'What, cunt?'

'Yes.'

'Does Deborah say cunt?'

'You must be joking,' he said, chuckling.

'Are you going to fuck my cunt, Rod?'

'Oh, yes. I'm going to fuck your sweet cunt so hard.'

Sheena knew that Deborah would be a stuck-up prude, and Rod obviously loved the idea of screwing a teenage slut behind her back. Fucking a dirty little whore was probably his way of rebelling against his posh family. Pulling a young whore and screwing her in her seedy bedsit was far removed from the prim and proper life he was used to with his family. He'd think about his teenage slut the next time he screwed Deborah, Sheena thought happily. He'd think about licking her tight little hole, sucking her erect clitoris and pushing his solid cock deep into her writhing body.

She imagined him having sex with Deborah. He'd be on top of her, saying nothing as he pumped his spunk into her posh pussy. The act would be cold and clinical with no words of lust, no passion. In defiance of his family, he obviously loved the idea of fucking a dirty little slut who used expletives and had no finesse. A common slut with greasy blonde hair, she thought as her orgasm neared. That's what Rod wanted.

Arching her back as her clitoris exploded in orgasm, she cried out and writhed on her bed as he sustained her ecstasy. He was good, she thought dreamily – wasted on a stuck-up prude like Deborah. Her vaginal muscles contracting, gripping his thrusting finger, her clitoris pulsating wildly beneath his wet tongue, she again cried out as her orgasm peaked and shook her teenage body to the core. Again and again, waves of ecstasy crashed though her trembling body as she rode the crest of her climax. She knew she'd be seeing a lot more of Rod.

Her young womb rhythmically contracting, she could feel her vaginal muscles spasming, her clitoris pumping waves of pleasure throughout her young body as her orgasm rode on. Rod was very good, she thought again as he massaged the inner flesh of her sex-dripping pussy. Most of the men she'd been with were only out to satisfy themselves and hadn't given a thought to Sheena's needs and desires. Rod was different.

'Fucking hell,' she gasped as her pleasure finally began to wane. 'Fucking hell, Rod. That was – that was amazing.'

'You liked it?' he asked, chuckling as he withdrew his wet finger from her tight vagina and lowered his trousers.

'Liked it? It was fucking brilliant. But I want more.'

'Let's see whether you like this.'

Slipping his purple knob between the wet inner lips of her vulva, he massaged the solid nub of her clitoris with his thumb. He was teasing her, she knew, as he ran his swollen knob up and down the open valley of her wet pussy. He was making her wait for the feel of his hardness deep inside her young vagina. She begged him to fuck her as he massaged her erect clitoris with his firm cock. Her sex milk flowing in torrents from her neglected vagina, her womb contracting, she punctuated her words of desire with crude expletives.

Finally ramming the entire length of his rock-hard penis deep into her tight vagina, he lifted her feet and placed her legs over his shoulders. She gasped, her eyes rolling, her head lolling from side to side, as he withdrew his solid cock and then rammed into her again. The bed rocking, creaking loudly, he found his rhythm and repeatedly battered her ripe cervix with his firm cock. Writhing in the grip of her ecstasy, she could feel the engorged inner lips of her pussy rolling back and forth along his veined shaft as he repeatedly drove his rock-hard shaft deep into her squirming body. Her lower stomach rose and fell with every thrust of his beautiful cock. This was what she'd craved.

Her erect clitoris massaged by the wet shaft of his thrusting cock, Sheena knew that she'd soon be writhing in the grip of her second orgasm. She'd lost count of the men she'd taken back to her bedsit for sex, but she knew that Rod was the best in a long time. By the expression of sheer sexual bliss on Rod's face, she also knew that she was far better than Deborah. Did the woman fake her orgasms? she wondered. Or didn't she even bother to make out that she was enjoying Rod's intimate attention? Rod needed a real woman, she thought as he breathed heavily and his body became rigid. He needed a common slut.

'Here it comes,' he gasped, throwing his head back.

'Fuck me hard, Rod,' she cried, her clitoris teetering on the verge of a massive orgasm. 'Yes, yes ... Fuck me senseless and fill my dirty little cunt with your spunk.'

'You're beautiful, Sheena. You've been sent to me from heaven.'

'From hell, more like. Stop talking crap and spunk into my tight little cunt.'

His sperm gushing from his throbbing knob and bathing her rhythmically contracting sex sheath, he rammed his length deep into her writhing teenage body again and again as he drained his swinging balls. Sheena reached her second climax, wailing and squirming on her bed as she felt his male cream flooding her tight vagina. Her orgasm gripping her, her vaginal muscles pulsing in waves, she shook uncontrollably as the squelching sounds of sex resounded around the room.

He really was good, she thought in the grip of her sexual delirium, and she imagined seeing him every evening and enjoying hours of crude sex. He knew how to treat a girl, how to treat a dirty little common slut. Looking forward to nights of hot fucking as her clitoris pulsated in orgasm, pumping waves of pleasure deep into her young pelvis, she wondered how often she'd see him. She also wondered how much money he'd give her.

'You really are amazing,' he gasped, finally slowing his thrusting rhythm. 'You're everything a man could ever want.'

'I'm still coming,' she breathed. 'Don't stop, I'm – I'm still coming.'

Massaging her pulsating clitoris with his thumb, he grinned. 'You're my dirty little slut,' he said as he sustained her climax and she writhed uncontrollably in her ecstasy. 'You're my dirty little teenage whore.'

'Yes, yes,' she murmured, her young body convulsing.

'I'll fuck you senseless every day, Sheena. Would you like that?'

'God, yes, fuck my tight little cunt every day.'

'OK, relax now,' he whispered, massaging the last ripples of sex from her deflating clitoris. 'Just relax, my horny little angel.'

'Was I – was I better than Deborah?' she asked him hopefully.

'You were a million times better.'

'Good, that's good. Fuck me, you were amazing. That was the best fuck I've had in ages.'

'I'd better get going,' he said, rising to his feet and tugging his trousers up.

'No, no . . . I want more, Rod. Please, don't go yet.'

'I have to, sweetheart. There's a family meeting later and I must be there.'

'Will *she* be there?'

'Deborah? No, no, she won't be there.'

'Who fucks best, me or Deborah?'

'It's Deborah or me.'

'I'll never get it right, will I?'

'Of course you will. Anyway, you fuck best, Sheena. You're by far the best. Now, I really must go. Do you have a phone?'

'Don't talk crap. How the hell can I afford a poxy phone?'

'How can I contact you, then?'

'Give me your number, Rod. I'll call you and . . .'

'No, no, I can't do that. Look, I'll meet you in the pub tomorrow evening. Say, six o'clock?'

'OK, I'll be there. Does Deborah live on the private estate?'

'Why this preoccupation with Deborah?'

'I – I want to know, that's all.'

'Yes, she lives on the estate. Until tomorrow, my angel.'

'Yes, OK. Bye, Rod.'

Waiting until he'd closed the door behind him, she slipped off the bed and pulled her knickers up her long legs to cover her sperm-oozing sex crack. Punching the air with her fist, she reckoned her future was looking good. Rod had money, he was good in bed . . . Looking around her room and imagining the day when she'd be leaving her bedsit to move in with Rod, she grinned. Deborah was about to become history, she thought happily, grabbing her handbag and leaving the room.

The evening sun warming her as she walked to the back-street pub, she felt positive for the first time in her life. She'd made a little money now and then by screwing dirty old men, but she was going to leave all that behind her and move on to better things. She'd have a house with a fitted kitchen, she mused happily. A nice bathroom and a huge bedroom and . . . But she realised that she had a long way to go before walking down the aisle with Rod.

Wandering into the pub, she noticed her friend standing at the bar. 'Hi Nat,' she said, her pretty face beaming.

'Where the fuck have you been?' the girl asked her.

'Getting fucked by a rich man,' Sheena replied with a giggle. 'Sorry I'm late.'

'Dirty little bitch. Did he pay you?'

'Of course he did. Fifty quid.'

'Wow! You can get the drinks in, then.'

Ordering two lagers, Sheena couldn't stop grinning. 'He's not just a one-nighter,' she said. 'He gave me fifty quid, but not for sex. He wants me to buy some new clothes, a black dress.'

'You mean he's going to be a regular punter?'

'No, no . . . We're together, as a couple.'

'Don't talk out of your arse, Sheena.' Nat sighed. 'He gave you fifty quid for a fuck.'

17

'Think what you like, Nat. But me and him are an item. Him and me, I mean.'

'What?'

'He's going to teach me proper English, teach me to talk right.'

'Now you really are talking out of your arse,' the girl breathed, taking the drinks from the bar. 'Pay the man, and then come over here.'

After paying for the drinks, Sheena joined her friend at the table and sat opposite her. Nat was jealous, she thought as she took a gulp of her beer. They were the same age, both lived in bedsits, and both were stone broke. And Nat was jealous because Sheena had a chance of some sort of future, at long last. Eyeing the girl's long black hair, her huge dark eyes, Sheena smiled at her.

'We'll always be mates,' she said. 'Even when I live in a big house and . . .'

'Fuck off, Sheena,' the girl cut in. 'You're living in a dream world. This bloke, whoever he is, is taking you for a ride – literally.'

'No, no . . . Me and Rod went to the Castle Club.'

'He took you there?'

'Yes, he did.'

'You mean they let you in?'

'Why shouldn't they let me in?'

'Well, you're not exactly classy. Did you wear that skirt?'

'Yes.'

'I'll bet the snobs were laughing at you.'

'No one laughed at me. Rod introduced me to Elizabeth, a friend of his. She was really nice.'

'Get real, Sheena. She probably felt sorry for you. You're a trollop, like me, and you'll never change. We're losers, and always will be.'

'Say what the fuck you like, I don't care.'

'Did you walk around the club saying fuck all the time? I'll bet that went down well with the snobs.'

18

'Of course I didn't. It's a posh place, people don't swear.'

'Sheena, every other word that leaves your mouth is fuck. Fuck this, fuck that . . .'

'Not when I'm with Rod. You're just jealous.'

'You daft bitch, of course I'm not jealous. Anyway, I saw Jenny earlier.'

'Oh?'

'She's pregnant.'

'Fuck me.'

'See, you said fuck. You can't say anything without saying fuck.'

'Yes, but . . . I'm not with Rod now, am I?'

'You really are a silly cow, Sheena. Anyway, Jenny has been stuffed and she doesn't know who the father is so she won't be able to get child benefit.'

'They'll have to pay her something, won't they?'

'I don't know, I suppose so. Is that your plan?'

'What do you mean?'

'Like that slut did in the bedsit below yours. Get stuffed by some rich bloke with a wife and then . . .'

'Nat, me and Rod have talked about marriage. He lives on the Golden Beach private estate and . . .'

'What the fuck are you on, Sheena? You're not doing drugs, are you?'

'Of course I'm fucking not. Me and Rod . . . Rod and me have talked about marriage.'

'I think it's Rod and *I*,' Nat corrected her.

'What?'

'I remember from school . . . Never mind. So, a rich bloke who lives on the Golden Beach estate wants to marry a slut like you? How old is he, eighty?'

'He's in his twenties, actually.'

'Actually? Oh, I say, you do sound posh.'

'Fuck off, Nat. Why aren't you pleased for me?'

'Sheena, Sheena . . . You have so much to learn, babe.'

'I suppose you know everything?'

19

'I know more than you, that's pretty obvious. This bloke . . .'

'Rod.'

'OK, this Rod bloke . . . How long have you known him? When did you meet him?'

'Earlier, in here.'

'Fucking hell, Sheena. You met him this evening, and he wants to marry you?'

'Well, we've only talked about it. He has this stuck-up girlfriend and . . .'

'And you're his bit on the side? Yes, I get the picture.'

'It's not like that.'

'I've known you since we were five fucking years old, Sheena. I always knew you weren't the sharpest knife in the box, and now you've proved it. This bloke, Rod or whatever . . . You met him in here this evening, he fucked you and gave you fifty quid, and you reckon that he wants to marry you? Oh, and he already has a girlfriend.'

'You wouldn't understand, Nat. Anyway, there's a fiver so go and get the drinks.'

Sighing as her friend left the table and ambled up to the bar, Sheena began to wonder whether she was right. Rod had mentioned marriage, she reflected. But he'd been talking about marrying Deborah. He obviously liked Sheena, but was he only using her for sex? Was he lining her up as his permanent slut on the side to help him endure his marriage to a stuck-up prude? Sheena bit her lip as her friend walked back to the table. Nat was attractive and very sexy, she thought, eyeing her mini-skirt, her long, shapely legs. Would Rod have gone for her if Sheena hadn't been in the pub first?

'That barman is a cunt,' Nat said, plonking the drinks on the table. 'He tried to rip me off with the change.'

'That would go down well at the Castle Club,' Sheena said with a giggle. 'Calling the barman a cunt would go down very well.'

'I'm not at the Castle Club, am I? What's it like there?'

'It's really nice. There's a thick carpet and everyone's nicely dressed and . . .'

'Apart from you.'

'Fuck off, Nat. I look OK, don't I?'

'You look OK for this dump, but not for a posh club.'

'I need some new clothes,' Sheena sighed. 'I'm meeting Rod tomorrow so I'll have to buy something.'

'Are you meeting him at the club?'

'No, I'm seeing him here at six o'clock.'

'Here? You're going to come here all dressed up? They'll throw you out.'

'Don't be daft, of course they won't. Anyway, we won't be staying here. I expect we'll go to the club or out for a meal.'

'He'll buy you a few drinks and then take you back to your pit and fuck you, Sheena. I'd put money on it, if I had any.'

Sheena lowered her head and gazed into her beer glass. Nat was probably right, she reflected. Rod only wanted her as a bit of rough on the side, and there was no way he'd take her to the club again. A tear rolling down her cheek, she knew that she could never compete with the likes of Deborah. She could contact the woman, tell her that Rod had been screwing her . . . But where would it get her? Deborah had money, and she was well in with Rod's father. Her dream shattered, she looked up at her friend and frowned.

'You're right,' she agreed. 'We're both trollops, and always will be.'

'You've had your dream, babe,' Nat said, smiling at Sheena. 'Now get back to the real world, OK?'

'OK.'

'Let's get pissed.'

'Yeah, let's get pissed,' Sheena echoed. 'Let's blow the money on booze and get totally fucking wrecked.'

21

Two

Sheena felt despondent as she dragged herself out of bed the following morning. Her room was a mess and the usual musty smell brought home the stark reality of her situation. There'd be no big house with a fitted kitchen and a nice bathroom; there'd be no money, no escaping poverty. She walked on to the landing and tried the bathroom door, but someone had beaten her to it. The water would take hours to heat up again, she thought broodily as she wandered back to her room.

She grabbed her handbag and checked her money. Sighing as she realised that she'd spent thirty pounds in the pub, she filled the kettle and made a cup of coffee. *So much for a new dress*, she thought sadly, dropping her bag on to the floor. Taking her coffee back to bed, she slipped beneath her quilt and pondered her future. Water dripping through the ceiling told her that it was raining, but she didn't place the bowl on the floor to catch the drips as she usually did. All she wanted to do was get out of the slum she called home and search for a better life.

'Fuck it,' she breathed, finishing her coffee and leaping out of bed as she heard the bathroom door open. 'I'm going to change my life if it's the last fucking thing I do.'

After a cold shower, she dressed in her red miniskirt and walked into town. Nat was probably right about Rod, she reflected for the umpteenth time as she wandered into a clothes shop. But she wasn't going to give up without a fight.

Sorting through the dresses hanging on a rail, she found a black one that she liked and checked the price tag. Thirty-five pounds. The woman behind the counter was on the phone, so Sheena grabbed the black dress and rolled it up into a ball. She'd never done this before, she thought apprehensively as she glanced at the woman. She was many things, but not a thief. Three girls wandered into the shop, distracting the woman, and Sheena slipped out into the street and walked down an alleyway. Breathing a sigh of relief as she looked at the dress, she felt swamped with guilt. Never again, she decided, taking a carrier bag from a dustbin and concealing the dress.

Walking along the street, she looked up at the huge office block and grinned. Gibson-Brown Architects. Was Deborah in the building? she wondered as she pushed the glass revolving doors and stepped on to the plush carpet inside. The security man looked up at her as she walked towards his desk, and she felt her heart banging hard against her chest. She had no idea what she was going to say as he asked her whether he could help her.

'Is Miss Gibson-Brown in?' she said softly.

'Do you have an appointment?' he asked her, grabbing a phone and punching in a number. 'What name is it?'

'Er . . . Johnson, Elizabeth Johnson.'

'Security here,' he said. 'Is Miss Gibson-Brown available, please? There's a Miss Johnson here to . . . Oh, I see. Thank you.' He replaced the phone and gazed at Sheena. 'I'm afraid she's out, Miss Johnson. What time was your appointment?'

'I – I didn't have an appointment. You see, I'm supposed to deliver a package to her house and . . . I know the road, on the Golden Beach estate, but I forget the house number.'

'You could leave the package with me.'

'No, no . . . I have to deliver it to the house.'

Opening a book, he sighed. 'I shouldn't be doing this,' he said. 'But as you know the road ... It's twenty-five Beach Lane.'

'Oh, thank you,' Sheena breathed. 'You've saved the day.'

After leaving the building, Sheena walked to the private estate with a spring in her step. So far, so good, she thought as she found the road. The detached house was huge, and Sheena stood at the end of the drive gazing at the Porsche parked by the double garage. A different world, she contemplated dreamily, imagining the beautiful kitchen. Wandering up the drive, she gazed at the Porsche and sighed. A world a million light years away. She crept up to an open window, then hid behind a bush when she heard someone talking, and listened.

'Pick me up at seven,' a woman said. 'Seven, Rodney, and don't be late. Well, you'll just have to cancel your meeting. Look, if your meeting is at six, you can be here by seven. Yes, of course. On the dot, Rodney.'

Slipping away, Sheena wondered whether Rod was going to turn up at the pub. A meeting at six? Had he meant the meeting with Sheena at the pub? Walking home, she felt butterflies in her stomach as she hoped that Rod had lied to Deborah about a business meeting. *He must think something of me to lie to her*, she thought happily. But she knew in her heart that he only wanted her young body.

Wearing her new dress, Sheena arrived at the pub at six and sat at a table with a pint of lager. She'd done her hair and applied a little makeup and felt good, as one of the regulars asked her whether she'd come into money. Ignoring him, Sheena kept her eyes on the door. Her heart raced, her stomach fluttering. She'd never felt so apprehensive in all her life. What if Rod didn't turn up? What if he really did have a business meeting and ... Her pretty face beaming as the door opened, she waved at Rod.

'Hi,' he said, walking over to her table. 'Wow, you look great.'

'Thanks,' she breathed. 'And thanks for the money.'

'I'm afraid I don't have a great deal of time,' he sighed, sitting next to her. 'I have a business meeting at seven.'

'Oh, right. Aren't you having a drink?'

'No, I've got the car outside. Do you fancy going for a drive?'

'Where to?'

'Let's go somewhere quiet, where we can be alone. How about going up to the forest?'

'Rod, I'm wearing my new dress. I thought we were going for a meal or . . .'

'Yes, yes, I know. This damned meeting is a pain, and I can't get out of it.'

'OK,' she said, finishing her beer. 'Let's go.'

Sheena didn't know what make Rod's car was as she settled on the leather seat, but it was big and obviously expensive. She imagined Deborah sitting in the car, sitting next to Rod later that evening, and she vowed to destroy their relationship. She didn't like the idea of Rod lying to her, but she was happy to think that he'd also lied to Deborah. He'd also turned up on time and she was now the other woman in his life, which was a start. But she knew that she had a long way to go before she stepped into Deborah's shoes.

'I like it here,' Rod said, parking on the grass edging the forest. 'I used to come here when I was a kid.'

'Yes, it's nice,' Sheena said softly. 'But I'm not really dressed for a walk in the forest.'

'You could take the dress off,' he suggested, grinning at her.

'I don't think there's time, Rod. I mean, you're picking Deborah up at seven so . . .'

'She won't mind if I'm a few minutes . . . How do you know that?'

'It was a guess, Rod. You've brought me here to fuck me, haven't you?'

25

'No, I . . .'

'Come on, Rod. I may be a dumb blonde, but I'm not totally thick. You only want me for sex.'

'Sheena, that's not true.'

'Isn't it?'

'You know it's not. As I said last night, I like you as a person.'

'Prove it.'

'What? How?'

'Where are you taking Deborah later?'

'She wants to go to that new restaurant down by the river.'

'Take me there instead.'

'Sheena, I – I can't.'

'Why not? All you have to do is tell Deborah that you're at a meeting. She'll understand, won't she?'

'Well . . . No, no, I can't. You don't appreciate the situation I'm in, Sheena. Deborah's father owns . . .'

'Gibson-Brown Architects, yes, I know.'

'How the hell . . .'

'Take me to the new restaurant, Rod. You can see Deborah later.'

'Sheena, be reasonable.'

'I am being reasonable, Rod. You want my cunt, and I want to go out for a meal.'

'Don't put it like that, sweetheart.'

'That's the way it is, isn't it? If you want me as your bit of cunt on the side, you'll have to look after me. Don't worry, I won't cause trouble. I won't go to twenty-five Beach Lane and talk to Deborah.'

'Christ, Sheena . . . How the hell do you know where she lives?'

'As I said, I may be a dumb blonde, but I'm not totally thick.'

'Just give me a minute,' he said, taking his mobile phone from his jacket pocket and leaving the car.

Sheena watched as he paced the ground in front of the car. He was talking to Deborah, lying to her about a

26

business meeting, and Sheena felt smug. She hadn't wanted to threaten him, but she did want to spend the evening with him and didn't see that she'd had a choice. Nat would ask her about the evening, and she didn't want to have to say that Rod had fucked her in the forest and then dumped her off at the pub. Gazing at Rod, Sheena noticed his pained expression as he slipped his phone back into his pocket.

'It's OK,' he said, joining her in the car and starting the engine. 'But I have to pick her up at nine.'

'That's good,' Sheena breathed. 'You see, it wasn't that difficult.'

'No, but . . . Sheena, you're not out to cause trouble, are you?'

'*Me?* Of course I'm not. It's just that, when you arrange to spend time with me, I expect you to keep your promise.'

Rod said nothing as he drove to the restaurant, and Sheena knew that she was going to have to take the pressure off the situation if she was going to see him again. Her threat might make him think twice about seeing her, but she had something between her legs that he wanted. Deborah had finesse and money, but Sheena had her teenage body.

'Have you noticed something about me?' Sheena asked him as he parked the car.

'The dress, yes, it's nice.'

'No, no . . . Something else.'

He looked her up and down and frowned. 'Tell me,' he said. 'I'm afraid I'm not very observant.'

'I haven't said fuck once this evening.'

'Oh, right,' he said, chuckling as they left the car. 'Whatever you do, don't swear in this place,' he added, leading her into the foyer.

'Good evening sir, madam,' a man greeted them.

'I've booked a table for two. The name's Robertson.'

'Certainly, sir. This way, please.'

Sheena gazed at the white cloths and candles adorning the tables as she followed Rod. This certainly wasn't the sort of place to swear. The thought made her giggle inwardly as the man pulled a chair out for her. *If only Nat could see me now*, she thought as Rod sat opposite her and ordered a bottle of wine from a waiter who appeared from nowhere. Sheena would have preferred a pint of lager, but decided not to say anything. Smiling at Rod, she realised that she was sitting in the very chair that Deborah would have occupied. *One up to me*, she thought happily.

'It's nice here,' she said. 'There aren't many people around.'

'Just as well,' he replied. 'It only opened last week and Deborah's been on and on . . . You look lovely with the candlelight sparkling in your eyes.'

'I expect you think I'm even lovelier with my knickers pulled down and my legs open.'

'Shush, people might hear you.'

'Sorry.'

'Sheena, we need to talk. I'm marrying Deborah soon and . . .'

'And I'll be your bit of pussy on the side?' she whispered.

'Yes, but . . . I can't have you causing trouble.'

'Rod, I won't cause trouble. I know what I am, I know my place, so don't worry.'

'How the hell did you get Deborah's address?'

'I asked someone.'

'Christ, who the hell was it?'

'Don't worry, Rod.'

'What else have you discovered?'

'Nothing, I promise.'

'Here comes the waiter.'

Sheena said nothing as Rod tasted the wine and nodded his head at the waiter. She'd never been out for a sit-down meal before, and thought it best to keep her mouth shut in case she embarrassed Rod. But she was learning all the time, she realised as the waiter passed her a menu. She was learning how to behave in posh company. The last time she'd eaten out was when she'd had fish and chips on a park bench. Far removed from this upper-class restaurant, she thought as the waiter filled her glass. Frowning as she looked at the menu, she waited until they were alone before asking Rod why it was written in a foreign language.

'It's French,' he replied. 'What sort of food do you like?'

'I like fish and chips.'

'You are lovely,' he said, smiling at her. 'The more I get to know you, the more I like you. They don't have chips, sweetheart.'

She frowned and cocked her head to one side. 'Why not?'

'Because . . . Chips aren't posh.'

'Oh, I see. So, what can I have?'

'If you like fish, there's trout or . . .'

'Steak and chips? I mean, steak and something posh?'

'Steak with boiled potatoes?'

'Yes, that sounds good. What made you say that I'm lovely just now?'

'Because of the way you are. You're worldly wise and yet – and yet you're as innocent and naïve as a little girl. Oh, I almost forgot. I have a present for you.'

'Really?' she trilled as he reached into his jacket pocket.

'There, it's a mobile phone.'

'Wow, thanks. What's the number?'

'I've written it on the instruction book. Now I'll be able to ring you and arrange to see you.'

'Thanks, Rod. But how do I pay the bill? I mean, is there a top-up card or something?'

'It's a contract phone. Which means that I pay the monthly bills, so don't go calling Australia every five minutes.'

'It's lovely, Rod. No one's never given me a present before.'

'Don't lose it, whatever you do.'

'No, no, I won't,' she said, her face beaming as she slipped the phone into her bag. 'Thank you so much.'

'It's also a camera.'

'Wow, that's amazing. Can I take a picture of you?'

'No, it might end up in the wrong hands. And if we're going to come to places like this, you'll need a new handbag,' he said, reaching for his wallet. 'Take this and buy some shoes and a bag and anything else you want.'

Taking the cash, she gasped. 'Rod, there's over two hundred quid here.'

'Two hundred and fifty. That should be enough to get you a few decent clothes.'

'I – I don't know what to say.'

He chuckled and leaned across the table. 'Just don't say fucking hell, OK?' he whispered.

'OK,' she said, stuffing the cash into her bag as the waiter returned.

Rod ordered the meals and Sheena again kept quiet for fear of embarrassing him. She was doing well, she thought. She hadn't sworn or said anything out of place, and she looked good in her new dress. Thinking of her friend, Nat, she could hardly wait to tell her that she'd been out for a meal with Rod. Nat wouldn't believe her, but she'd show the girl her mobile phone and tell her about the money and . . . It was probably best not to say anything to Nat, she decided. They were good friends and she didn't want to upset her.

'Will you bring Deborah here?' she asked as the waiter left.

'I'll have to,' Rod sighed. 'She's been on about this place since it opened.'

'It would be funny if you had this table and she sat where I am. What if the waiter says something to her?'

'Waiters don't speak out of turn, Sheena.'

'Rod, the money and the phone . . . Why did you do it?'

'Because I like you and I hope to see you again.'

'Do you think the day will come when we . . .'

'Don't think about the future. I hope that we'll be seeing each other for a long time, but . . .'

'Just seeing each other?'

'That's all we can do, Sheena. My life, my work, Deborah . . . It's all mapped out.'

'And I'm not on the map?'

'You are, but you're not in the centre of the map. You're sort of hovering nearby.'

'OK.' She sipped her wine and then forced a smile. 'I might get a little bit closer to the centre one day.'

'Sheena, I can never . . . Yes, maybe one day.'

Sheena enjoyed the meal, but the time was passing by quickly and she knew that Rod would soon be with the woman he'd planned to marry. Sheena would go back to her bedsit or to the pub, and the dream would be over for another day. She didn't dare ask Rod whether she could see him the following evening. She knew that she came second to Deborah and she might have to wait several days before Rod took her out again. Once Rod was married, she doubted whether she'd see much of him at all. Of course, if Rod didn't marry Deborah . . . That was her priority, she thought again. She had to destroy their relationship.

Finally, after leaving the restaurant, Sheena sat in the car beside Rod and thanked him for a lovely evening. He checked his watch before driving her back to her bedsit, and she knew that he was wondering whether he had time for sex. After all, that was all he wanted her for, she mused as he pulled up outside her place. The money, the phone, the meal . . . It was all payment for sex.

'I'd better get going,' he said. 'I'd like to have stayed but . . . Well, you know how it is.'

'Will you take her to the restaurant?'

'No, not tonight. The waiter wouldn't say anything, but I can hardly go back there with another woman. Besides, I haven't booked a table. I'll ring you, OK?'

'OK.'

'Don't look so sad, sweetheart. I'll ring you tomorrow.'

Reaching over and squeezing the crotch of his trousers, she smiled. 'Will you give her that tonight?' she asked him.

'She won't want that, I can assure you.'

'I want it,' she breathed, tugging his zip down and hauling out his flaccid penis.

She leaned over and took his purple knob into her hot mouth, then sucked gently as his cock stiffened. He gasped, holding her head as she took his swollen knob to the back of her throat and sank her teeth gently into his hard shaft. She knew that Deborah wouldn't suck his cock, and she reckoned that this was a sure way to hang on to him. All the time she gave Rod what Deborah couldn't or wouldn't, she'd hang on to him.

Working her wet tongue around the rim of his bulbous cockhead, she wanked his shaft slowly. The longer it took him to come, the longer he'd stay with her, she thought as he trembled and breathed deeply. She'd had a lovely evening with him, and she didn't want him to leave her. She didn't want to be cooped up in her bedsit alone while he spent the rest of the evening with another woman. Deborah didn't deserve Rod, she mused as she licked and sucked on his hard prick.

'God, I'm coming,' he groaned as she snaked her tongue over the silky-smooth surface of his engorged knob and ran her hand up and down his firm shaft. 'Sheena, I – I'm coming.' As his fresh spunk jetted from his throbbing cock and filled her cheeks, she sucked hard and swallowed repeatedly. She was good at blow-jobs, she reflected. After all, she'd lost count of the men who'd fucked her mouth and spunked down her throat, so she'd had more than enough practice. 'You're amazing,' Rod groaned as she sucked the remnants of his spunk from his deflating knob. 'You really are a beautiful little slut.'

Sitting upright and licking her sperm-glossed lips as he zipped his trousers, she mulled over his words. *You really are a beautiful little slut.* That's all she was to him, she thought sadly as he started the engine. She was nothing more than his little slut, his bit of cunt on the side. He checked his watch and complained about the time, so Sheena left the car without saying a word and closed the door. Watching him drive off, she felt an ache in her heart. The dream was over, for now.

Rather than go up to her room, she walked to the back-street pub, hoping that Nat would be there. She wasn't going to tell the girl about her evening; she just wanted a friend to get drunk with. Rod would be with Deborah by now, she thought forlornly. He'd be taking her out, spending money on her and . . . It was better to be Rod's slut on the side than to be the cheated woman, she decided as she pushed the pub door open. Nat was there, sitting alone at their usual table, and Sheena bought two pints of lager and joined her.

'Where the fuck have you been?' Nat asked her. 'And where did you get that dress from?'

'I bought it,' Sheena replied. 'Do you like it?'

'It's OK. So, where have you been?'

'I saw Rod,' she said softly.

'And he fucked you?'

'No, no, he didn't. We just talked and stuff.'

'Why didn't he fuck you? I mean, that's all he wants you for, so why didn't he . . .'

'It's not like that,' Sheena cut in angrily. 'I told you last night, it's not like that.'

'Whatever you say. Oh, Tommy was in earlier. He was looking for you.'

'Did he say why?'

'He wants to screw you again. I would have obliged, but he only had a tenner so I told him to piss off and have a wank instead.'

'I don't know why he don't do something with his life.'

'Because he's like us, babe. He's a born loser.'

'He's not bad-looking, so why don't he . . .'

'Sheena, Tommy is a waster. He drinks all day and tries to fuck all night. That's his life, booze and girls. I dread to think where he gets the cash from.'

'I think his parents are loaded.'

'And they give it to him? Fuck me, they must be mad. You see, having money doesn't change people. If this rich bloke of yours did marry you and you had money, you'd still be a slut like me.'

'No, I wouldn't, Nat. I'd get out of this stinking life and do something worthwhile.'

'Such as?'

'Well, I'd – I'd have a nice house and make nice meals in my posh kitchen.'

'Fuck off, Sheena. You'd soon get bored with that and come sneaking in here looking for fun. I wish you'd get it into your thick head. We're losers, babe, and we always will be. You've had a taste of the high life by going to the Castle Club and . . .'

'I went to that new restaurant with Rod this evening,' Sheena blurted out. 'The one down by the river.'

'He took you there? And he didn't fuck you afterwards?'

'There's more to life than fucking, Nat.'

'Christ, I never thought I'd hear you say that. You must have had a hundred cocks up your cunt, and you loved every one of them.'

'People change, Nat.'

'Yeah, right. Remember this, babe. Once a slut, always a slut.'

'That's not true.'

'OK, so this bloke marries you. What about his family? There's you, at the reception, getting pissed out of your head and staggering around saying fuck me all the time. Maybe you'd lay off the booze and make out you're posh and get away with it for a while. But how long before you start swearing in front of his mum or his old man? How long before they see the real you, Sheena?'

Sheena gulped down her beer, then walked up to the bar and bought another pint. She knew Nat was right, but she felt that she had to at least try to drag herself out of the mire and get a decent life. *Once a slut, always a slut.* Was that true? she wondered, wishing she'd had a better upbringing. If her father hadn't been a drunken slob who walked out on her mother, things might have been different, she reflected. She might have gone to school rather than bunking off and . . . It was no good looking back, she decided as she retook her seat.

Grinning as her phone rang, she opened her bag. 'Hello,' she said, pressing her new mobile to her ear as Nat stared at her in disbelief.

'Sheena, it's me,' Rod said. 'I've managed to get away for a few minutes.'

'Hi, Rod. I'm really pleased you phoned.'

'Are you OK? Only, you went off without saying anything.'

'Yes, I'm OK. I'm in the pub with a friend.'

'A boyfriend?'

'No, no.'

'I don't want you giving your little pussy away,' he said with a chuckle.

'No, I wouldn't do that. So, where are you?'

'I'm . . . I have to go. I'll call later, if I can.'

'OK, bye.' Dropping the phone into her bag, she grinned at Nat. 'That was Rod,' she said triumphantly.

'Where the fuck did you get that phone from? Is it new?'

'Yes. Rod bought it for me.'

'Fucking hell, he must really like what you have up your skirt.'

'Nat, I've told you, it's not like that.'

'I'm beginning to believe you. So, he took you to the

35

Castle Club, and that new restaurant, and now he's bought you a mobile phone?'

'And he gave me two hundred and fifty quid to buy clothes.'

'What the fuck have you got up your skirt? I don't know why I'm asking you that, seeing as I've licked your pussy out.'

'People might hear you,' Sheena whispered, looking around the pub.

'So, we both like a little bit of lessie sex now and then. What's wrong with that?'

'Nothing, but . . . I just don't want you telling the world about it.'

'What would Rod say if he found out that we've spent many nights licking and . . .'

'He won't find out, Nat.'

'Well, I won't tell him. I think you might be on to something here, babe. I mean, there's plenty of cunt around here going for a few quid. The money and things he's given you . . . He must want more than the odd fuck.'

Sheena hung her head as she recalled Rod's words. *My life, my work, Deborah . . . It's all mapped out*. There was no place on the map for her, she thought as she sipped her beer. Rod's life was planned, and his plans didn't include Sheena. But she wasn't going to give up, she told herself for the umpteenth time. Even Nat was beginning to think differently. As the girl said, there was plenty of cunt around going for a few quid. Why would Rod spend a fortune on Sheena if that was all he was after?

'Fancy an early night?' Nat said, breaking Sheena's reverie.

'What, you mean . . .'

'Yes, back at your place.'

'I don't know,' Sheena sighed. 'My head's all mixed up now, I don't know what to think about Rod.'

'That's why I'm suggesting we chill out in your bed, Sheena. Come on, finish your drink and I'll take you to bed and relax you.'

'OK.'

Leaving the pub with her friend, Sheena decided to forget about Rod for the time being and enjoy a night of lesbian sex. She'd first had sex with Nat when they were at school together. They'd gone back to Sheena's house and had been playing around on her bed when their hands had begun to roam and their hormones course through their veins. They'd kissed and rubbed between each other's legs, and a new and exciting side of their relationship had begun. Although Sheena had never considered herself a lesbian, she enjoyed the loving sex she'd found with her best friend.

When they arrived at her bedsit, Sheena poured two glasses of wine as Nat sat on the bed and talked unashamedly about pussy-licking and clit-sucking. Sheena felt her clitoris swell and her juices of arousal flow into the crotch of her tight knickers as she imagined Nat parting her fleshy sex lips and exploring her wet inner folds with her tongue. Sipping her wine, she was about to join her friend on the bed when her phone rang.

'Hi, Rod,' she said, holding her phone to her ear and grinning at Nat.

'Sheena, we need to talk,' Rod said mysteriously.

'What, now?'

'Yes, if that's all right? Where are you?'

'Well, I – I'm at home and I have a friend here at the moment.'

'I'll pick you up and we'll go for a drive.'

'It will have to be quick because . . .'

'Half an hour, no more.'

'OK, I'll wait outside.'

Dropping the phone into her bag, Sheena gazed at Nat. 'I won't be long,' she said.

'What does he want?' Nat asked.

'He wants to talk. You wait here and I'll be back soon, OK?'

'OK.'

Sheena left her bedsit and hovered on the pavement outside the house wondering what Rod wanted to talk about. Thinking that it must be important, she wondered whether he was going to dump her. Perhaps he'd decided to call it a day as he was going to be married to Deborah soon and didn't want Sheena hanging around in the background. When his car pulled up, she opened the door and sat beside him, expecting the worst. She could smell perfume, and she reckoned he'd only just dropped Deborah off.

'I haven't got much time,' she murmured as he drove down the road.

'Half an hour,' he said, smiling at her. 'That's all I need.'

'Rod, what's this all about?'

'As I said before, Deborah is a prude. I've been thinking about you all evening, Sheena. And I want you.'

All he wanted was sex, she thought with a heavy heart. That's what had been so important, getting his cock into her young pussy and fucking her. But this was her role. She had to be available when he wanted sex; that was obviously the deal he had in mind. The money, the phone, the meal . . . He'd kept his side of the bargain and she had to keep hers. If only Deborah wasn't around. If only Sheena had met Rod before Deborah had come on to the scene . . .

'Are you going to dump Deborah?' she asked him hopefully as he pulled up on the grass by the forest.

'No, I can't do that.' Slipping his hand between her thighs, he kissed her cheek. 'I want your sweet little pussy,' he breathed huskily.

'Rod . . . Have you brought me here just to fuck me?'

'Yes, of course.'

'But . . . I was with my friend. I've left her alone at my place because I thought you wanted to talk about something important.'

'I do, Sheena. I want to talk about your wet pussy. Now that's what I call really important.'

38

'So, you dropped Deborah off and . . .'

'What's the matter?' He moved back and stared at her. 'Don't you want to be with me?'

'You know I do. But I don't want you to go out with her and then come to me for sex because she won't fuck you.'

'You're complicating things,' he sighed. 'I wish you'd forget about Deborah and enjoy our times together.'

'And I wish you'd forget about her and spend more time with me.'

'Sheena, we've been through all this before. As it is, I'm taking a huge risk by going out with you. Don't make things difficult for me.'

'What about me? I mean, it's not exactly easy for me having to . . .'

'Maybe we should call it off? My brother, Charles, is already suspicious.'

'What do you mean?'

'I was talking to him earlier. Someone told him that they'd seen me with a young blonde girl in my car. If he finds out that . . . He's also a member of the club.'

'So, we ain't going to the club again?'

'It was a mistake to go there, Sheena.'

'What about the restaurant? Ain't we going there again, neither?'

'How can we, Sheena? Deborah wants to go there, and Charles wants to take his wife there, so I can't take you again. Why don't you slip your knickers off and . . .'

'I might go to the restaurant by myself,' she cut in, lifting her firm buttocks clear of the seat and tugging her knickers down. 'I might even see you there with Deborah.'

'That wouldn't be a good idea, Sheena.'

'I might go to the club, too.'

'You have to be a member or be taken there as a guest.'

As he slipped his hand between her naked thighs and massaged the fleshy swell of her teenage pussy lips,

39

Sheena reclined in the seat and thought the situation over. She wasn't a fool – she'd realised from the outset that he only wanted her for sex. But he'd given her money and she reckoned he'd give her more. Was it money he would have spent on Deborah? His fingers delving into the wet heat of her tight vagina, he kissed her succulent lips passionately and drove his tongue into her wet mouth. He was really nice, she reflected as his tongue met hers. But it was obvious that she'd never be anything more than his bit of rough on the side.

'I need somewhere better to live,' she said as he opened her blouse and lifted her bra clear of her firm breasts. 'Rod, I need . . .'

'How can you move?' he asked her. 'You don't have any money.'

'You could rent a flat for me.'

'What? You mean . . .'

'If you want to fuck me, we'll need somewhere nice to go.'

'Sheena, I can't . . .'

'That's what they do in films. The rich married man sets his slut up in a flat so he can fuck her whenever he wants to.'

'This isn't a film, Sheena,' he sighed. 'I'll give you money to help you out, but I can't pay the rent on a flat. I hope you're not going to start threatening to cause trouble?'

'I won't, I promise. But there is one thing I want.'

'What's that?'

'I want to be a member of the Castle Club. Don't worry, I won't talk to Charles or . . .'

'OK, I'll get you membership and I'll help you out with cash. But I want you to give me what I want in return.'

'It's a deal,' she said happily.

Sheena knew that she'd never get anywhere by sitting in the back-street pub every evening. But if she went to the Castle Club she'd meet a better class of people, people with money. Giggling inwardly as she thought about taking Nat to the club, she imagined her friend calling the barman a cunt. It was best to keep Nat well away from the club, she decided as Rod unzipped his trousers and hauled out his hard penis. Nat was a good friend, and a great lesbian lover, but it wouldn't be a good idea to take her to the Castle Club.

Lifting Sheena's leg over the back of the seat, Rod moved closer and rammed his solid cock deep into her tight vagina. Sheena was extremely uncomfortable with her legs open as far as they would go and the back of her head pressed hard against the door, but she wasn't going to complain. Rod had money and, unbeknown to him, he was also her way into the family. That was her quest in life, she decided happily as he repeatedly battered her young cervix with his bulbous knob – to marry into the rich family.

'You're a tight little whore,' he breathed, gasping as he rocked his hips. 'You're my little teenage slut, Sheena.'

'I'll always be your little slut,' she replied, deciding that the time had come to be rid of Deborah once and for all. 'Even when you're married, I'll always be here for you.'

'And my cock will always be hard for you, my angel.'

Listening to the squelching sounds of crude sex as Rod's firm cock slid in and out of her contracting vagina, she wondered how to get rid of Deborah. It would be fatal to cause trouble, she realised as her clitoris swelled against the wet flesh of his thrusting shaft. Deborah had to be dealt with subtly, with no obvious connection to Sheena. Perhaps Nat could speak to her? If Nat made out that she was Rod's bit of rough on the side ... This needed some serious planning, she thought as Rod squeezed her small breasts and pinched the ripe nipples of her sensitive teats.

She reached between her splayed thighs to fondle his huge balls as he increased the speed of his shafting rhythm. She grabbed the base of his cock, feeling the slippery wetness of his shaft as he drove into her again and again. This was raw sex, she thought, her inner lips rolling back and forth along his veined shaft. But there was more to it than that. There was something more than an illicit fuck, wasn't there?

'Here it comes,' Rod gasped. 'I'm going to pump your dirty little cunt full of spunk.'

'I'm coming,' Sheena cried. 'Don't stop, I'm – I'm coming.'

'Talk dirty to me, you filthy little slut. Talk dirty.'

'I can feel your hard cock in my cunt. Fucking my wet cunt and . . . God, I'm coming. Fuck me, Rod. Fuck my dirty little cunt and fill it with your spunk.'

Shaking uncontrollably as her orgasm erupted within the solid nub of her clitoris, Sheena cried out as she felt Rod's fresh sperm flooding her pulsing cunt. Imagining Nat sucking Rod's spunk from her inflamed vaginal sheath, she knew that she could never give up crude sex. It was a way of life, she mused dreamily as her clitoris throbbed and shook her young body to the core. She'd been brought up on crude sex, selling her pussy to men, and enjoying every minute of it. She craved Nat's wet tongue between the puffy lips of her pussy, she yearned for hard cocks driving deep into her tight vagina. If she did become Rod's wife, would she change her ways?

'God, you're amazing,' Rod groaned, finally resting with his spent cock deep within the heat of her sperm-brimming vagina. 'I could never live without you, Sheena. You know that, don't you?'

'You won't have to,' she sighed, her vaginal muscles spasming, squeezing the last of Rod's sperm from his deflating penis.

'You're a beautiful girl. I want us to be together for always.'

'That's what I want, too. If Deborah . . .'

'Don't talk about Deborah,' he sighed.

'OK, I'm sorry. Can you go to the Castle Club on your way home and get my membership sorted out?'

'There's a form to fill in, but I'll deal with it for you. I know the manager, so it won't be a problem. I'll leave your membership card with the doorman, OK?'

'Thanks, Rod, that's great.'

'I doubt you'll see Charles there,' he said, finally sliding his flaccid penis out of her tight vagina and zipping his trousers. 'You wouldn't know him anyway.'

'I won't cause trouble, I promise. Even if I do meet him, I won't say nothing about us.'

'There is just one thing. Elizabeth only goes to the club on Wednesday evenings. As you've discovered, she can be a right little bitch. Don't go there on Wednesdays, OK?'

'OK, I'll remember that. You can trust me, Rod.'

'I know that, sweetheart. Right, let's get you back to your friend and then I'll go on to the club.'

Sheena was going to leave her knickers in the car in the hope that Deborah would find them, but she thought better of it. Deborah had to be dealt with subtly, she thought again as Rod drove her back to her bedsit. An anonymous letter about Rod screwing Elizabeth might do the trick, she thought in her rising wickedness. Then again, a photograph of Rod screwing Nat would be even better. That would certainly put an end to the relationship.

Leaving the car with sperm filling the crotch of her tight knickers, she said goodbye to Rod and went up to her room. She sighed as she read the note from Nat saying that she'd gone home. Maybe it was just as well, she thought, pouring herself a glass of wine. With Rod's sperm oozing from her inflamed pussy, it might be best not to have Nat lick her. Looking around her room, she felt despondent. The place was a dump, she thought, flopping on to her bed. But she was beginning to make plans to change her young life, and she knew that she wouldn't be living in a seedy bedsit for much longer.

Three

Sheena went into town the following morning and bought some new clothes and a decent pair of shoes. After a trip to the hairdresser, she felt good as she walked home. To have money in her purse was a new experience, and she was all the more determined to leave the mire of her bedsit and change her life. Crossing the park, she turned as someone called her. It was Tommy, a stark reminder of the rut she was in.

'Hi,' she said as he approached her.

'Fuck me, I hardly recognised you,' he said, looking her up and down. 'Have you come into some dosh, or what?'

'No, no, I – I'm moving on, Tommy. I'm changing my life, which is something you should do.'

'Change my life? What for?'

'Because we're losers and we can change that. Drinking and fucking all day is . . .'

'That sounds good to me,' he cut in with a chuckle.

'Don't you want to get a job and earn decent money?'

'My old man's loaded, so why should I bother?'

'Because . . . Oh, never mind.'

'Fancy a drink? I'm off to the pub, if you want to join me?'

'No, I can't. I'm going out this evening and I have to get ready.'

'Where are you going?'

'I'm going to the . . . I'm just going out with a friend.'

'Come on, Sheena, I need someone to get pissed with.'

'Tommy, I'm going out this evening. I don't want to get pissed in the middle of the fucking day.'

'Fuck me, you have changed. How about a quick fuck at your place?'

'No, Tommy.'

'I hope you're not going to leave your mates behind when you move on and change your life?'

'Of course I'm not, Tommy. It's just that I'm going out this evening. I'll see you in the pub tomorrow, OK?'

'And we'll go back to your place afterwards?

'Maybe.'

'OK, I'll be there.'

As she walked away, Sheena turned and smiled at Tommy, who stood slouching with his hands in his pockets. He was a loser. He was eighteen, and spent all his days drinking and trying to fuck girls. There had been many times when she'd spent all day in her bed with him, drinking and screwing because there was nothing else to do, but things were different now. That was her old life, she mused, walking back to her bedsit. Things were different now.

Having spent the afternoon cleaning her room and getting ready for the evening, Sheena felt good in her new dress and shoes. The dress was fairly short but not tarty, and she reckoned she'd be accepted at the club. But she'd have to speak properly, she realised as she neared the back-street pub. Stopping outside, she glanced through the grimy window and noticed Tommy sitting at a table with Nat. They were both losers, she thought, realising that she'd been stuck in a rut for far too long. Drinking and screwing was all very well, but it wasn't the kind of life Sheena wanted any more.

Reaching the club, Sheena smiled at the doorman and gave him her name. She felt relieved as he returned her smile and passed her a membership card. Rod hadn't let her down, she thought happily as she made her way to the bar. And she wasn't going to let him down. There were a dozen or so people standing at the bar, and she felt a little self-conscious as she ordered a vodka and tonic. But she knew that she was well-dressed and that her hair looked lovely, so there was no need to worry. Thanking God that Elizabeth wasn't there, she sat at a corner table and wondered what the evening had in store for her.

Fiddling nervously with her long blonde hair, she sipped her drink and did her best to look relaxed. But this was a different world from the pub and, even though she looked nice, she felt out of place. The people at the bar were laughing and joking, and they obviously knew each other, but Sheena thought it best to stay at her table rather than try to join in. The last thing she wanted was to start chatting to people and make grammatical errors.

'All alone?' one of the young men asked her as he walked to her table.

'Yes, I'm . . . I'm waiting for a friend,' Sheena replied awkwardly.

'You're new here, aren't you? Oh, sorry, I'm Brian.'

'I'm Sheena, pleased to meet you. Yes, I've only just joined.'

'There have been a few newcomers recently, which is a good thing as the numbers have been dwindling. May I ask . . . Is your friend male or female?'

'Er . . . Male.'

'Well, he won't want to find me talking to you when he arrives. Enjoy your evening. And welcome to the Castle Club.'

'Thanks.'

Breathing a sigh of relief as he walked back to the bar, Sheena wondered whether she should have got to know him. She couldn't sit alone at a table every time she went to the club, she realised, wondering what Tommy and Nat were doing in the pub. They were probably getting pissed and having a laugh, she thought, again thinking that she was out of place in the club. But she realised that this was a new start and it was bound to be difficult at first. She didn't look common, she thought, peering down at her new dress. As long as she didn't open her mouth, she'd be all right.

Looking up as the barman said, 'Good evening, Charles,' Sheena gazed at a young man walking up to the bar. Was he Rod's brother? she wondered. She reckoned there was a likeness. He was very good-looking, she thought, sipping her drink and trying to appear relaxed. He was wearing dark trousers and a white shirt and tie. He'd probably called in for a drink on his way home from the office. He was talking to one of the men at the bar, but repeatedly glanced in Sheena's direction. She'd promised Rod that she wouldn't talk to Charles or cause trouble, and decided that it was best to steer clear of him.

'Haven't I seen you somewhere before?' he asked her when he finally walked over to her table.

'I – I don't think so,' she murmured, hoping that he hadn't seen her with Rod.

'I'm Charles. Mind if I join you?'

'Er . . . No, that's fine. I'm Sheena.'

'I've seen you somewhere, I'm sure.' he persisted, smiling at her. 'But I can't think where. Are you new here?'

'Yes, this is my first time.'

'I don't get in here very often, pressure of work and all that.'

'What sort of work do you do?' she asked him, hoping to discover a little more about him, and about Rod.

'I'm a director of the family business.'

'That sounds interesting.'

'It's not, Sheena, believe me. Families are funny things at the best of times. Put several brothers together with their father in business and . . . I won't bore you with that. Let's talk about you.'

'No, no, I'm interested.'

'Why's that?' He frowned and then chuckled. 'You don't even know me.'

'I've always been interested in people, their stories and stuff.'

'OK, if you're sure? There's my brother, David, who's terrified of his wife. There's Raymond, who's looking for a wife, and then there's Rod who ... Rod is due to be married soon but I don't think ... Then there's my father. His name is George but he's known as the Boss. He's a formidable man and no one dares to disagree with him.'

'Wow, four brothers. Do you get on OK with each other?'

'Most of the time, yes.'

'So, Rod is the one who's getting married soon?'

'That's right. The Boss – I mean, my father – believes that Deborah is a goddess and would be good for Rod. Deborah is Rod's intended.'

'Do you think that she's a goddess?' she probed.

'She ... No one knows this, but she has a chequered past.'

'Really?' Sheena leaned forward and grinned. 'Tell me more.'

'She comes from a decent family and she's had a good education. I shouldn't say anything but, seeing as you don't know her ... When Deborah was at university, she did a series of porn photos.'

'Porn photos?'

'She was a rebel, into drugs and all sorts. It's a long story but I have several of the photographs. She don't know that I know, but the photos say it all.'

'Does Rod know?'

'No, he doesn't. Deborah is a prude now, you'd never think that she ... Well, I suppose that's all in the past. We all have skeletons in the cupboard, Sheena.'

'Do you have skeletons?'

48

'A few,' he replied, chuckling as he winked at her. 'How about you?'

'I have loads of cupboards full of skeletons.'

'Have you done naughty things?' he asked her, gazing at the firm mounds of her teenage breasts.

'Yes, I have. I've done very naughty things.'

'You're a pretty little thing, Sheena. This place needs some new life pumping into it. I'm pleased I've met you. Sorry, I've barged in on you. Are you waiting for someone?'

'No, no, I'm all alone.'

'No boyfriend?'

'Er . . . No, not really.'

'In that case, I'm very pleased I've met you.'

'I'm pleased I've met you too, Charles. I must admit, I was feeling like a spare prick at an orgy sitting here all alone. I was going to bring a girlfriend but . . . Well, she couldn't make it.'

'That's a bit of luck. For me, I mean. Is she the same age as you? Don't get me wrong, I'm not asking you your age.'

'We're both eighteen. Me and her . . . Her and me have been friends since school. We've always done everything together. We go to the pub together, get pissed together . . . I mean . . .'

'Sounds like a good friendship. Would you like another drink?'

'Oh, thanks. It's vodka and tonic.'

Sheena realised that she'd never be able to speak properly, as she watched Charles walk across the plush blue carpet to the bar. Her hair looked nice, and her new dress and shoes were expensive, but she could never hide the fact that there was a common slut hiding behind the façade. She didn't have too much trouble controlling her language when she was sober but, after a couple of drinks, she found herself slipping back into her old ways. At least she'd discovered something about Deborah, she reflected happily as Charles returned with the drinks.

She felt comfortable chatting with Charles but, after her fifth vodka, her head was spinning and she was beginning to reveal her true character. Charles thought she was deliberately speaking badly when she said that she'd never had no proper boyfriend. She laughed it off, but she was acutely aware of her mistake, and she knew that she'd never fit in with a posh and very well-off family. She was a common slut, she reminded herself as Charles asked her where she lived. Once a slut, always a slut.

'It's a dump,' she blurted out. 'I hate it.'

'It's not that bad, surely?'

'It's worse,' she sighed. 'I suppose you've got a big house?'

'Well, it is fairly large. Do you live with your parents or . . .'

'I live on me own. It's a poxy bedsit and I hate it.'

'Oh, I see.' He forced a smile. 'Sheena, I really am pleased that I've met you.'

'Why, because I'm a . . . I mean . . .'

'What were you about to say?'

'Nothing. I think I've had too much to drink. I should have eaten something before coming here. I'm sorry if I sound a bit . . .'

'Don't apologise, Sheena. You're good company. I mean that. It makes a nice change to meet someone who – who isn't all airs and graces.'

'Someone common, you mean?'

'No . . . Look, we're all different. I must admit that I get fed up with etiquette. My family are all terribly prim and proper when they're together. Many times I've wished that we could just relax and have a laugh for a change.'

'I think I need some fresh air,' Sheena sighed, downing the last of her drink. 'I think I'd better get home and . . .'

'I can give you a lift,' he offered as she rose to her feet and swayed on her unsteady legs. 'Here, take my hand.'

Sheena hated herself for getting drunk, and she wondered what Charles thought of her as he led her to his car. To make matters worse, she had a bout of hiccups as he pulled out into the traffic. When he suggested that they go for a walk down by the river to clear her head, she knew what he was after. He even placed his hand on her knee, but she was beyond caring. She'd tried to speak properly and behave like a refined young lady. But the alcohol had stripped away her flimsy disguise and revealed her true colours. She might as well take his money and fuck him, she decided.

'Are you married?' she asked him as he parked by the river.

'Well, yes but . . .'

'Your wife don't understand you?' she said with a giggle.

'Something like that. I like you, Sheena. You're my type of girl.'

'What is your type of girl, a slut?'

'No, no, I . . .'

'Be honest, Charles. You like me because I'm a common slut.'

'I like you because you're you.'

'That's what I meant. You like me because I'm a common slut.'

'You're not common, Sheena. And you're not a slut. Your voice is . . . Well, it's a little husky and rough around the edges, but I like that.'

Sheena got out of the car, walked along the river bank and sat on a bench. The sun was low in the sky and the evening air was warm, and she wondered whether Charles would suggest that she strip naked as he joined her on the bench. He was a nice man, she thought, wondering what Rod would say if he knew that she was out with his brother. Rod knew that she was a slut and he'd realise that she was using Charles to glean information. But there was no way she could use Charles to get her foot into the door of the family home. Like most married men she'd met, he only wanted to use her for sex.

'It's nice here,' Charles said.

'I used to bunk off school and come here with boys,' she breathed. 'We'd have a smoke and then ... It was fun.'

'What were you doing in the club?' he asked her. 'How did you become a member?'

'What's a slut like me doing in a place like that, you mean?'

'No, no, I didn't mean that.'

'What did you mean, then?'

'You don't seem the type to ... I'm not making a very good job of this.'

'I know what you mean,' she sighed. 'Won't your wife be wondering where you are?'

'No, no. I often have to work late, so she won't be bothered. My father will probably wonder what I'm up to, though. He likes the family to get together in the evenings. We have the evening meal at the big table in the dining room, then we retire to the study and talk business. Mind you, Rod is hardly ever there. He's usually out and about somewhere.'

'Oh? What does he get up to?'

'He's very much like me, Sheena.' He chuckled and placed his hand on her knee. 'Rod likes beautiful teenage girls. I really can't see his marriage working out.'

'You said that Deborah did porn stuff? If she was a slut in her teens, she can't of changed that much.'

'It's can't *have* changed ... Never mind. According to Rod, she's a prude. To be honest, I think she only wants him for his money. Her father's very well off, but he's also very tight and she wants her own money.'

'Yes, but ... Why is she a prude? I mean, if she wants to marry him for his dosh, she could at least drop her knickers and open her pussy.'

'I'll let you into a little secret. Deborah does drop her

knickers and open her pussy, as you so beautifully put it. But not for Rod.'

'Who for, then?'

'Deborah is still in touch with the chap from the university, the one who used to take the porn photos of her.'

'You mean . . . She's fucking him on the side? How do you know all this?'

'Father likes me to vet girlfriends and future wives. You know, check them out and make sure they're not just after money. He likes Deborah very much and he's been pushing for the marriage, but – I've done a little homework, and I've discovered a few interesting things about young Deborah.'

'Ain't you told your old man?'

'No, not yet. She comes from a wealthy family and my father is well in with her father so – I suppose I'll have to talk to him at some stage.'

'If the grabbing bitch is only after Rod's money, you'll have to say something.'

'I know, but my father does business with her father. It's a difficult situation, Sheena. I've been thinking of doing away with her without mentioning it to my father.'

'What, you mean killing her off?'

'No, no,' he returned, laughing. 'I mean, having a chat with her and telling her to leave Rod. Once she sees the photos, hopefully she'll slip away and that will be that. The last thing she'd want is her father discovering the incriminating evidence of her wanton behaviour.'

'I think you should do it, Charles. Do it now, before it's too late.'

'Yes, you're right. I'll speak to her tomorrow. So, my little beauty, what about us?'

Sheena smiled impishly. 'Us?' she said, cocking her head to one side.

'Well, I'd like to see you again.'

'OK.'

'Really? You don't mind that I'm married?'

'Most men I meet are either married or have a girlfriend. Anyway, I want to help you to get rid of Deborah.'

'Why, when you don't even know her?'

'Because I don't like gold-diggers. If Rod is anything like you, then he'll be a nice man. I'll help you to get rid of the money-grabbing bitch, if I can.'

'Thanks, but – I really don't see how you can help me.'

'I'll think of something.'

Sheena got up from the bench, stood before Charles and unbuttoned the front of her dress. The idea of helping him to get rid of Deborah appealed to her, and she decided to use her young body to discover more information about his family. Allowing her dress to fall down her long legs and crumple around her ankles, she grinned as he focussed on the bulging crotch of her tight knickers. He reached out to take hold of her shapely hips, then pulled her towards him and kissed the smooth plateau of her stomach.

'You're a beautiful little thing,' he whispered. 'I hope we'll be seeing a lot of each other.'

'I hope so too,' she replied softly as he pulled her knickers down to her knees.

He leaned forward and ran his tongue up and down her moist sex crack. 'You taste like heaven,' he murmured.

'You sound just like your . . .' Her words tailed off as she realised that she was going to have to be careful not to mention Rod.

'I sound just like my what?' he asked her.

'I was just wondering what heaven tastes like.'

'Like a teenage girl's pussy,' he replied.

He slid off the bench and knelt before her to part the fleshy lips of her young pussy and sweep his wet tongue over the sensitive tip of her erect clitoris. Sheena quivered as her juices flowed and her clitoris pulsated. She loved sex, and had always found new relationships exciting and rewarding. Sex had been her escape from reality, she reflected as Charles tongued her creamy-wet vaginal entrance. She'd used sex to escape and earn money. Now she was using sex to get her foot in the door of a very rich family.

Sure that meeting Charles in the club had been fated to happen, she wondered where their relationship would take her. She knew that she'd be nothing more than his bit of rough on the side, but that didn't bother her. She wanted information from Charles, updates on Deborah, and she decided that she might as well take his money as an added bonus. He was obviously happy to use her for sex, she thought, looking down as he lapped up her copious pussy milk. Would he also be happy to pay her?

'You're beautiful,' he murmured as he drank from her teenage vagina.

'You like a bit of rough on the side, then?' she asked him with a giggle. 'You want a dirty little whore as a plaything?'

'You're not a whore, Sheena. You're beautiful.'

'I'm a beautiful whore, then,' she returned. 'Is your wife a prude?'

'That just about sums her up.'

'And you like the idea of a dirty little teenage slut to satisfy you?'

'Definitely.'

'And if you're happy with me, you'll help me out financially?'

He looked up at her and smiled. 'Of course I will.'

'I ain't a prostitute, Charles. It's just that I'm short of dosh and ... Well, you know how fucking expensive things are these days.'

'Let's start as we mean to go on,' he said, taking a wad of notes from his pocket. 'There's fifty, will that keep you going until I see you again?'

'You're very kind, Charles. That will really help me out. Now, why don't you drop your trousers and sit on the bench and let me show you how grateful I am?'

Sheena knelt on the ground as he slipped his shoes and trousers off and sat on the bench. She parted his knees, rested her elbows on his thighs and took the shaft of his solid penis in her hand. His cock was huge, she mused happily as she kissed his heaving balls and breathed in his male scent. Licking his scrotum, she knew that she only had to please him and he'd want to see her again. All she had to do was give him more than his wife could or would give him, and she'd have him hooked. But Rod was her way into the family – he was her goal. If she could persuade him to marry her ... It was early days, she thought as Charles gasped and his solid cock twitched.

Licking his rock-hard shaft, her tongue moving dangerously close to his swollen knob, she wondered how many cocks she'd sucked during her young life. She was good at giving head, she reflected as Charles held her head and begged her to suck his cock. She'd lost count of the men who'd praised her for her oral expertise and called her a come-slut. Wondering whether Charles enjoyed fucking his wife's mouth, she finally took his purple plum to the back of her throat and sank her teeth gently into his veined shaft.

Charles let out a low moan of pleasure as she kneaded his rolling balls and almost swallowed his bulbous knob. He muttered something about deep throat, and Sheena knew that he'd part with more money the next time they met. She knew how to please men, she reflected. She knew how to use her young body, her mouth, her vagina, her tight bottom-hole. But she'd met very few men who'd satisfied her. Perhaps the brothers would give her what she wanted, she thought as she raised her head, sliding his cock out of her mouth and licking its purple crown.

'You're fantastic,' Charles praised her. 'I've never known a girl take my knob down her throat the way you did.'

'I love doing that,' Sheena breathed huskily. 'I love men fucking my mouth as if it's me cunt.'

'You're beautiful, Sheena. I've never heard a girl use that word before and . . . God, it's such a turn on.'

'Cunt?' she repeated. 'You like me to say cunt?'

'Yes, I do. To hear that word coming from a young girl is so horny. How far can you take my cock down your throat? Can you take all of it?'

'I'll show you,' she replied, grinning at him.

Again sucking his swollen knob into her hot mouth, she angled her head, aligning her neck and taking it into her throat. Easing his solid cock further into her mouth, she breathed heavily through her nose as his knob slid down her throat and her lips pressed against his pubic mound. Charles grinned as her wide eyes looked up at him, and she knew that she had a satisfied customer as she felt his knob swell deep within her throat.

Holding her head and rocking his hips, he again let out a low moan of pleasure as his swollen knob glided back and forth along her hot throat. She knew that she wouldn't even get a taste of his spunk as his body trembled and he neared his climax, but she wasn't bothered. This was for his enjoyment, she thought as his balls battered her chin. This was in return for the fifty pounds, and the information he'd given her.

His spunk finally jetting from his throbbing knob and gushing down her throat, he gasped and shuddered in his adulterous orgasm. Sheena could feel his creamy liquid sliding down her throat as he repeatedly rammed the entire length of his cock into her full mouth, and she imagined both brothers simultaneously sharing her young body, one cock shafting her tight vagina and the other spunking down her throat. His balls drained, he kept his cock deep within her mouth, his knob absorbing the heat of her throat as he recovered.

'That was the best blow-job I've ever had,' he breathed, finally sliding his cock out of her mouth. 'I suppose it was a throat-job,' he added, chuckling as he gazed into Sheena's blue eyes.

'Call it what you like,' she said. 'As long as you enjoyed it, that's all that matters.'

'You really are amazing, Sheena. As I said earlier, you're my type of girl. I'm glad I found you before Rod did. He's often in the club and ... Well, I found you first.'

'What if he sees me in the club and chats me up?' she asked, rising to her feet as he tugged his trousers on. 'That would be funny, wouldn't it?'

'I don't think you should get to know him,' he replied, frowning at her. 'If he does see you in the club and ... Keep away from him, Sheena.'

'Why?' she asked, grabbing her dress. 'Do you want to keep me all for yourself?'

'No, no, it's not that. Deborah is insanely jealous. If she finds out that ... It's just best not to tangle with Deborah.'

'If I got to know her, became friendly with her ...'

'For God's sake, don't get involved with the woman.'

'I could help you to get rid of her, Charles.'

'No, leave it to me. She's dangerous, Sheena. You leave it to me. Look, we'd better get going. I'll drop you off at your place, OK?'

'OK,' she said, slipping into her dress. 'Do you want my mobile number?'

'Yes, that would be great.'

She took a pen and paper from her bag and scribbled the number. 'There, now you can ring me when you need me.'

'You're great, Sheena. I'll ring you tomorrow. Right, let's get out of here.'

Pondering the situation as she gave Charles directions to her bedsit, Sheena reckoned it might be fun to get to know Deborah. If the woman was a slut, they'd have something in common and might even become friends. Coming up with an idea, she asked Charles the name of the photographer that Deborah was screwing on the side.

He laughed and shook his head, and she didn't think that he'd tell her.

'You're not thinking of going into the porn business, are you?' he asked her.

'You never know,' she replied. 'If the money's good and . . .'

'He's not a photographer and he's not in the porn business. The university thing with Deborah was a one-off, as far as I know.'

'If I get to know him, I might be able to find out more about Deborah. That would help you to get rid of her.'

'I don't want you involved, Sheena,' he warned as he turned into her road.

'Drop me here,' she said as he slowed down. 'You will phone me, won't you?'

'Yes, of course I will. Look, this thing about Deborah. I don't want you contacting Sam and . . .'

'Ah, so that's his name.'

'You bring out the worst in me,' he said, chuckling as she opened the car door.

'I thought I brought out the best in you, Charles. Does Sam live locally?'

'His name is Sam Brookes and, yes, he lives locally. Happy now?'

'Thanks, Charles. Ring me, OK?'

'OK, I will. Take care.'

There was still time to go to the pub, Sheena decided as Charles drove off. Hoping that Nat and Tommy were still there, she walked briskly down the road. Charles had a wife to go home to, but Sheena was free and the evening was young, and she had fifty pounds in her purse. Life was looking good, she thought happily as she reached the pub. With two rich men on the go and money in her purse, life was looking better than ever.

'Oh, it's the little rich kid,' Nat said as Sheena walked into the pub and headed for the bar. 'Been out with your future husband, then?'

'You getting married?' Tommy asked Sheena after she'd bought a drink and joined them at the table.

'Yes, I am,' Sheena replied. 'To a lovely man with lots of money.'

'Silly cow,' Nat mocked. 'He won't marry you.'

'Of course he will.'

'You had your hair done?'

'Yes, I have. By the way, do either of you know Sam Brookes?'

'Who's he?'

'I know of him,' Tommy offered. 'He's a photographer. He did some work for . . .'

'I need to contact him. Do you know where he lives?'

'No, but he did some work for Ian, who's up at the bar. Why don't you ask him?'

'Is this for your wedding photos?' Nat asked, grinning at Sheena. 'I can just imagine you in your white dress surrounded by the rich family. Don't go telling the vicar to fuck off, though. And try not to call the best man a cunt if he . . .'

'Someone mention my name?' Ian said, wandering towards the table.

'Sheena wants to contact Sam Brookes,' Tommy said. 'He did some work for you, didn't he?'

'He was going to, but I couldn't afford it. He charges a fucking fortune.'

'Sheena is getting married,' Nat said sarcastically. 'She wants wedding photos.'

'You'll need a fucking bank loan to get Sam to do the pics.'

'Her future husband is loaded.'

'Shut up, Nat,' Sheena hissed. 'Ian, do you have his phone number?'

'It's at home. I'll bring it in, OK?'

'Thanks, that would be great.'

Grinning as he walked back to the bar, Sheena reckoned that her plan was coming together well. If she could get in with Sam and find out some information about Deborah, maybe even get copies of the porn photos, she'd be well on her way to causing trouble. Once Deborah was out of the way, she could work on Rod and take the first few steps towards marrying him. Her final hurdle would be Rod's father, she mused as she went up to the bar and stood beside Ian.

'Any chance that you could get Sam's number tonight?' she asked him.

'No, it's at home,' he replied as she ordered a vodka and tonic. 'What's the rush?'

'I just need to get the photos arranged, that's all.'

'Photos?' the barman said. 'Are you talking about Sam Brookes?'

'Yes,' Sheena said. 'I need his phone number.'

'Hang on, I'll get it for you.'

Sheena turned to Ian and frowned. 'How come everyone knows Sam?' she asked him. 'I've never heard of him.'

'He used to come in here a lot. That was before your time.'

'Oh, right.'

Ian smiled and looked Sheena up and down. 'We've never really got to know each other,' he said. 'We've spoken often enough but . . . How about coming back to my place later?'

'I can't, not tonight.'

'You're not going to screw Tommy, are you?'

'I'm not going to screw anyone, Ian.'

'There you go, Sheena,' the barman said, passing a piece of paper to her.

'Wow, thanks. I'll ring him now.'

Moving to the end of the bar, away from other people, Sheena took her phone from her bag and dialled the number. She had no idea what she was going to say, and decided to play it by ear. A thousand thoughts ran through her mind as she listened to the ringing tone. She could make out that she knew Deborah or . . . Her heart racing as he answered the phone, she took a deep breath.

'Hi, my name's Christine,' she said softly. 'I – I used to be friends with Deborah and . . .'

'Deborah Gibson-Brown?' he cut in.

'Yes, that's right. I heard that you were still in touch with her.'

'Who told you that?'

'Just a friend. I'm trying to contact her and wondered whether you could help me?'

'No, sorry. I lost contact with Deborah years ago.'

'Oh, OK. It's just that she's getting married soon and . . . Oh well, never mind.'

'You know that she's getting married?'

'Yes.'

'I might be able to help you. I can't explain on the phone because . . . The situation is rather difficult. Perhaps we could meet some time?'

'Yes, right. I'm free now if . . .'

'No, I'm in a pub with some friends.'

'I'm a pub with some friends, too. Perhaps we could . . .'

'Which pub are you in?'

'The worst pub in town. I call it the scumhole, but its real name is the Green Man.'

'I'm only down the road, I'll be there in five.'

'Oh, right. That's great.'

'See you soon.'

Slipping her phone into her bag, Sheena hoped that Nat and the others wouldn't start blabbing when Ian arrived. Knocking back her drink, she decided to wait outside and told Nat that she'd be back soon. She thought how quickly things were moving as she hovered on the pavement outside the pub. Charles had revealed the photographer's name, the barman had given her his phone number . . . But what the hell was she going to say to Sam?

62

Watching a young man walking towards her, she reckoned it was Sam. He was wearing tight jeans and a T-shirt, and his brown hair was long. He looked like a hippy, she thought as he approached. Then again, she imagined that all photographers looked like hippies. What on earth did Deborah see in him? Perhaps she liked a bit of rough on the side like Rod did. Seeing as Deborah was soon to marry Rod, she was playing a dangerous game by seeing Sam behind his back. Sheena felt her stomach churn as the young man introduced himself, and she again wondered what she was going to say.

'I'm Christine,' she lied, holding her hand out.

'So, you want to contact Deborah?' he asked her, shaking her hand.

'I heard that Deborah was getting married and I'd like to get in touch with her.'

'What for?'

'Well, I – I suppose to wish her luck and . . .'

'Tell me the truth, Christine,' he cut in. 'You're crap at lying, so tell me the truth.'

'I have some photographs,' she breathed, hanging her head. 'They belong to her and I thought she might want them back.'

'What sort of photographs?'

'When she was at uni, she had some dirty pics taken.' She hesitated, wondering what to say. 'Deborah told me all about it and . . . I want to get into the business.'

He looked her up and down and grinned. 'You want to do porn pics?' he asked her. 'So why come to me?'

'I haven't come to you, Sam. I want to speak to Deborah about it.'

'Oh, right.'

'Why all this mysterious stuff? I just want to contact a friend I haven't seen for a while.'

'I have to be careful because . . . It's a long story.' He took a business card from his pocket and scribbled something on the back. 'I'm a photographer, so if you want to do porn pics, get in touch with me.'

'Oh, thanks,' she said as he passed her the card. 'But what about Deborah?'

'Her number is on the back of the card. Don't tell her that I gave it to you, OK?'

'No, no, I won't. That's brilliant, thanks a lot.'

'You look good,' he said, stepping back and again looking her up and down. 'Have you done porn stuff before?'

'No, not exactly.'

'How old are you?'

'Eighteen.'

'And you'd be OK getting fucked in front of the camera?'

'Yes, yes, of course.'

'OK, give me a ring tomorrow.'

'Yes, I will. Thanks very much.'

Imagining herself a porn star as she watched him walk away, she crossed the road and sat on a low wall. A porn star, she thought, wondering how much money she could earn. Taking her phone from her bag and dialling Deborah's number, she wondered whether the woman was at home. She also wondered what to say to her. Deciding that she couldn't go through with it, she was about to hang up when a man answered.

'Is Deborah there, please?' she asked him.

'Hang on,' came the abrupt reply.

'Er . . . Thanks.' Her heart banging hard against her chest, she bit her lip as a woman asked who was calling. 'My name's Hannah,' Sheena said. 'I'm phoning to tell you about Rod.'

'Rod? What about him?'

Images of Alison, the girl in the bedsit below hers, flashed into her mind. 'I'm pregnant,' she whispered. 'With his baby.'

'You're what?' Deborah gasped. 'Say that again.'

'I'm pregnant, with Rod's baby.'

'Don't be ridiculous. Rod wouldn't . . .'

'He was telling me that you're getting married soon. I just thought you'd better know that he will have me and the baby to support.'

'I don't believe you. I have no idea what your game is, but it won't work.'

Sheena grinned as the woman hung up. That was a start, she thought happily as she walked home. Deborah would tell Rod about the phone call and he'd deny all knowledge of Hannah and a baby and – and the seed of doubt would be sown. The next step would be to let Rod know that Deborah was once a porn slut, Sheena decided as she reached her bedsit. Driving a wedge between the couple would eventually split them up. Nothing could go wrong. Could it?

Four

Sheena was woken at eight o'clock by someone banging on her door. She leaped out of bed, grabbed her dressing gown and ran her fingers through her dishevelled blonde hair. She was a mess, she thought, catching her reflection in the dressing-table mirror. Wondering whether it was Alison from downstairs, she opened the door to find Rod pacing the hallway. He looked haggard, his expression pained. Inviting him in, she asked him what the problem was.

'Deborah is the problem,' he snapped.

'What do you mean?' she asked him, filling the kettle.

'Did you phone her last night?'

'Why would I do that? I don't even have her number so . . .'

'Some girl rang her and said that she was pregnant with my baby.'

'You haven't been a naughty boy, have you?' She giggled and kissed his cheek. 'Who have you been fucking?'

'No one, apart from you. Who the hell would have phoned her?'

'It weren't me,' Sheena sighed.

Rod laughed. 'You are lovely,' he said. 'I love the way you talk.'

'What do you mean? Anyway, I don't have her number. Besides, I'm not pregnant. What did she say? Did she go mad?'

66

'Mad? She went mental. She said that the wedding's off and . . .'

'Is that such a bad thing? You're not in love with her, are you?'

'No, but – if this gets back to my father . . .'

'The Boss?' she said, giggling again.

'How do you know we call him the Boss?'

She averted her gaze. 'Er . . . You told me the other day.'

'Did I? Anyway, she was fuming and threatening to tell my father.'

'I wouldn't worry about it,' Sheena said nonchalantly as she poured the coffee. 'It's your word against hers, isn't it? Anyway, where is this pregnant girl? Without her, Deborah's story is crap.'

'There is no pregnant girl,' he sighed. 'But I can't prove that. She believes that I've been screwing some slut on the side and . . .'

'And you have, haven't you?'

'No, I mean . . . God, what a bloody mess this is. To make matters worse, if that's possible, Charles has been dropping hints about Deborah screwing around.'

'Charles?'

'My brother. He's not actually said anything but he's been dropping subtle hints.'

'Why don't you dump her, Rod? You don't love her, your brother reckons that she's screwing around, and now some girl has phoned her . . . She's becoming a problem, so just forget about her.'

'I can't do that. The wedding is arranged and . . .'

'I thought she'd called it off?'

'That's what she said, but she didn't mean it. Look, I'm sorry to come round here and burden you with all this.'

'It's OK, that's what I'm here for. I'll always be here for you, Rod.'

'You're great, Sheena. I wish Deborah was more like you.'

'A slut, you mean?'

'No, I mean . . .'

'Why don't you come to bed with me?' she offered huskily, slipping her dressing gown off her shoulders. 'I'll make you feel better.'

'I have to get to the office,' he replied with a sigh, gazing at the small mounds of her firm breasts, the brown peaks of her erect nipples.

'You can spare a few minutes, can't you?'

'Well, I suppose so.'

Slipping beneath her quilt, Sheena felt her clitoris swell as Rod unbuttoned his shirt and dropped his trousers. His cock was rock-hard, she observed as he stripped naked and joined her in the bed. Now, all she had to do was please him and she'd be a step closer to marrying him, she thought as she dived beneath the quilt and sucked his swollen knob into her hot mouth. Once Deborah was out of the way . . . But Sheena knew that she had a long way to go yet.

'Ever had a throat-job?' she asked him.

'Well, I've heard of deep throat,' he replied, pushing the quilt aside and gazing at her long blonde hair cascading over his stomach. 'To be honest, I don't think it's possible.'

'Want me to show you how it's done?'

'You'll never get my whole cock in your mouth,' he said, chuckling.

'No? OK, watch this.'

Taking his cock deep into her mouth, she aligned her head with her neck and slid his knob down her throat. He gasped and stared wide-eyed at her, obviously unable to believe that she'd taken the entire length of his cock into her mouth as she pressed her lips hard against his pubic bone. Recalling kneeling before Charles and taking his knob down her throat, she wondered what Rod would say if he discovered that his brother had beaten him to it. She also wondered what he'd say if he found out that she was the one who had called Deborah. It didn't bear thinking about, she mused as she moved her head up and down, repeatedly taking his bulbous knob deep into the hot tube of her throat.

'God, that's incredible,' Rod groaned. 'I've never fucked a girl's throat before.' Sheena bounced her head up and down faster. She was desperate to feel his lubricious sperm sliding down her throat, but she hoped that he could also manage to pump her contracting pussy full of spunk once he'd filled her stomach. Deborah wouldn't want to do this, she reflected as Rod's knob swelled within her throat. Even if she did want to, she'd probably gag on his cock.

Rod gasped, his naked body trembling and his cock shaft swelling as his throbbing knob pumped spunk into Sheena's throat. Rocking his hips, driving his knob deep into her throat as she bounced her head up and down, he let out a low moan of pleasure. Sheena pondered her plans as she swallowed his creamy offering. Although she wanted to ring Deborah again, she didn't want to push her luck by making too many phone calls to the woman. Subtlety was the answer, she decided as Rod finally begged her to stop.

After slipping his cock out of her throat, she moved up the bed and placed her knees to either side of his head. Lowering her young body, pressing her open vaginal slit over his gasping mouth, she threw her head back and ordered him to push his tongue deep into her dripping pussy hole. Rod complied, licking deep inside her tight cunt as she rocked her hips and ground her vaginal flesh hard against his face.

Her clitoris swelling, her pussy muscles convulsing, she breathed heavily and shook her young body, her nipples tightening as she neared her orgasm. Massaging her teenage breasts, twisting and pinching her sensitive milk teats, she cried out as her orgasm exploded within the swollen bulb of her erect clitoris. Her copious juices of arousal streaming from her open vaginal duct and flooding Rod's mouth, she lowered her head and lifted her breast and sucked her nipple into her wet mouth. Biting the sensitive teat, riding the crest of her climax as Rod slurped and sucked between the swollen lips of her young pussy, she knew that she could never be faithful to one man.

There was no way she could decline the offer of a hard cock, no matter who it belonged to. Her orgasm peaking, her juices flooding Rod's face, she also knew that she could never be without Nat. She'd had some wonderful nights of lesbian passion with her friend, and there was no way she could say no to her succulent pussy. She pictured them putting on a show. Rod would probably enjoy watching two teenage lesbians licking and sucking and writhing in orgasm.

Again imagining having Rod and Charles attending to her feminine needs, she envisaged one hard cock driving deep into her tight vagina as another filled her mouth with spunk. She was a common slut, she reflected as her orgasm hit another peak and her hot milk gushed from her tight sex sheath. Her young womb contracting, her hard clitoris pumping waves of pure sexual ecstasy through her naked body, she wondered whether she'd ever set foot in Rod's family home. Once a slut, always a slut.

'That was brilliant,' Sheena panted, looking down at Rod's pussy-wet face.

'I could stay here all day,' he said lazily as she lay next to him on the bed. 'But I have work to do. I also have Deborah to appease.'

'I don't understand this at all,' Sheena said, snuggling up to Rod. 'Deborah seems to be nothing but a pain in the arse, and you don't love her, but you insist on marrying her. She'll tie you down, Rod. Once you're married, she won't let you out of her sight.'

'I know, I know,' he admitted, leaping off the bed and

grabbing his clothes. 'One thing is for sure, I'll still see you when I'm married.'

'Do you know anything about her past?'

'How do you mean?'

'Ex-boyfriends, what she did during her teens, that sort of thing.'

'She went to university, she never had any real relationships or ...' He frowned at her as he dressed, then sat on the edge of the bed. 'What are you getting at?'

'Nothing, it's just ... Nothing.'

'I know you've been digging around, finding out where she lives and ... What else have you discovered?'

'I haven't discovered nothing, Rod. It's just that you said that Charles had been dropping hints. I wondered whether you knew about her past.'

'Deborah's squeaky clean, I can be sure of that. Look, I'd better get going.'

'Will I see you this evening?'

'Er ... No, no. I'll have to spend some time with Deborah and try to sort this mess out. I'll ring you, OK?'

'OK.'

'Be a good girl for me,' he said, kissing the top of her head.

'Maybe I will,' she replied, giggling. 'Maybe I won't.'

'Sheena, are you ... I know that it's none of my business but ... Are you seeing other men?'

'I've had offers,' she confessed, smiling up at him from her pillow. 'I enjoyed the meal we had, Rod. You bought me a phone and gave me money and ...'

'Are you OK for cash?'

'Well, I bought some clothes and I had to pay the rent.'

'You need more?'

'I can probably get by.'

'I really like you, Sheena. I don't ever want to lose you, even when I'm married.'

'You won't lose me.' Smiling again, she giggled. 'Not unless another rich man comes along.'

71

'That's what worries me. I'm not trying to buy you, but I have a proposition.'

'Oh?'

'Promise me that you won't see other men, and I'll . . .' He reached into his pocket and pulled out a wad of notes. 'There's a hundred. If I give you a hundred every week, whether I've seen you or not, will you be faithful to me?'

'I can't guarantee anything, Rod,' she said, taking the cash. 'You might think that I'm a gold-digger, but I do need to survive.'

'There's another fifty,' he said. 'Will that keep other men out of your knickers?'

'Yes, I think it will. Thanks, Rod.'

'I'll ring you.'

'OK.'

Sheena sighed as he left the room and closed the door. She felt another bout of despondency coming on as she leaped out of her bed and stuffed the cash into her handbag. Screwing married men and then being left alone had become a way of life for her, but this was different. Rod wasn't just another man who paid her for sex, he was something special. Did she have a place on his map? She crossed the landing to the bathroom and took a shower.

Dressed in her red miniskirt and white blouse, she brushed her long blonde hair and left her bedsit. She had no idea where she was going as she walked aimlessly down the street. At least she wasn't stone broke, she thought as she found herself in town and wandered into a café. Ordering a cooked breakfast, she gazed out of the window at the people passing by. Where were they all going? Then again, where the hell was she going? Answering her phone as the waitress brought her coffee over to the table, she was pleased to hear Charles.

'How are you, sexy?' he asked her. 'What are you up to?'

'I'm having breakfast in a café,' she said proudly. 'Thanks for the money, Charles.'

'That's OK, you're worth every penny. I thought I'd update you on the Deborah front, seeing as you're so interested.'

'Oh?'

'She's had a phone call from some girl.'

'What about?'

'This girl reckons that she's pregnant with Rod's baby. Can you believe it?'

'Well, I – I don't know what to say. Did she tell you this?'

'No, Rod told me this morning. He left early but he's not in his office. God knows where he's gone. Anyway, I rang Deborah at her office and told her that I knew about the porn pics.'

'Fucking hell.'

'I think that's what she wanted to say, but she didn't.'

'So what did she say?'

'She called me a liar and a bastard. Then I told her that I had some of the photos and she went quiet. I described what she was doing in the photos, just to prove that I had them, and . . . I tried to talk to her about it, but she hung up.'

'At least you've started the ball rolling.'

'Yes, but I'm not sure it was a good idea.'

'Why not?'

'She's a dangerous woman, Sheena. I dread to think what she'll do now.'

'There's nothing she can do.'

'Don't you believe it. Even though I have the photos, she'll lie her way out of it somehow and I'll end up as the bad guy.'

'Charles, give me a couple of the photographs.'

'What? You must be joking.'

'No, no. I have an idea. Trust me, OK?'

'Look, I'll – I'll give you one photo, Sheena,' he agreed

73

hesitantly. 'But I don't want you to . . . I'm in my office and there are people about so I can't talk now.'

'Meet me somewhere.'

'How about this evening? I'll meet you at the club, OK?'

'Yes, I'll be there.'

'I should be able to make it by seven, but I won't be able to stay.'

'OK, no problem. Bring the photo, promise me.'

'Yes, yes, I'll bring it. I've got to go, bye.'

Placing her phone in her bag as the waitress brought her breakfast over, Sheena couldn't stop grinning. Things couldn't have worked out better, she thought as she enjoyed her food. But she was going to have to be careful. It would cause no end of trouble if she was to show the photograph to Rod. And if Deborah was a dangerous woman . . . This needed some serious planning, she decided. At least now she'd have some hard evidence of Deborah's whoredom.

Finally leaving the café, Sheena decided to ring Sam. The evening was a long way off and she needed something to do to while away the hours. She took her phone from her bag, found his business card and dialled his number. She dreaded making mistakes, and reminded herself that he knew her as Christine. She didn't dare mention Rod or Charles, she thought as she listened to the dialling tone. When he finally answered his phone, Sam seemed pleased when she said that she wanted to talk more about posing for porn photos.

'Come over now, if you like,' he said. 'My studio is above the camera shop in the high street.'

'I'm in town now,' she said. 'I just want to talk, OK?'

'That's fine. We'll have a coffee and a chat.'

'Good, I'll see you in a minute.'

Sheena found the entrance next to the camera shop and made her way up a flight of steps. Had Deborah been to the studio? she wondered as she pushed a door open and found Sam fiddling with some lights. Was she still posing for porn shots? If Rod knew what she got up to, he'd be bound to send her packing. There was no way that Rod's father would be happy if he discovered that his son was marrying a slut. Sheena was a slut but ... Sam grinned as he looked Sheena up and down, and she knew exactly what he had in mind.

'Want to do a few test shots?' he asked her.

'No, I just want to talk about it,' she replied, settling on an old sofa and looking around the scruffy studio. 'What's the money like?'

'That depends on what you do,' he said, walking to a dirty sink in the corner of the room and filling a kettle.

'If there's a man involved ... I mean, who would the man be?'

'I have a couple of friends who fuck the girls. I'll be honest, Christine. There's not a great deal of money in it. Fifty for a series of fuck pics and a hundred for a video. By the way, did you get in touch with Deborah?'

'No, I haven't phoned her yet. I'll bet she don't do porn stuff.'

'That's where you're wrong,' he said, laughing as he poured the coffee. 'I shouldn't have said that, seeing as she's getting married soon.'

'Don't worry, I won't say anything. It seems strange, though.'

'What does?'

'Well, Deborah doing porn pics. I mean, she's so refined and ...'

'That's just a front,' he cut in. 'Her old man's loaded and ... I think I've said enough.'

'Does she come here, to your studio?'

'She's been here a few times.'

'Is she your bit on the side?' Sheena ventured to ask him.

'I suppose you could say that. I was rather cagey with you yesterday because she's getting married and ... As

75

you put it, she's my bit on the side. Not knowing you, I wasn't sure about you so I didn't want to say too much. Right, let's forget about Deborah and talk about you. Do you shave your pussy?'

'No, I don't. Why do you ask?'

'That's the in thing these days. Smooth and bald and . . . Actually, I need a blonde schoolgirl look-alike for a private customer. I reckon you're just what he wants. If I could show him a couple of your pics, I think he'd pay well.'

'You want me to shave, then?'

'If you want the job, yes.'

Sheena realised that she'd not only discover information about Deborah if she posed for Sam, but she'd earn money. Shaving wasn't a problem, she mused as Sam placed a roll of film into a camera. She'd shaved in the past and hadn't had a problem with the bald look. In fact, she'd rather liked the feel of her smooth pussy lips. Her thoughts turning to Nat as she recalled her friend talking about shaving, she wondered whether Nat would like to earn some money by posing for Sam. Perhaps Sam would like a lesbian couple? Two bald-pussied schoolgirl look-alikes licking each other would go down very well, she felt sure, as Sam took a towel and a tube of cream from a shelf.

'I offer a shaving service,' he said.

'What?' Sheena frowned as he stood before her. 'What do you mean?'

'Twenty quid to shave you. Well, to use the cream.'

'Hang on, you mean that I have to pay you? Fuck off, Sam. You should pay me.'

'The cream is expensive, Christine.'

'And I'm expensive.'

He chuckled. 'Oh well, it was worth a try. OK, I won't charge you for shaving your pussy.'

'You're too kind.'

'Are you going to take your knickers off, then? The camera is ready, so . . .'

76

'OK,' she sighed, lifting her bottom clear of the sofa and sliding her knickers down her long legs. 'But I want the cash up front for the photos.'

'Minus the cost of the cream.'

'OK, OK.'

Watching as Sam knelt before her and parted her legs wide, she reclined on the sofa and allowed him to tug her short skirt up over her stomach. He was all right, she reflected as he massaged the cooling cream into her pubic fleece. She'd been wary of him at first, but he was fun to be with and she figured that they were going to get on well together. He talked about her young body as he caressed her swelling pussy lips and rubbed the cream into the fleshy mound of her pubic bone, and Sheena knew she'd end up screwing him.

'You have a very photogenic pussy,' he said, smiling at her as he wiped his hands on the towel.

'I'll bet you say that to all the girls,' she returned with a giggle, wondering what photogenic meant.

'No, no, it's true. Some girls' lips are sort of flat with no shape to them. Yours are full and puffy, just what the punters want. The cream will take a few minutes to work and then . . .'

'What are Deborah's pussy lips like?'

'Her lips are puffy, but not as nice as yours.' He moved to a filing cabinet and took out several photographs. 'That's her,' he said, passing the photos to Sheena. 'And that's my cock up her.'

Sheena gazed at the blonde woman and grinned. She was posing on the sofa, completely naked, with her slender legs wide open and a huge cock embedded deep within her pussy. Sam's face wasn't in the frame, but Deborah was smiling. The photos were all much the same, apart from one where Deborah was sucking a hard cock. The pictures were perfect, she thought, wondering whether she could get away with stealing them. Sam took the photos and slipped them back into the filing cabinet, then began to fiddle with the lighting again as Sheena thought about breaking into the studio that night.

'How come Deborah's getting married?' she asked him. 'I mean, if she's seeing you and doing this porn stuff . . .'

'Money,' he cut in. 'The guy she's marrying is loaded. We're going to set up in business together once she's got her hands on some cash. I'll have a proper studio with decent equipment instead of this junk.'

'Sounds like a good plan.'

'It's perfect. OK, wipe the cream off and we'll get started with a few upskirt shots.'

Sheena grabbed the towel, wiped the cream away and gazed at the full lips of her hairless pussy. Would Rod like her new look? she wondered. What would Charles think? Following Sam's instructions and reclining with her thighs parted just enough to reveal her hairless pussy, she cocked her head to one side and donned an impish smile. This was easy money, she thought as the camera shutter clicked. And it was nice not to have to rely solely on Rod and Charles for cash.

Sheena chatted to Sam as he took the photos, but she didn't learn any more about Deborah. At least she'd now had a good look at the woman, she thought, eyeing the filing cabinet and wondering again how easy it would be to break into the studio. Charles was supposed to be giving her a photograph, but she doubted it would show Deborah's face. Breaking into the studio was imperative, she realised as Sam asked her to open her blouse and show her tits.

'How many models do you have?' she asked him as he focussed on her ripening nipples.

'Not as many as I'd like,' he murmured. 'Ever thought about doing voiceovers?'

'What's that?'

'Making audio recordings. Introducing websites, advertising sex toys, that sort of thing. You have a good voice, Christine. It's husky and common, just right for . . .'

'Are you saying that I'm common?'

'Yes. Do you have a problem with that?'

'No, I suppose not.'

'You speak OK, grammar and that, but you sound so . . . I don't know. You sound like a common slut.'

'Oh, thanks very much.'

'I'm not putting you down, Christine. You have the voice of a common slut, and that's just what people are looking for. You could read dirty audio stories for websites. There are very few English girls doing that.'

'I suppose being a common slut isn't all bad, then,' she sighed. 'Anyway, I can't hang around here all day. Have you finished with me?'

'Yes, unless you fancy a quick fuck?'

'You couldn't afford it,' she said, giggling as she pulled her knickers on and buttoned her blouse.

'I like to try out my models, so . . .'

'Next time, maybe. OK, where's the money?'

He passed her fifty pounds and made a note of her mobile-phone number. His dark eyes lit up when Sheena mentioned that she had a girlfriend and asked him about lesbian shots. He wanted to meet the girl and take a few test shots, and Sheena knew that Nat would be up for it. At least her friend would have some money to buy the drinks for a change, she thought as she grabbed her handbag and moved to the door.

'Ring me and we'll arrange something,' Sam said. 'It's not easy to get lesbians to pose. I reckon we could both make some decent cash if it works out.'

'I'll talk to her about it,' Sheena said, looking at the door lock, still thinking about breaking in. 'OK, see you some time.'

'Cheers, Christine. Take care.'

Leaving the studio, Sheena pondered Deborah's plan to set up in business with Sam once she'd got her hands on Rod's money. She was a right little bitch, she decided as she walked home. Reaching her bedsit, she began to think about meeting Charles at the club that evening. He'd said that he wouldn't be able to stay for long, which was a shame. Sheena didn't want to have to sit at a table alone, but then again she didn't want to go to the back-street pub either. She needed some excitement, she decided as she wondered what to wear.

The afternoon dragged by, and Sheena realised what a boring existence she'd been leading. Deborah had a good job and drove a Porsche, Rod and Charles were directors of their family business, Sam was trying to make it as a photographer . . . Again vowing to change her life for the better, she sorted through her new clothes and decided on her black dress. Eyeing her reflection in the mirror as she changed her clothes, she focussed on her bald pussy lips. What would Rod and Charles think? she wondered as she dressed. What would Nat think? Her makeup impeccable, her long golden locks shining in the light, she grabbed her handbag and left her bedsit.

The club was quiet and Sheena began to wonder whether she should stay later one evening. Most people wouldn't go out until later, she realised as she sat at her usual table with a vodka and tonic. But she couldn't stay too late that evening as she was hoping to break into the studio and steal the photographs of Deborah. Sam would probably guess that she'd taken them but there'd be nothing he could do about it.

'Are you all right for a drink?' Charles asked as he approached.

'Oh, er . . . I didn't see you come in. I'll have a vodka and tonic, please.'

He said something to the barman and then joined Sheena at the table. 'I can't stay long,' he said, taking an envelope from his jacket pocket. 'Here, have a look at that.'

Sheena opened the envelope and gazed at the photo of Deborah. 'Fuck me,' she murmured. 'Look at the size of that cock in her mouth.'

'Keep your voice down,' Charles whispered as the barman brought the drinks over. 'So, what do you reckon?'

'I reckon that she's a lucky girl. How many photos are there?'

'I have half a dozen. The others are larger. I brought that one because it fitted in my pocket.'

'If Rod was to see this . . .'

'He'd have a fit. I wish I had more time, Sheena. I'd love to spend an evening with you.'

'You must keep your wife happy,' she said with a giggle. 'What are you doing this evening?'

'I think we're going out for a meal, I'm not sure. You look lovely, as always.'

'Thank you.'

'So, what are your plans for the evening?'

'I don't have any plans,' she complained, slipping the envelope into her handbag. 'I don't fancy sitting in my poxy room all evening, but I haven't got much money.'

'What have you done with the money I gave you?'

'Charles, it don't last five minutes. I have the rent and . . .'

'You'd better have a little something to keep you going,' he said, taking his wallet from his pocket. 'There's a hundred, OK?'

'Wow, thank you so much. I don't know what I'd do without you.'

'You're my special girl, Sheena. I figure that if I look after you, you'll look after me.'

'Deep throat, you mean?'

'Well, yes. The way you did that was amazing. I haven't stopped thinking about it.'

'You can do more than just think about it if you take me out one evening.'

'I'll arrange something.'

'Do you like shaved pussies?'

'God, yes I do.'

'I thought you would. I shaved my pussy for you, Charles.'

'For me?'

'Just for you. Do you want to see?'

'No, not here. Look, I really have to be going.'

'Just feel it, then.'

She parted her legs beneath the table, and grinned as he slipped his hand between her naked thighs. He moved the tight crotch of her damp knickers to one side, breathing heavily as he stroked the smooth flesh of her bald pussy lips. Sheena knew that no man could resist her as his fingers drove deep into the hot sheath of her vagina. She also knew that spending time with rich men was the way to go. Wasting her life by drinking with the likes of Nat and Tommy had been crazy.

'I must go,' Charles declared, slipping his fingers out of her creamy-wet pussy. 'God, I wish I had more time.'

'I'll always be here for you, Charles,' she offered huskily.

'You're beautiful,' he said, downing his orange juice. 'I'll ring you. OK?'

'OK.'

Sipping her drink as he left the club, Sheena felt her clitoris swell and her juices of arousal seep into her knickers. She could pull a man for sex, she thought, looking at the customers standing by the bar. Reminding herself that this wasn't the seedy pub, she returned her thoughts to breaking into Sam's studio. She opened her handbag and gazed at the photograph of Deborah. She had enough evidence of the woman's whoredom. There was no point in risking getting caught.

Looking up as someone walked into the club, she found herself gazing wide-eyed at Rod and Deborah. Her hands trembling as they went up to the bar, she thanked God that Charles had left. Rod was ordering the drinks and Deborah began chatting to someone, and Sheena wondered whether to slip away before she was noticed.

As Rod turned and looked around the club, he caught sight of Sheena and almost choked on his drink. Nodding towards the door as if indicating for her to leave, he turned and faced Deborah as she spoke to him.

This could be fun, Sheena thought, deciding to stay. Looking Deborah up and down, she imagined her in Sam's studio with his cock embedded deep within her mouth. If only Rod knew, she mused dolefully as he walked across the club to the toilets. Perhaps the time had come to show him the evidence of his future's wife's whoredom. Her phone rang, and she knew that it was him as she answered the call.

'What the hell are you doing here?' he asked her.

'I'm a member of the club,' she returned. 'I'm allowed to come here for a drink.'

'Look, Sheena . . . Go now and I'll ring you later, OK?'

'Rod, I don't want to go. I'm not going back to my poxy bedsit just because you've brought your whore here.'

'She's not a whore.'

'Isn't she?'

'What do you mean by that?'

'She's into porn photos, Rod.'

'Don't be ridiculous, she's the biggest prude going.'

'She's a slut, Rod. And I have a photograph, here in my handbag.'

'Sheena, I don't know what your game is, but I don't like it.'

'It's not a game.'

'You promised me that you wouldn't cause trouble, and now you're going on about photographs and . . .'

'Come over to my table. I'll show you a photograph of your innocent little Deborah with a fucking great cock stuck in her mouth.'

As he hung up, Sheena bit her lip. She shouldn't have mentioned the photo, she reflected as Rod walked back to the bar. Repeatedly glancing in her direction and making odd facial expressions, he seemed to be very angry. Sheena sipped her vodka slowly while Rod downed at least three drinks. He obviously wanted to talk to her, and his opportunity came when Deborah went to the ladies'.

'What are you playing at?' he hissed through gritted teeth as he approached her table. 'What's this photograph you have?'

Sheena held up the photograph. 'This,' she whispered. 'It's one of many filthy pictures of that slut.'

'Where the hell . . .' he began, staring open-mouthed at the photo. 'Where did you get that?'

'She's after your money, Rod. That's the only reason she's marrying you.'

'She's got money. Her father's loaded.'

'She wants her own money so she can set up in business with a photographer.' Sheena stuffed the photo back into her bag. 'She's using you, Rod.'

'I – I don't know what to say. Where did you get that?'

'It don't matter where.'

'We need to talk. I'll get rid of her, OK?'

'OK.'

As he dashed back to the bar, Sheena reckoned she'd done the right thing. Even if she didn't end up marrying him, at least that bitch wouldn't become his wife. Charles wanted to see the back of Deborah, and now Rod would dump her. Sheena had done the family a favour, she realised as Deborah joined Rod at the bar. No matter what happened, the family would be better off without the slut. And with her out of the way, the door would be wide open for Sheena.

After several more drinks, Rod and Deborah seemed to be arguing. Sheena bought herself another vodka and tonic and waited patiently at her table as the unhappy couple left the club. Rod would be back, she was sure of that. He'd probably dump Deborah off at her house and then come back to the club. Sheena downed several vodkas and made her plans as she waited. But after an hour, she began to wonder whether she'd been wrong. Maybe Rod wasn't going to come back. Had he told Deborah about the photograph? Had the woman lied her way out of trouble? Her phone rang. Sheena didn't get a chance to say anything as Rod ordered her to meet him outside the club. He sounded really angry, she thought as she grabbed her bag and left.

'Are you OK?' she asked him as she sat next to him in his car.

'Where did you get that photograph from?' he asked her as he drove off.

'A friend,' she replied. 'I happen to know someone who knows Deborah. We got talking and . . .'

'Who is this friend?'

'No one you know, Rod. She was at university with Deborah and . . .'

'What's all this about Deborah going into business with someone?'

'That's what my friend told me.'

'I knew you'd be trouble,' he sighed.

'Don't blame me,' Sheena returned angrily. 'Blame that slut of yours. If anything, you should be thanking me for saving you from that money-grabbing slut.'

'I'm not blaming you, Sheena. It's just that ever since you came on the scene there's been trouble. The phone call from some girl telling Deborah that she's having my baby, Charles has been dropping hints, and now you present me with that bloody photograph.'

'Did you ask Deborah about it? I could see that you were arguing.'

'We were arguing about something else.' Pulling up outside Sheena's bedsit, he sighed. 'I can't see you again,' he announced.

'Why not? What the fuck have I done wrong?'

'I can't explain, Sheena. I'm marrying Deborah and . . .'

'Rod, I – I love you,' she whimpered.

'Don't be daft. Look, the meal at the restaurant was a mistake. Getting you membership for the club was a mistake and . . .'

'So, getting to know me was a mistake? I thought we had something?'

'We had sex, Sheena. That's all it was, I told you that from the start.'

Sheena left the car, and walked the short distance to the pub. Hoping that Nat wasn't there as she pushed the door open, she ordered a large vodka and tonic and sat at a corner table. Fortunately there was no sign of Nat, and Tommy wasn't there either. This had been the worst evening of her life, she thought sadly as she sipped her drink. Her plans were in ruins. She couldn't understand why Rod had dumped her. Would he stay with Deborah even though he knew that she was a slut? All she needed now was for Charles to dump her too. But she wasn't going to allow that to happen. This was just a minor setback, she tried to convince herself. She'd get Rod, if it was the last thing she did.

Five

Woken by the phone the following morning, Sheena hoped that Rod had changed his mind and wanted to see her. By the time she'd leaped out of bed and grabbed her handbag, the phone had stopped ringing and there was no number left so she couldn't call back. After a shower, she dressed in her miniskirt and blouse and decided to go out for breakfast. Things wouldn't be easy now that she'd lost Rod's financial contributions, but she couldn't spend another minute cooped up in her small room.

Her phone rang as she was about to leave. She felt her stomach churning. 'Hello,' she said, hoping that it was Rod.

'Sheena,' Charles said. 'What are you doing today?'

'Er . . . Nothing, I suppose.'

'I should have said, what are you doing tonight?'

'I'm not doing nothing. Why?'

'Fancy a night in a hotel with me? I have business in London tomorrow morning and I'm staying in a hotel tonight, if you're interested?'

'Wow, yes, I'm very interested.'

'OK, I'll pick you up outside the library at six.'

'Yes, yes, I'll be there. Thanks, Charles.'

'No problem. By the way, there's been a huge bust-up between Rod and Deborah. God knows how, but he's discovered that she's been doing porn pics.'

'Really? So, is the wedding off?'

'Everything's off. I'll tell you more this evening.'

'OK, I'll see you later.'

Dropping her phone into her handbag and punching the air with her fist, she reckoned that there was a real chance of getting Rod back now that Deborah was out of the way. A night in a hotel with Charles would be great, she thought happily, but it was Rod that she really wanted. Sleeping with Charles was a means to an end, she decided as she pulled her tatty suitcase out from beneath the bed. If she kept in contact with Charles, then she'd get updates on Rod. As she packed her new black dress and some clean underwear, a knock sounded on the door.

'Rod?' she breathed, opening the door to find him hovering in the hallway. 'Er . . . Come in.'

'Are you going away?' he asked, eyeing the suitcase on the bed as he walked into the room.

'Well, I – I'm just sorting out some clothes. It's really nice to see you.'

'Sheena, I'm sorry about all this. You're a lovely girl and . . . Well, I just came round to say that I'm sorry.'

'Oh, I thought . . . So, you've finished with me then?'

'I have no choice. I'm marrying Deborah and that's that. I spoke to her about the photograph and she admitted that she did some porn pics when she was at university. That was years ago so . . .'

'Since when was last week years ago?'

'Last week?' he echoed, frowning at her.

'Rod, that picture was taken last week. There are dozens more like it, and worse.'

'No, no, you're wrong.'

'Sam, the photographer, took them. He's the man she was at university with and he's the man she's going into business with.'

'I don't believe you, Sheena.'

'I'm a common slut, Rod.'

'And?'

'I hang out in rough bars and I get fucked against walls in dark alleyways. I'm in with the pond life, and I know

88

what's going down. You with your money and your big house and posh friends ... You don't know what goes on. You don't know what Deborah gets up to with Sam or anyone else.'

'Where is this Sam? Where can I find him?'

'I'm not getting involved, Rod. You go off and marry your two-timing slut and learn for yourself.'

'Sheena, I need to know whether this is all true. If it is, I'll dump her.'

'The way you dumped me?'

'No, I mean ... Look, I really want to see you. If this is true, I'll dump Deborah for you.'

'Rod, I might be a common blonde slut, but I'm not totally thick. I'd be your tart on the side until another posh woman comes along who suits your father and then you'd marry her and I'd be ...'

'OK, if you don't want me ...'

'You have to prove that you want me, Rod. Prove that you want me, and I'll be yours. Marry me.'

'Marry you?' He shook his head and laughed. 'Sheena, what the hell would my family say if I took you home and announced that we were to be married? You're great fun and really horny, but ...'

'But I'm a common slut. Get out, Rod. Fuck off back to your other slut.'

'Sheena, I ...'

'There's one thing you'll discover in time, and that's that Deborah is a common slut. In fact, there are two things. The other thing you'll realise is that I'm an honest slut. I would never treat you the way she has.'

'Sheena ...'

'Get out, Rod.'

A tear rolling down her cheek as he left the room and closed the door, she recalled the meal they'd had in the restaurant. It had been a wonderful evening, and she'd hoped for many more. 'I'm not fucking good enough,' she sighed, kicking the suitcase off the bed before leaving the room. She walked down the street, heading for the park, where she sat on a bench beneath the summer sun. Her arms folded, she stared at the ground as she fumed in silence. What was it about Deborah? What did the slut have that Sheena didn't? Money and a posh voice? The woman wasn't exactly stunning, and she was a porn slut, so what was it about her that attracted Rod like a magnet?

Nat had been right. Once a slut, always a slut. Why would a rich and successful man like Rod want to marry a teenage whore like Sheena? It wasn't that he'd used her for sex; she was used to taking money from men in return for opening her legs. Stupidly, she'd thought that she meant more to Rod than a quick fuck. He hadn't led her on, she reflected. He'd said from the start that there could be no future. Was she in love? She'd never been in love before and had no idea how it felt. But judging by the way she felt now, she reckoned she was.

'All alone?' a middle-aged man asked her as he approached the bench.

'Looks like it,' she returned.

'Mind if I join you?'

'Please yourself.'

'You don't seem too happy.'

'Don't I?'

'Want to talk about it?'

'Not really,' she sighed, unfolding her arms. 'Why does life fucking stink?'

'Life is what you make it. I'm Danny, by the way.'

'And I'm Sheena. I suppose you're looking for a slut?'

'Well, I . . .'

'It's OK, you don't have to lie to me.'

'I've been wandering around town looking for a girl. They're thin on the ground these days.'

'So why did you come up to me?'

'You look the type. Sorry, I mean . . .'

'I know what you mean, so don't apologise.'

'Are you ... What I mean is, are you on the game?'

'What do you want and how much are you willing to pay?'

'I'd like to strip you naked, for a start. You see, my wife is ...'

'You don't have to explain,' Sheena cut in, leaving the bench. 'There's a nice spot in the bushes over there. I've been there many times and it's quite safe, we won't be disturbed. Fifty quid, up front.'

He passed her the cash and followed her across the park, eyeing the backs of her naked legs as she walked towards the bushes. Sheena discreetly slipped the cash into the bushes as she entered the small clearing. She was an old hand at entertaining men, and she knew from experience that there was a chance that he'd take the money back once he'd used her. Turning to face him, she wondered what he'd think of her bald sex lips. Most men preferred a hairless pussy, she reflected as he unbuttoned her blouse.

Grinning, he opened her blouse and slipped it off her shoulders, then unhooked her bra and pulled it away from the petite mounds of her firm breasts. Her nipples rising, standing proud from the darkening discs of her areolae in the relatively cool air in the shaded clearing, she felt her clitoris swell and her juices of lust flow into her tight knickers. Poor old sod, she thought as he squeezed each firm breast in turn. All he wanted was a teenage slut to bring back memories of his youth, and he had to pay for it.

She wondered what he'd been about to say about his wife as he leaned over and sucked an erect nipple into his hot mouth. Was it that she didn't understand him? That was the usual story. Assuming that the flame of passion must burn low after years of marriage, she thought of Rod. He was having to turn to a teenage slut for sex even before he was married. What the hell would it be like for him when Deborah was his wife?

Looking down at the man's balding head as he knelt before her and tugged her skirt down, she knew that there were a lot of lonely men walking the streets looking for teenage sluts. Realising that this was the only way she could ever earn decent money, she wondered whether she should forget about Rod and Charles and their family. She'd only ever dabbled in prostitution, making a few pounds here and there, and now she wondered whether to go into business properly. She could earn money from porn photos, build up a list of paying clients and possibly rent a decent flat. Would she ever have a beautiful fitted kitchen and drive a Porsche? she wondered as the man pulled her knickers down to her ankles.

'God,' he breathed, focussing on the bald lips of her teenage pussy, her sex slit tightly closed, as she stepped out of her skirt and knickers. 'You've shaved.'

'Do you like it?' she asked him as he stroked each smooth lip in turn.

'Yes, yes, I do. I often fantasise about the girl who lives over the road from me. I imagine her hairless little slit and . . .'

'What's her name?'

'Kirsty.'

'OK, I'll be Kirsty. Imagine that I'm Kirsty and you have me here in the bushes. You can do anything you want to me.'

He moved forward, trembling as he kissed the gentle rise of her smooth mons and breathed in the scent of her young body. His cock would be as hard as rock, she thought as he ran his wet tongue up and down the tight crack of her hairless pussy. Parting the fleshy pads of her outer lips, he breathed heavily as he lapped up the hot milk flowing from her open vaginal entrance. Sheena felt her young womb contract as his wet tongue swept over the solid protrusion of her sensitive clitoris, and she realised how desperately she needed an orgasm.

'You've been a naughty little girl, Kirsty,' the man

whispered. 'You've been playing with your pussy, haven't you?'

'I put my finger in it,' Sheena said, playing out his fantasy. 'I fingered my tight little cunt.'

'Did you rub your clitty?'

'I rubbed it hard and I had a big orgasm.'

'That's very naughty, Kirsty. I'm going to have to punish you.'

'What will you do to me?'

'I want you to do a little pee for me. I want to see it running down your legs and splashing on your feet.'

Grinning as she squeezed her muscles, she watched her golden liquid rain down over his face. He was an old pervert, she thought as he pressed his mouth hard against her open hole and drank from her young body. But he was paying for the pleasure, so she was happy to comply with his every perverted whim. Her golden flow finally stopping, he parted her puffy lips wide and slipped his tongue deep into her sex hole to lick the creamy walls of her tight vagina.

Fifty pounds wasn't bad for half an hour or so, Sheena mused as her copious sex juices flowed freely from her open vaginal duct. Satisfying a couple of men each day would earn her seven hundred a week, and she could easily afford to rent a decent flat with that sort of cash coming in. She hadn't wanted to become a professional prostitute, but she could think of no other way of digging herself out of the rut she was in. Although there was still a chance that Rod could give her a respectable life, she had to make contingency plans.

'Kneel down and bend over that log,' her client instructed her.

'OK,' she said, placing her handbag by the log and taking her position with her rounded buttocks jutting out.

'I'm going to give you the fucking of your life, Kirsty.' He knelt behind her and unzipped his trousers. 'I've been

93

dreaming about this,' he murmured. 'I've been dreaming about fucking your little virgin cunt until you scream.'

Sheena gazed at the ground, watching an ant scurrying through blades of grass as her client slipped his swollen knob between the hairless lips of her pussy and drove his solid shaft deep into her contracting vagina. The ant disappeared as the man grabbed Sheena's hips and began his fucking motions. The squelching sounds of sex filling the air, her mind began to wander. She'd wanted an orgasm, but her thoughts turned to spending the night with Charles in a hotel.

What if Rod phoned her while she was away? What if he wanted to meet her? Maybe it was best not to be at his beck and call and go running to meet him whenever he phoned her. Her ripe cervix repeatedly battered by the man's thrusting knob, she tightened her vaginal muscles as he began to gasp. Maybe getting away for the night would do her good, she thought as his sperm jetted from his throbbing cock and lubricated their illicit union. Crying out, faking orgasm, she knew she should at least make out that she was enjoying the crude act.

'You're a beautiful little whore,' he panted, his groin meeting her naked buttocks with loud slaps. 'Whores like you need fucking hard every day.'

'More, more,' Sheena gasped as his sperm overflowed from her tight vagina and ran in rivers of milk down her inner thighs. 'Give me more.'

'Dirty little bitch,' he murmured.

Mumbling obscenities as his swinging balls emptied, he repeatedly rammed his solid cock deep into her inflamed sex sheath. Sheena could feel her engorged inner lips rolling back and forth along his veined shaft as his knob pummelled her cervix. The sensitive tip of her erect clitoris massaged by his creamy-wet cock, she was finally nearing her climax, but he stopped pumping his deflating knob deep within her sperm-bubbling sex sheath. That was an easy fifty pounds, Sheena thought, wishing she'd reached her orgasm.

'You didn't come,' he said, sliding his flaccid penis out of her spermed vaginal sheath.

'I did,' she returned. 'It was amazing.'

'How much longer have I got?' he asked her. 'I mean, what else do I get for my money?'

'Anything you like,' she said softly. 'I can spare a little more time.'

'Do you like having your arse licked?'

'I like having anything licked,' she returned, giggling. 'Give me a good tongue bath.'

He parted the firm orbs of her naked buttocks, and licked the delicate brown tissue surrounding her tight anal hole. Sheena gasped as he stretched her buttocks wider apart and his tongue entered her hot rectum. Her young womb contracting, she knew that she could never remain faithful to one man. Even if she did marry Rod, she'd be screwing the gardener, the window cleaner and anyone else who called at the house. Wondering what she really wanted from life, she closed her eyes as her client locked his lips to her anal hole and sucked hard. Her clitoris swelling, a cocktail of sperm and vaginal milk streaming from her inflamed sex sheath, she felt a quiver run through her pelvis. This was what she wanted, she thought dreamily – money and crude sex.

His fingers parting the wet lips of her vulva and slipping deep into her contracting love duct, he massaged her hot inner flesh as he continued to suck on her anal hole. Would he fuck her again? she wondered, parting her knees wider to allow him better access to her sex holes. Was his cock hard and ready for another screw? His tongue felt very long, she thought as he licked deep inside her rectal duct.

'I love an anal tongue-fucking,' she breathed shakily. Saying nothing, he pushed his tongue further into her tight tube. Sheena grinned as she heard her phone ringing. She gazed at her handbag, wondering whether Rod was trying to contact her. She'd promised to be faithful to him, she reflected as more fingers forced their way deep into her tight vagina. But seeing as he'd dumped her, she could do what she liked. The phone finally stopped ringing, and she was pleased that she hadn't been able to answer it. That'll teach him, she thought as the man behind her forced half his fist into her greedy vaginal cavern.

'Have you ever been fisted?' he asked her.

'Many times,' she gasped as her vaginal muscles stretched to capacity.

'How many men do you have each day?'

'As many as I can. Why do you ask?'

'I have a couple of friends who might appreciate a filthy little slut like you.'

'I'll give you my phone number,' she said, her eyes rolling back as he drove two fingers deep into her hot rectal tube.

Her sex holes stretched painfully open, she reached behind her naked body and yanked her buttocks apart as far as she could. She knew what men wanted, she reflected as he managed to force his fist into her pussy. Driving more fingers into her inflamed rectum, he again murmured obscene comments as she whimpered and writhed uncontrollably. She could hear her sex juices squelching as he fisted her tight vagina. Her clitoris massaged by his twisting hand, she let out a moan of pleasure as the birth of her orgasm stirred within her contracting womb.

'I'm coming,' she moaned, her naked body shaking fiercely. 'Keep going. I'm – I'm coming.'

'I'll make you come, you dirty little slut,' he said, chuckling as he pummelled her swollen sex ducts. 'I've got my fist right up your dirty little cunt and my fingers deep in your tight arsehole, and I'm going to make you scream in orgasm.'

'Yes, yes,' she whimpered as her orgasm exploded within the pulsating nub of her erect clitoris. 'Now, now . . . I'm coming.'

Her long blonde hair veiling her flushed face, her sex milk spewing from her fisted vagina, she cried out in the grip of a massive orgasm. This was what she wanted out of life, she thought dreamily – payment for the pleasure of crude sex. She also wanted the excitement of going with different men every day, and she thought again that she could never remain faithful to Rod. Her climax finally beginning to subside, she lay quivering over the log as his fist left her vaginal cavern with a loud sucking sound and he yanked his slimed fingers out of her burning rectal duct.

Before she'd recovered from her mind-blowing orgasm, he drove the entire length of his solid cock deep into her rectum. His knob embedded within the dank heat of her bowels, her tight tube stretched to the extreme, she could feel the delicate tissue of her anus gripping the base of his huge cock. He grabbed her hips, withdrawing his massive organ slowly as she quivered and breathed heavily. Ramming into her again until his balls were pressing against the hairless lips of her vulva, he let out a low moan of pleasure.

He was certainly getting his money's worth, she thought as he began his crude anal thrusting. Wishing that she'd charged him more as her naked body rocked back and forth and her erect nipples scraped against the rough bark of the log, she reckoned she'd put the price up once he became a regular customer. She was going to have to set her prices, she decided as his lower stomach repeatedly slapped the rounded cheeks of her firm bottom.

Sheena imagined Rod and Charles sharing her young body as the man increased the pace of his shafting rhythm. One solid cock embedded deep within her rectum, the other shafting her tight vaginal sheath . . . Sheer sexual bliss, she thought dreamily. But she knew that her fantasy would never see the light of day. She was lucky to be clinging on to Charles, let alone enjoying both brothers. Her client gasped as he neared his second climax. She squeezed her muscles and gripped his cock tightly. She could feel his creamy sperm lubricating the burning walls of her rectum as he repeatedly rammed his throbbing knob deep into her bowels. His swinging balls battering her hairless pussy lips, he gripped her hips and pulled her against him to meet his hard thrusts as she gasped and squirmed.

Sheena thought that she should pay him for the immense pleasure he was bringing her as he drained his balls for the second time. He had staying power, she thought happily. If his friends were as good, she'd enjoy crude sex and earn some decent money for a change. Finally stilling his spent cock, he leaned over her trembling body, gasping for breath. It was over, Sheena realised, squeezing her muscles again to extract the last of his spunk from his cock. Would Charles be as good that night?

'That's it,' he breathed, sliding his creamed cock out of her inflamed rectal sheath. 'I can't do any more.'

'You were amazing,' she praised him, hauling her quivering body upright. 'Was I worth the money?'

'Every penny,' he replied, grinning at her. 'I'd like to see you a couple of times a week, if that's OK?'

'That's fine,' she said, grabbing her clothes and dressing. 'I'll give you my phone number before I leave.'

'What made you get into this sort of thing? You're attractive, you're young and . . .'

'Money,' she replied honestly. 'And I love sex.' She wrote down her phone number as he finished dressing, then passed him the piece of paper. 'I'm usually available,' she said, smiling at him.

'I've had quite a few sluts in my time,' he said, returning her smile. 'And you're the best.'

'I know I am,' she replied with confidence. 'Anyway, you'd better get back to your wife.'

'Yes, of course. I'll be in touch.'

Before leaving the clearing, Sheena ran her fingers though her long blonde hair and grabbed the money from the bushes. Walking across the park, she wondered what to do for the rest of the day. Charles wasn't picking her up until six, and she had several hours to kill. Deciding to go to the pub, she vowed not to get drunk. She wanted to be bright and breezy that evening, not suffering from a hangover.

Apart from one old man who was chatting to the barman, the pub was empty. Sheena ordered an orange juice and became acutely aware of her sperm-wet knickers as she sat at her usual table. Wondering where Nat was, she noticed the barman nodding in her direction as he chatted to the old man. They were probably talking about her young body, she thought, grinning as the old man turned and gazed at her. What was he thinking? Was he picturing her tight little pussy crack and her firm breasts? More than likely.

Sheena felt sorry for the old man, sure that he hadn't the pleasure of seeing a naked teenage girl for decades. It was a shame, she thought as he again turned to look at her. It was old men who appreciated young girls, but it was the younger men got their hands on them. It wasn't fair. She giggled inwardly as she sipped her orange juice. Teenage lads just wanted a grope and a fuck, whereas old men appreciated the young female form. All he had to do was slip her a twenty-pound note, and she'd not only allow him to slip his finger into her tight pussy but she'd give him a discreet wank beneath the table.

'Want to make an old man happy?' the barman asked her as he approached her table.

'The one at the bar?' she asked him. 'I noticed him looking at me.'

'I was telling him that you earn cash on the side. If you want to go and sit round the corner where you can't be seen, I'll send him over.'

'Fifty quid,' she said.

'Fuck me, Sheena. You've put your prices up, haven't you?'

'Yeah, well, you'll want your cut. I wanked off the last old man for twenty quid, and you took half of it.'

'Forget my cut this time, do it for thirty.'

'OK, send him over.'

Moving around the L-shaped bar to the secluded table, Sheena knocked back her orange juice as she waited for the old man. More easy cash, she thought happily. She was going to have to come to an arrangement with the barman, she decided. He met all the ageing perverts who wandered into his seedy pub, so he could set them up with Sheena. Trying to work out what twenty per cent of thirty pounds was, she reckoned she could do quite well.

'Hi,' the old man said as he wandered towards Sheena. He placed a drink on the table. 'The barman said that you like vodka and tonic.'

'Oh, thanks,' she said, grabbing the money as he placed it on the table. 'So, you'd like a horny teenage girl to give you a nice wank?'

'Yes, I would.' He sat beside her and grinned. 'You're very pretty.'

'Thank you. I'd better get you a little excited first, just to stiffen you up,' she whispered, unbuttoning her blouse. Lifting her bra clear of her teenage breasts, she grinned. 'Help yourself.'

Moving closer to her, he squeezed each firm breast in turn. Toying with her erect nipples with one hand, he slipped the other up her short skirt and felt the wetness of her tight knickers. He commented on how wet she was, but Sheena didn't let on that it was her previous client's spunk. Pulling the crotch of her tight knickers to one side, he massaged the fleshy swell of her hairless love lips.

'There's no hair,' he said, frowning at her.

'Is that all right?' she asked him. 'Don't you like bald pussies?'

'I love bald pussies,' he returned, his face lighting up. 'I wish I could take a look.'

Lifting her buttocks clear of the chair, she pulled her knickers down. 'There,' she said proudly, parting her slender thighs and displaying her smooth vulval flesh.

'God, you look like . . .' His words tailing off, he slipped his finger into the heat of her contracting vagina and massaged her inner flesh.

He was in his seventies, and Sheena wondered whether the male libido ever diminished. Would he be wanking when he was in his eighties? Her vaginal muscles tightening around his thrusting finger, her clitoris swelling, she breathed heavily in the grip of her rising arousal. Again commenting on her wetness, he drove a second finger into her dripping love hole.

'You must be incredibly aroused,' he murmured, before leaning over and sucking her ripe nipple into his hot mouth.

'I love being fingered,' she whispered. 'It makes me so wet and horny.'

'Your tits are so hard, and so is my cock.'

'That's what I like to hear,' she breathed, giggling as she grabbed the crotch of his trousers. 'It feels so big.'

'And you feel so tight. Do you . . . What I mean is, could we arrange to meet somewhere? I'd like to feel your tight little cunt hugging my cock.'

'I'll give you my phone number later. I know a nice little place in the park where we can fuck. How does that sound?'

'It sounds wonderful. You're so young and tight and fresh . . .'

'Why don't you get your cock out and let me deal with it?'

Sliding his fingers out of her sperm-bubbling vagina, he unzipped his trousers and hauled out his penis. Sheena wrapped her fingers around the warm shaft, amazed by the sheer size of his organ as she retracted his foreskin and exposed the purple globe of his cockhead. She'd earned eighty pounds so far, and she couldn't understand why she hadn't become a professional prostitute before. Rather than spending half the day in bed and then sitting in the pub until midnight, she could have been earning money.

'I'm going to shoot,' the old man muttered shakily as she rubbed her thumb over the silky-smooth surface of his solid knob.

'Naughty boy,' she whispered. 'I suppose you'd like to spunk in my mouth?'

'God, yes.'

'I normally charge more for this but . . .' She leaned over to suck his knob into her wet mouth and rolled her tongue around the rim.

'Yes, yes,' he gasped, clutching her head. 'It's been so long since . . . I'm going to shoot, don't stop.'

Bouncing her head up and down, repeatedly taking his huge knob to the back of her throat, she breathed in the heady scent of his organ as he gasped and trembled. Fondling her petite breasts, squeezing her mammary spheres and pinching her elongated nipples, he swivelled his hips, propelling his knob deep into her throat as his spunk jetted. Sheena repeatedly swallowed hard, drinking his fresh cream as he shook uncontrollably and gasped with pleasure.

Sinking her teeth gently into his veined shaft, she snaked her tongue over the velveteen surface of his throbbing cockhead, moaning softly through her nose as she sucked out his creamy spunk. She liked to give her clients their money's worth, she thought as his sperm-flow ended. He'd become a regular client for sure, she thought as she sucked the remnants of his orgasmic cream from his deflating knob, and she'd soon be able to rent a decent flat.

'All right?' she asked him, sitting upright and licking her sperm-glossed lips.

'Yes, yes,' he breathed, his eyes rolling back as he shuddered. 'That was amazing.'

'I do my best,' she whispered, giggling as she pulled her wet knickers up and adjusted her skirt. She wrote her phone number down and passed him the piece of paper. 'Give me a ring any time,' she said as he zipped his trousers. 'It'll cost you fifty for a fuck.'

'I'll phone you as soon as I can. Thanks, you've made an old man very happy.'

Watching as he went to the bar, Sheena brushed her dishevelled blonde hair away from her pretty face and sipped her vodka and tonic. He returned with another drink, and she thanked him before he left the pub. Although she'd vowed not to get drunk, she was feeling pleased with herself. Eighty quid, she thought happily as she took her drink to her usual table. The barman grinned at her and held his thumb up, and Sheena again contemplated coming to an arrangement with him.

'Hi,' Nat called as she breezed into the pub and went up to the bar.

'Hi,' Sheena said. 'Where have you been?'

Nat bought herself a large vodka and tonic and sat opposite Sheena. 'Into town,' she replied. 'Looking at the clothes in shop windows and wishing I had some money. What have you been up to?'

'I've just sucked off an old man for thirty quid,' Sheena replied unashamedly.

'What, in here?'

'Yes, just now. And I got fucked by an old man in the park earlier. He gave me fifty quid.'

'Dirty cow,' Nat whispered. 'I thought you were getting married?'

'I am, but I can still earn a bit on the side.'

'I suppose I should open my legs and earn some dosh. But I just don't seem to be able to find anyone willing to pay. Where did you meet the bloke who gave you fifty?'

'I was sitting in the park and he came up to me. Nat,

do you fancy earning some cash by doing lesbian porn photos?'

'With you?'

'Yes, lesbian licking and stuff.'

'It's about time I gave your wet cunt a good licking-out,' she said rather too loudly.

'Language, Nat,' the barman called out. 'This is a respectable pub, isn't it, Sheena?'

'Respectable, my arse,' Sheena returned with a chuckle.

'Tell me more about the porn photos,' Nat whispered.

'It's a photographer I know.'

'The one you were after in here the other day?'

'Yes, I went to see him. He's looking for a couple of girls to do lesbian shots. It's easy money, Nat.'

'OK, I'm up for it.'

'Right, I'll ring him later and arrange something.'

'Will you be in here this evening?'

'No, I'm going to London for the night. I'll be staying in a posh hotel,' Sheena announced proudly.

'Fuck me. Are you going with your future hubby?'

'Er . . . Yes, that's right.'

Downing her drink as Nat tried to put her off marriage, Sheena began thinking about Rod. He was good-looking, he had money and he was fun to be with and – and all he'd wanted was her young body. Prostitution was her only option, she concluded. If she wanted money and a decent flat, she was going to have to work the streets. Taking her empty glass to the bar and ordering two vodka and tonics, she heard her friend rambling on, and turned and nodded appropriately. But she wasn't listening – her mind was on Rod.

Returning to the table, she wondered about the brothers she hadn't met yet. Charles had mentioned David and Raymond, she remembered. Recalling his words, she grinned. *There's Raymond who's looking for a wife* . . . Maybe he was the one to go for, she mused, sipping her drink. But how was she going to meet him?

Her goal had been to marry Rod, but marrying Raymond would at least get her into the family.

'You're not listening to me,' Nat said, breaking Sheena's reverie.

'Sorry, I was miles away.'

'I was saying that we should rent a flat together. If we work as prossies, we could easily afford a flat.'

'Good idea,' Sheena agreed, wondering how she could meet Raymond.

'We could go halves on everything. We'll need a deposit, but that should be easy enough if we do the porn pics. How about starting in business together now?'

'There aren't any men in here,' Sheena complained.

'No, I mean go down to town and . . .'

'Tomorrow,' Sheena cut in. 'I'm going to London for the night, and I have to get ready.'

'I wish I was going with you,' Nat said despondently. 'I suppose I'll be sitting here all fucking evening.'

'Find us some punters,' Sheena said, writing her mobile number down. 'There you are. Give them my phone number, and tell them to ring when they need us.'

'Yes, good idea.' Watching Sheena finish her drink and leave the table, she frowned. 'Where are you going?' she asked.

'I've got to get ready for tonight. I have to pack a case and stuff.'

'OK, well, good luck.'

'Thanks, Nat. I'll see you tomorrow.'

Sheena left the pub and headed home with butterflies fluttering in her stomach. The hotel would be posh, she thought, vowing not to let Charles down by swearing or speaking badly. Rod wouldn't bother to phone, she realised as she reached her bedsit. He'd be arguing with Deborah and wishing that he'd never met Sheena. Was he looking forward to his wedding day? Deciding to take a shower, Sheena again thought it best to forget about Rod and look forward to her night with Charles.

Six

Charles picked Sheena up at six and remarked on how nice she looked. She was wearing her black dress and new shoes, and she felt good. Clutching her handbag as Charles talked about the hotel, she wondered whether Rod would phone her. He was probably with Deborah, she mused as Charles said that he had some bad news.

'My brother, David, will be turning up at the hotel,' he said. 'I tried to put him off but he insisted on attending the meeting tomorrow.'

'I'll have to keep out of the way,' Sheena breathed.

'It's all right, he won't be arriving until nine o'clock. We'll have time to enjoy a meal and have a few drinks in the bar. You go up to the room just before nine and I'll do my best to join you as soon as I can.'

It was a shame that Rod wasn't going to the hotel. Then again, perhaps that wouldn't have worked out too well. Deciding to sit in the bar and take a look at David rather than go up to the room, she knew that he wouldn't realise she was with Charles. She was getting closer to meeting the family, she realised as Charles chatted about his father. But her aim now was to meet Raymond.

When he finally pulled up at the hotel, Charles ushered her up the steps as a boy dressed in a burgundy uniform lugged the cases in and a man in a peaked cap parked the car. The foyer was amazing, Sheena thought, looking around at the plush furniture as Charles went over to the reception desk. There was background music playing and extremely well-dressed people milling about, and Sheena realised that she'd stepped into another world. Feeling self-conscious, she was relieved when Charles took her into the bar and bought her a drink.

'We'll take a look at the room later,' he said, pulling a chair out for her at a table.

'This place looks so expensive,' she exclaimed as she sat down.

'It is expensive,' he returned with a chuckle. 'Still, the company is paying for it. So, how's your day been?'

'Quite good,' she replied, concealing a grin as she recalled her clients. 'How's Rod getting on with his problems? You said you'd tell me about it.'

'Well, the wedding is still off. God only knows how he discovered that Deborah had been involved in porn pics. All I can think of is that he must have got a private dick on to it.'

'He must have had his suspicions, then?'

'I've been dropping hints for some time now so he knew that something had been going on. I don't know what Deborah said, but she obviously didn't have a leg to stand on. The camera doesn't lie.'

'What a mess. I hope your wife don't find out about me.'

'No chance, she's too busy with her stuck-up friends. I'm looking forward to this evening, Sheena. Are you going to do your deep-throat trick later?'

'Of course I am. That's why you brought me here, isn't it?'

'Yes . . . Well, not only for that. I like you as a person, you're good company. Are you hungry?'

'Yes, very.'

'OK, let's go through to the restaurant.'

Sheena was delighted when Charles said that she could have steak and chips. Even though she downed six glasses of red wine during the meal, she behaved herself.

Although it was a five-star hotel, the waiter didn't hover relentlessly, allowing Sheena to chat to Charles without having to choose her words too carefully. But when Charles received a call on his mobile phone, Sheena suspected the evening might be going to change dramatically.

'Damn it,' Charles swore. 'David has changed his mind. He won't be coming to the hotel.'

'That's good, isn't it?' Sheena said, frowning at him.

'It would have been, but Raymond is coming instead.'

'How does that change things?'

'Raymond is single and he likes a good time. I'll probably be stuck in the bar with him for hours. I'll do my best to escape, but . . .'

'Don't worry, we'll still have time together in the room.'

'It gets worse, I'm afraid. David was due here at nine. Raymond will be here in ten minutes. You'll have to go up to the room and . . .'

'I'll sit in the bar,' Sheena cut in. 'Raymond won't know who I am, so I'll sit in the bar.'

'Well, I suppose it will be all right. There's no time for coffee, I'm afraid. I'd better go into the bar and wait for Raymond.'

'OK, I'll find a table out of the way and sit there quietly.'

'Take this,' Charles said, passing her the key to the room. 'You go up when you're ready and I'll join you as soon as I can.'

Charles led Sheena into the bar, ordered her a vodka and tonic and suggested that she sit at a table by the window. She hadn't expected the evening to turn out like this, she thought as she settled at the table. But it might be interesting to see the two brothers together. Hoping that she wouldn't be left alone for too long, she took her phone from her handbag and placed it on the table. Would Rod call? She wondered what he was doing. Or would he be too busy trying to keep Deborah happy?

'Hi, Charles,' a good-looking young man said as he breezed into the bar. He smiled at the barman. 'Large scotch, please.'

'Why the change of plan?' Charles asked him.

'Something cropped up, but David wouldn't say what it was. Anyway, it gives me a chance to have some peace. What with the way Rod and Deborah were going at each other, I was pleased to get out of the house.' Noticing Sheena, Raymond smiled at her and whispered something to Charles.

'We're here on business,' Charles said, glancing at Sheena.

'We can still have a little fun. She's rather tasty and . . .'

'Leave it, Raymond.'

Returning Raymond's smile, Sheena thought how much he looked like Rod. He was wearing dark trousers and a white shirt with the tie loose. Maybe Raymond was her way into the family, she mused, remembering what Charles had said. *There's Raymond who's looking for a wife* . . . Smiling at her again as Charles talked about the business meeting, Raymond obviously wasn't listening. This was an awkward situation, Sheena thought, sure that Raymond would make a move towards her at some stage.

Charles looked anxious as a middle-aged man walked into the bar and spoke to him. Forcing a smile, he shook the man's hand and checked his watch. Gazing at Sheena, he mouthed something and made an odd facial expression, but she had no idea what he meant. Sheena couldn't hear what they were saying, but guessed that it had something to do with business as Charles followed the man out of the bar. Raymond wasted no time, wandering over to Sheena's table to ask her whether she'd mind if he joined her.

'Er . . . No, that's fine,' she allowed.

'I'm Raymond,' he said, sitting opposite her.

'I'm Sheena. Where have your friends gone?'

'I'm here with my brother on business. He's gone to sort out some problem or other. Are you staying here?'

'Well . . . No, no, I'm not. I'm meeting a friend here.'

'In that case, I'll leave you in peace.'

'No, no, it's all right. She won't be here for an hour or so.'

'Oh, that's good. Do you live locally?'

'No, I'm from . . . I live in Sussex.'

'Really? Whereabouts in Sussex?'

'Nutwood,' she replied, biting her lip.

'What a coincidence, that's where I live. Well, they do say that it's a small world. What do you do for a living?'

'I'm a secretary but . . . I'm between jobs at the moment.'

'I'm looking for a secretary, if you're interested?'

'Well, I . . .'

'Here's my card,' he said, opening his wallet. 'Give me a call.'

Sheena took the card and dropped it into her handbag. 'Yes, yes, I will,' she breathed, imagining working for the family business.

'Let me get you another drink.'

'Thanks, vodka and tonic.'

This was a nightmare, she thought as he went up to the bar. She wished she hadn't told him where she lived, and dreaded the thought of Charles walking into the bar and catching her with Raymond. But she'd done nothing wrong. It wasn't her fault that he'd introduced himself and joined her. Again imagining working for the family business, she grinned. Maybe the situation wasn't so bad. A job would certainly be a step further to getting her foot in the door of the family home, she thought as her phone rang.

'Hello,' she said, hoping it was Rod.

'Sheena, it's Charles. Look, I'm sorry about this. Everything's gone wrong.'

'That's OK,' she whispered, glancing across the bar at Raymond.

'Has my brother started talking to you yet? Knowing Raymond, he'll . . .'

'Yes, he has,' she cut in. 'But don't worry.'

'I do worry, Sheena. Whatever you do, don't mention me.'

'Of course I won't,' she sighed. 'I'm not totally thick, Charles. We're just chatting, so don't worry. When will you be back?'

'I'm stuck with a business colleague who's also an old friend. I hadn't arranged to meet him. He'd heard that I was coming up to London and . . . I'll try to get away as soon as I can. I'll ring again later, OK?'

'OK.'

It was just as well that she had Raymond to keep her company, she thought as he returned with the drinks. Hoping that this wouldn't end in tears, she imagined Charles questioning Raymond and then Rod discovering that she'd been screwing his brothers and . . . She could hardly tell Raymond not to say anything to Charles, she realised as he talked about the business meeting he'd had in the morning. Then again, they were only talking. It wasn't as if Raymond had taken her up to his room and stripped her naked – yet.

'We'll have to meet up when we get home,' he said, smiling at her. 'Maybe go out for a meal or something.'

'Yes, I'd like that,' she said. 'You're not married, then?'

'No, no. What about you, is there a boyfriend lurking somewhere?'

'Not at the moment. I'm between jobs and between relationships.'

'It's almost as if we were meant to meet,' he said with a chuckle. 'I'm looking for a secretary, you're between jobs and . . . It would be great if we became friends.'

'Yes, I'd like that. When do you think your brother will be back?'

'Knowing Jordan, the chap he left with, he'll keep Charles out half the night. So I'll have plenty of time to get to know you. Oh, your friend will be here later. I forgot about that.'

'She won't be here for a while,' Sheena said.

'In that case, would you like to come up to my room for a drink?'

'Yes,' Sheena said without hesitation.

She finished her drink before following Raymond to the lift, making her plans. She'd spend some time with Raymond and then go to her room and wait for Charles, she decided. Neither brother would know anything about her time with the other, so she'd get away with it. Then again, if Raymond began boasting to Charles about pulling a girl in the bar ... She'd have to cross that bridge when she came to it, she thought as Raymond led her into his room. He opened the small fridge and poured her a vodka and tonic. Not wanting to waste any time, Sheena lay on the bed and beckoned to Raymond to join her.

'This is relaxing,' she said huskily as he settled beside her. 'It's much better than sitting in the bar.'

'Am I reading you correctly?' he asked her, running his hand up her thigh.

'I think so,' she replied, grinning at him. 'After all, you did say that you wanted to get to know me.'

Closing her eyes as his fingers pressed into the swell of her tight knickers, she parted her thighs wide. Brother number three, she mused dreamily as he moved the crotch of her knickers aside and massaged the fleshy pads of her outer sex lips. At least Raymond wasn't married, she reflected happily as his finger slipped into the wet heat of her tightening vagina. He was free and single. He was also Sheena's way into the family.

'Have you shaved?' he asked, slipping his finger out of her tight vagina and pulling her knickers down.

'Yes. Is that OK with you?' she said.

112

'Very much so,' he muttered, easing her shoes and knickers off her feet.

After lifting her dress up over her stomach, he settled between her open legs and kissed the smooth flesh of her pubic mound, breathing in her female scent. Sheena let out a gasp as his wet tongue ran up and down her sex crack. Her clitoris inflating, her juices of lust seeping between the pink wings of her inner lips, she grabbed tufts of Raymond's dark hair and forced his face hard against her vulval flesh. Was this meant to be? she wondered as he parted the swollen lips of her pussy and licked the solid nub of her sensitive clitoris. She'd been looking forward to spending time with Charles but David had decided to come to the hotel. Then Raymond had turned up and Charles had gone away somewhere and . . . This was meant to be, she decided as Raymond's tongue entered her creamy-wet vaginal hole.

'You taste like . . .' he began.

'Don't say heaven,' she cut in, giggling.

'I was going to say you taste like paradise.'

'What does paradise taste like?'

'Like you, Sheena. Hot, creamy, sexy . . . I'm so glad that we met. And to think that you live in my home town . . .'

'It's meant to be,' she sighed as he sucked her erect clitoris into his hot mouth.

Sheena pulled her dress up further and managed to tug it over her head as Raymond licked the wet flesh between the succulent lips of her pussy. She slipped her bra off, spread the limbs of her naked body and arched her back as her young womb contracted. She'd never stayed in a hotel before, she realised as Raymond drove two fingers deep into her tight vaginal sheath. She'd enjoyed a nice meal, had a few drinks, and was now offering her young body to Raymond before going to bed with his brother.

Her first orgasm of the evening approaching, she threw her head back and breathed deeply as Raymond sucked and licked her swollen clitoris and massaged the inner flesh of her teenage vagina. Her naked body shaking uncontrollably, she cried out at the explosion of lust. She could feel her copious juices of arousal spilling from her inflamed vaginal sheath as her clitoris pulsated wildly beneath Raymond's sweeping tongue. Crying out in the grip of her massive orgasm, begging Raymond not to stop, she brought her knees up to her chest to allow him deeper access to her burning vaginal duct.

'My bum,' she gasped. 'Finger my bum.' He complied, thrusting a finger deep into her hot rectal duct as her orgasm peaked and rocked her young body to the core. Massaging deep inside her sex holes, he sucked hard on her pulsating clitoris and sustained her mind-blowing pleasure as she writhed and gasped on the bed. The squelching sound of her orgasmic juices resounding around the room, she wondered whether she'd ever come down from her amazing climax. Again and again, her vaginal muscles contracted and her clitoris pulsated, pumping waves of pure sexual ecstasy through her quivering body.

Gasping for breath as her pleasure finally began to recede, she lay convulsing on the bed as Raymond slipped his fingers out of her inflamed sex holes and lapped up her flowing milk. She could feel his tongue between the splayed lips of her pussy, sweeping over the pink flesh surrounding her vaginal entrance, as she began to drift down from her earth-shattering orgasm. She knew she'd be seeing a lot more of him.

'You're amazing,' she breathed shakily, trying not to use expletives. 'Raymond, that was incredible.'

'You're unbelievable, Sheena,' he said, lapping up her flowing cream. 'I'm so glad we met.'

'So am I. This is far better than – than spending the evening with my friend.'

'Will she wait for you in the bar?'

'No, she won't stay if I'm not there. I want you to – I'd like you to make love with me now.'

He leaped off the bed, slipped out of his clothes and again settled between her parted thighs. Sheena closed her eyes as she felt the bulbous globe of his firm knob slip between the wet petals of her inner lips. He was big, she thought happily as her vaginal entrance opened and her teenage sex sheath yielded to his massive shaft. Sinking his rock-hard cock deep into the heat of her trembling body, he let out a rush of breath as his knob pressed hard against the creamy mound of her ripe cervix.

'God, you're so tight,' Raymond gasped.

'And you're . . .' Remembering not to use an expletive, Sheena grinned. 'You're huge,' she said. 'You might tear me open.'

'You're obviously not a virgin. How many . . . Sorry, I shouldn't ask.'

'I've only had a couple of boyfriends,' she lied. A couple of your brothers, she thought. 'I'm really quite new to this.'

'I'll have to teach you a few things about sex.'

'Yes, I'd like that.'

Rocking his hips and finding his shafting rhythm, he looked down at his thick penis repeatedly driving deep into her contracting vaginal duct. Arching his back and lowering his head, he managed to suck one of her erect nipples into his hot mouth, adding to her incredible pleasure as she writhed on the bed beneath his naked body. His rock-hard cock stretching her sex sheath open to capacity, his swinging balls battering the firm mounds of her naked buttocks, he increased the tempo of his fucking rhythm. Sheena swivelled her hips and gasped as her sensitive clitoris met his massaging shaft, and she knew that she wasn't far from another mind-blowing climax.

She had Charles to fuck next, she mused in her wickedness. Once she'd been fucked and spunked in by one brother, she'd open her legs to the next and take his cock deep into her inflamed vagina. It was a shame that

Rod wasn't waiting in the sex queue. But she knew that Raymond was beginning to take his place. He was good company, and he was good in bed. If he took her out for meals and spent money on her . . . Trying not to think too far ahead, she wrapped her naked legs around his body and pulled him closer.

'Fuck me hard,' she said, the words falling from her pretty lips without her thinking.

'Naughty girl.' He chuckled as he grinned at her. 'I obviously bring out the worst in you.'

'You're amazing, Raymond. You're the best.'

'You're beautiful. Are you ready for my spunk yet?'

'Yes, yes. Give it to me now. Give it to me hard.'

Throwing his head back, he let out a moan of pleasure as his cock swelled and his creamy spunk jetted from his throbbing knob. Sheena reached her orgasm, her clitoris pulsating wildly as her vaginal muscles spasmed and gripped his thrusting organ. It was nice to be on a bed rather than in a car or on the ground, she thought as he again sucked on her erect nipple. Crying out as he sank his teeth gently into the sensitive protrusion of her milk teat, she tightened her grip with her legs and forced his cock harder and deeper into her convulsing vagina as his sperm flowed. This was amazing sex, she thought as her climax rocked her naked body to the core.

Her sex sheath overflowed with his sperm, the creamy liquid running down to the tight hole of her anus. She imagined his cock fucking her there, pumping spunk deep into her bowels. Recalling him saying that he'd teach her a few things about sex, she didn't think there was a single sexual act she hadn't experienced. But it was best that Raymond thought her innocent, she reflected as her orgasm began to recede and his sperm-flow ended. In his eyes, she wanted to be an innocent, naïve and refined young lady.

'That was fantastic,' he gasped, his naked body collapsing on top of her as he rested with his deflating cock deep

116

within her sperm-bubbling vagina. 'You really are beautiful, Sheena.'

'You took me to heaven,' she whispered as she recovered from her amazing come. 'That was wonderful, thank you.'

'We're good together,' he said, his cock sliding out of her burning vaginal duct as he lay beside her on the bed. 'I hope that we meet again. I mean, I hope that our relationship lasts.'

'So do I,' she breathed softly. 'I think we're going to be together for a long time.'

'To think that we live in the same town is amazing. I've lived there all my life and . . .'

Sheena's thoughts wandered as he talked about his younger years. She had to keep this secret from Charles, she mused. If Raymond started boasting about screwing a girl he'd picked up in the hotel bar and Charles said that he'd also been screwing her, she'd lose both brothers. But she didn't know what to say to Raymond. She couldn't ask him not to tell his brother about her. Of course, the day would come when all three brothers discovered what she'd been up to.

'Raymond,' she began. 'About your brother.'

'What about him?'

'Will you tell him about us? I mean . . .'

'No, no, I won't. He doesn't like it if I have fun when we're on a business trip. He doesn't believe in mixing business with pleasure.'

'Really?' she said, trying not to laugh.

'To be honest, I think he's jealous. You see, he's married and I'm free and single. I'm not saying that I have loads of girlfriends, but I think he's jealous of my freedom. I'm also the youngest of the four brothers, and he thinks that he has to keep an eye on me to look after me.'

'I'm not too young for you, am I? I mean, I'm only eighteen.'

117

'You're perfect for me, Sheena. I'm so pleased that we met.'

'I'll give you my mobile number,' she said, leaving the bed and grabbing her handbag. She jotted the number down and passed him the slip of paper. 'I'd better get going,' she sighed. 'It's a long way home, as you know.'

'Why don't you stay here for the night?'

'No, no, I can't. I have a busy day tomorrow.' Dressing, she wondered whether Charles was looking for her. 'Ring me tomorrow, Raymond. We'll arrange to meet and . . .'

'Yes, I will,' he cut in eagerly. 'How are you getting back?'

'I came up by train, and I have a return ticket. I'd better go now.'

He left the bed and stood before her. 'You're beautiful,' he said softly. 'I'll see you tomorrow, OK?'

'OK.'

Leaving the room, she took the key from her handbag and checked the room number. This was very risky, she mused, hoping that she wouldn't bump into Charles as she crept along the corridor. Finding the other room, she took a deep breath before slipping inside and closing the door behind her. Thanking God that Charles wasn't there, she opened the fridge and poured herself a much-needed large vodka and tonic. So far so good, she thought, wondering how long Charles would be as she knocked back her drink.

Her knickers sticky with Raymond's sperm, she slipped out of her clothes and stepped into the shower. She wasn't used to such luxury, she thought happily as she washed her long blonde hair. The bathroom was amazing and the shower had gold taps and . . . She'd soon be out of her seedy bedsit, she told herself as she pressed the shower nozzle between the hairless lips of her vulva. The hot water played on her erect clitoris, flooding her tight vaginal cavern. She let out a rush of breath. She'd have a bathroom like this one day, she vowed as her young body trembled and her arousal soared.

After drying her slender body, she poured herself another vodka and tonic and slipped beneath the quilt, making herself comfortable in the huge bed. This was so far removed from her bedsit, she reflected again as she sipped her drink. But she knew that, even though she was now well in with Raymond, she wasn't really any closer to stepping into the family home. She'd tried to behave properly in the restaurant and the bar, but her voice had let her down. It was a little husky and rough around the edges, she recalled Charles saying. But she couldn't change that.

She looked up as the door opened.

'Sorry I've been so long.' Charles breezed into the room. 'Have you been OK on your own?'

'I had a few drinks in the bar and then I came up here and had a shower,' she replied happily.

'My brother didn't annoy you for too long, then?'

'He didn't annoy me at all. I like him, he's a nice man.'

'He'll pull your knickers down as quick as . . .'

'Charles, he did not pull my knickers down,' she cut in, giggling.

'He didn't even try to chat you up?'

'Well, a little bit. Anyway, I've waited long enough so come to bed.'

'I'll be right with you,' he said, grinning as he went into the bathroom.

Toying with the smooth lips of her pussy, running her fingertips up and down her sex crack, Sheena realised how wet she was. Two brothers in one evening, she thought proudly, wishing that Rod was next in the queue. Again thinking that Raymond was her best bet as Charles slipped into the bed beside her, she closed her eyes and parted her legs wide. Charles stroked the hairless lips of her pussy and sucked one of her ripe nipples into his hot mouth, and Sheena imagined that she was with Rod.

119

What was he doing? she wondered. Was he with Deborah?

Sighing as Charles ducked beneath the quilt and licked the smooth lips of her vulva, she felt her juices of arousal seeping from her tight vaginal hole. Parting her outer lips and licking the wet flesh within her teenage valley of desire, he thrust a finger deep into her contracting pussy and massaged the creamy-wet walls of her hot vagina. Two brothers in one night, she thought again, wishing she could have had three brothers in one night.

'You're so wet,' Charles breathed. 'I can't believe that you shaved your pussy just for me.'

'It's true,' she lied. 'I shaved just for you.'

'What about other men? I mean, are you seeing anyone else?'

'I'm only seeing you, Charles. The way you licked me by the river was . . . I haven't stopped thinking about it.'

'And I haven't stopped thinking about you taking my cock down your throat. That was amazing, Sheena.'

'You haven't fucked me yet, Charles. You fucked my throat, but it's my tight cunt that needs your lovely cock.'

'When did you last have a cock up you?'

'God, I can't remember. It was months ago.'

'I'll give you a good licking, and then I'll fuck you senseless.'

'Mmm, I like the sound of that.'

Breathing heavily as he stretched her fleshy pussy lips wide apart and licked the solid nub of her sensitive clitoris, Sheena pinched and pulled on the brown protrusions of her young milk teats. Her naked body glowing as her arousal soared, she clutched tufts of her lover's dark hair and ground her open cunt flesh hard against his mouth. Imagining Raymond kneeling astride her young body, his purple knob sliding in and out of her hot mouth, she began to tremble uncontrollably as the birth of her orgasm stirred deep within her contracting womb.

Lost in her arousal, begging him to finger-fuck her tight arsehole, Sheena wasn't interested in refinement or speaking properly. Charles wanted a dirty little slut, and all she had to do was forget about coming across as a decent young lady and be herself. She'd play the role of a sweet and innocent teenage girl when she was with Raymond, and a filthy little whore when she was with Charles. Raymond was looking for a wife, whereas Charles wanted nights of crude sex with a common slut.

Letting out a rush of breath as Charles pushed his finger deep into the heat of her tight rectal duct, she felt her clitoris pulsate beneath his sweeping tongue. Ordering him to push more fingers into her tight bottom-hole, she arched her back as he complied with her demand. Her eyes rolling back, her head lolling from side to side, she breathed deeply as her arsehole tightened around his thrusting fingers and her vaginal milk spilled over his hand.

'Finger both my holes hard,' she gasped in her sexual delirium. 'Finger my cunt and my arse and suck my clit until I come.'

'You're a horny little slut,' he panted through a mouthful of vaginal flesh. 'I'm going to give you the best orgasm you've ever had, and then I'm going to fuck you until you scream.'

'Yes, yes,' she murmured as her climax neared. 'Don't stop, don't . . . I'm coming.'

Her naked body shaking fiercely, her solid clitoris erupting in orgasm, she wailed loudly as she came. Charles sustained her orgasm, fingering her hot holes and sucking hard on her pulsating clitoris as she writhed on the bed in the grip of her ecstasy. All three brothers knew how to please a young slut, she thought dreamily as he forced at least four fingers deep into her spasming rectal tube. The delicate tissue of her anus stretching to capacity, her vaginal cavern swelling with arousal, she cried out as her pleasure peaked.

'Bite me,' she gasped. 'Bite my clit.'

'You're insatiable,' Charles returned, sinking his teeth into the fleshy cushions of her hairless outer lips.

'My clit . . . I want you to bite my clit.'

Following her instructions, he bit gently into the hard bulb of her pulsating clitoris as she squirmed and whimpered. Forcing her thighs apart to the extreme with his elbows, he repeatedly thrust his fingers deep into her inflamed sex holes and sucked and bit on her clitoris until her powerful orgasm began to subside. Slowing his thrusting rhythm, nibbling her deflating clitoris gently, he brought her down slowly from her sexual heaven and finally slipped his fingers out of her burning sex ducts.

'Now fuck me,' she gasped shakily. 'Fuck me senseless.'

'My pleasure,' he breathed, moving up the bed and slipping his bulbous knob between the splayed inner lips of her vulva. 'Are you ready for this?'

'Yes, yes . . . Ram your cock deep into my cunt and fuck me like you've never fucked before.'

He rammed his cock fully home, his solid organ driving deep into the fiery sheath of her young pussy. Sheena threw her head back as he lowered his mouth and bit into the sensitive nub of her erect nipple. She could hear the squelching of her vaginal milk as he fucked her, and she knew that she was about to experience another massive orgasm. Again thinking about all three brothers attending to her crude sexual needs, she wondered what the fourth brother was like. She'd had Rod, Raymond and Charles. But would she ever feel the hardness of David's cock stretching her vaginal sheath wide open?

Lost in her fantasy as she imagined the four brothers in bed with her, their thick cocks thrusting and spunking, she reached another mind-blowing climax. Charles gasped, his creamy sperm pumping deep into her contracting sex duct as his balls swung against the rounded cheeks of her firm buttocks. Wrapping her legs around his naked body and pulling him hard against her, she rocked her hips to meet his thrusts. Her ripe cervix battered by his pounding knob, her pulsating clitoris massaged by his wet shaft, she hoped that he'd have the stamina to flood her rectal duct with spunk too.

This was Sheena's night of wanton lust in a beautiful hotel room, and she was determined to make the most of it. Charles would be shattered by the morning. She giggled inwardly at the thought as he slowed his thrusting motion. His sperm-flow reduced to a dribble, he finally collapsed over her naked body and panted for breath as she squirmed beneath him. Sheena was happy with her second cock of the evening, but she hadn't finished with Charles yet. As he pulled his spent penis out of her inflamed vagina and lay beside her on the bed, she rolled over on to her stomach and jutted her naked buttocks out. Ordering him to lick her bottom-hole, she reached behind her back and parted the rounded bum cheeks.

'I want your tongue in my arse,' she said unashamedly.

'Sheena . . . You'll have to give me a minute to rest.'

'Rest?' she echoed with a giggle. 'But we've hardly started yet. Give my arse a good tonguing and your cock will harden in no time.'

'All right,' he conceded, moving behind her and gazing at her open anal hole.

'I want your tongue deep in my arse,' she ordered. 'Make it nice and wet and then you can push your cock all the way into my bum and fuck me like a dog.'

Lapping at her tight hole, he pushed his tongue into her hot rectal tube and breathed heavily through his nose as she trembled and gasped. Reaching behind her naked body again, Sheena parted her firm buttocks as far as they would go, opening her anal hole wide and allowing deeper access to the dank heat of her rectum. Charles was good, licking the walls of her anal duct as ordered, but he hadn't seemed too keen to attend to her crude needs. Was his cock stiffening? she wondered as his tongue darted in and out of her gaping anus. If he was unable to perform again, she knew that she could always go back to Raymond's room.

Whimpering in the grip of her sexual delirium, her rectal sheath rhythmically contracting as he tongued her anus, she finally instructed him to push his cock deep into her bottom-hole. He knelt behind her, pressing his swollen knob hard against her well-salivated anal ring, then pushed his hips forward and propelled his solid shaft deep into her quivering body. Uttering filthy words, ordering him to fuck her senseless, she rocked her young body back and forth to meet his penile thrusts. This was more like it, she thought happily as her clitoris swelled and her juices of desire flowed in torrents from her neglected vaginal opening. This was real sex.

'You're so hot and tight,' Charles declared. 'I've never had anal sex before.'

'What?' Sheena said with a giggle. 'You've never done a girl's arsehole?'

'No, I haven't.'

'You haven't lived, Charles. Have you ever shared a girl with another man?'

'No, never.'

'You'll have to call Raymond in here to fuck my cunt while you do my arse.'

He chuckled. 'Is there no limit to your decadence?' he asked.

'I was only joking. It's you I want, Charles. I only want you. Now, fuck me senseless.'

Clutching her slender hips, he repeatedly rammed the entire length of his hard cock deep into the inflamed sheath of her hot rectum. Sheena reached beneath her naked body and massaged the solid nub of her sensitive clitoris, adding to her immense pleasure as Charles sped up his thrusting rhythm. Her orgasm nearing, she knew that Charles was about to lubricate their illicit union with his creamy spunk as he gasped and trembled.

Her orgasm erupting within her pulsating clitoris, she let out a cry of pleasure as she felt his spunk flooding her spasming rectal sheath. His swinging balls battering her hairless pussy lips, his throbbing knob repeatedly sinking deep into the dank heat of her bowels, he rammed into her with a vengeance as she rode the crest of her powerful climax. Charles was good, she reflected as his spunk oozed from her anal eye and ran down to the gaping entrance of her contracting vagina. Her face buried in the pillow, she rocked her naked body to meet his powerful thrusts as his moans of pleasure echoed around the room. Two brothers in one night, she reflected again, recalling Raymond's hard cock shafting her tight vaginal sheath. If only she could enjoy both brothers simultaneously.

'No more,' Charles gasped, stopping his thrusts and allowing his knob to absorb the inner heat of her spunked bowels. 'That was absolutely incredible, Sheena. You're the horniest little slut I've ever known.'

'You were pretty good,' she breathed, lifting her head off the pillow as he slid his flaccid cock out of her anal duct. 'Let's get you hard again so that you can. . . .'

'God, give me time to recover,' he said, laughing as he lay beside her.

'OK, you have ten minutes,' she conceded, leaping off the bed.

Pouring herself a large vodka and tonic, she wondered whether Charles was into water sports. Her arousal rising to frightening heights, she imagined squatting over his face, her open hole pressed hard against his lips, her golden liquid filling his mouth. She walked over to the bed, knocked back her drink and sighed. Charles was sleeping deeply, his soft penis snaking over his balls as he snored. Grabbing her ringing phone from her handbag, she slipped into the bathroom to answer it.

'It's me,' Rod said. 'Where are you? Can we meet up?'

'Rod,' she whispered. 'I – I'm away at the moment.'

'Away?'

'I'm staying at a friend's house. I won't be back until tomorrow.'

'Oh, that's great. I was hoping that we could ... Oh well, never mind.'

'Hoping that we could what? I thought you'd finished with me.'

'I just thought that we could talk things over.'

'Are you saying that we're not finished?'

'I don't know what I'm saying, Sheena. I miss you, I know that much.'

'I miss you too, Rod. Are you with that slut?'

'No, no. I'm at the club. So, who's this friend you're staying with?'

'Just a girl I've known since school. We're having a few drinks and a chat.'

'Are you missing my cock?'

'You know I am, Rod.'

'Are you wet?'

'Yes, very. Look, phone me tomorrow. We'll meet up somewhere, OK?'

'OK.'

'Take care.'

'And you. Bye, Sheena.'

Switching her phone off, Sheena sighed. She'd had a feeling that Rod would phone her, but she wasn't going to be messed about. He either wanted her or he didn't. She wasn't prepared to be picked up and dropped at Rod's whim. She left the bathroom, settled in the bed beside Charles and stared at the ceiling. At least there was a glimmer of hope, she thought, pulling the quilt over her naked body before drifting into a deep sleep.

Seven

Sheena woke to find a note and some money on the bedside table. Charles had gone to the meeting with Raymond and had given her two choices. She could either wait for him, or get the train home. Biting her lip, she wasn't sure what to do. She knew that she should wait for Charles, but she was keen to contact Rod and arrange to meet him. Had he dumped Deborah at long last? she wondered as she stepped into the shower. Charles might be hours, she thought as she lathered soap into the mounds and crevices of her naked body. With three brothers on the go, she knew that she was going to have to be careful.

After a shower, she dressed hurriedly and left the hotel without having breakfast. Heading for the station, she couldn't stop thinking about Rod. He'd been the first of the brothers. Charles was all right and Raymond was fun, but she knew that Rod was the one for her. The train was packed with school kids, so she found an empty first-class compartment and made herself comfortable. Why hadn't Rod phoned? she wondered as an elderly man sat opposite her. She checked her watch as the train pulled out of the station. He'd be at his office by now and might not be able to call her until later. Hoping that she'd be home by ten, she noticed the old man gazing at her naked legs and wondered what he was thinking.

'Hi,' she said, smiling at him. 'I'm Sheena.'

'That's an unusual name,' he replied. 'A very nice name, though. I'm Harry.'

'So, Harry, where are you off to?'

'I'm going home. I've been visiting my daughter in London, and now I'm going home.'

'I've been visiting a friend in London,' she said, parting her thighs and displaying the triangular patch of her white cotton knickers to give him a treat. 'And now I'm going home.'

'You're a very attractive girl, if you don't mind my saying so?'

'Thank you, that's very nice of you.'

'If I was forty years younger . . .' he began, chuckling as he gazed at her knickers.

'What would you do?' she asked him, deciding to have a little fun during the journey.

'I'd be chatting you up, asking you to come to a dance or something. Those were the days.'

'Chat me up now,' she said, patting the seat beside her. 'Pretend that you are forty years younger, and chat me up.'

'Well,' he breathed, getting up and sitting next to her. 'I'm out of practice, but I'll try.'

'Put your arm around me,' she invited. 'That's what boys did to girls in the back row of the cinema, isn't it?'

'Well, yes, yes, it is,' he said, placing his arm around her. 'This takes me back a few decades.'

'What happens next?'

'I used to . . . It's rather embarrassing.'

'Just pretend that you're my age and do it.'

His hand travelled down over her shoulder, and he tentatively squeezed the firm mound of her breast. She smiled at him, signalling that she was happy with his intimate touch as his fingers massaged the ripe protrusion of her elongated nipple. She thought that he'd feel embarrassed and move away after a while, but he slipped his free hand between her naked thighs and pressed his

128

fingertips into the warm swell of her knickers. Saying nothing, she parted her thighs and allowed him to pull the crotch of her tight knickers to one side. Three brothers and now an old man, she thought, wondering where her decadence would take her as he slipped a finger deep into the wet heat of her contracting vagina. She knew that she could never be faithful to one man, but that wasn't going to stop her from marrying Rod.

'It's been so long,' the old man whispered in her ear as he massaged the wet inner flesh of her tight vagina. 'You're beautiful, Sheena.'

'I'm a slut,' she said, turning her head and smiling at him.

'No you're not.'

'It don't matter what I am, just enjoy yourself.'

Slipping his finger out of her tight sex hole, he tugged her knickers down. She helped him, slipping the wet garment off and sitting with her legs parted wide as he slid off the seat and dropped to his knees. He came closer to lift her short skirt up and lick the wet crack of her young pussy. Moaning softly through his nose as he lapped up her flowing sex milk, he parted the fleshy lips of her vulva and exposed the hard bulb of her sensitive clitoris.

Sheena watched as he pressed his lips to her open vaginal hole and drank the hot milk. He hadn't expected this, she thought happily as her clitoris swelled still further and her juices of arousal flowed freely. Would he slide his hard cock deep into her tight cunt and fuck her? she wondered as he moved up her gaping sex valley and licked the pink tip of her swollen clitoris. The train rocking her young body, she closed her eyes as the old man licked and sucked her sensitive clitoris, bringing her close to orgasm.

Thrusting two fingers into her tight vagina, stretching her inner flesh, he sucked harder on her aching clitoris as her young body shook uncontrollably. Her eyes closed, she threw her head back as her orgasm erupted. Her sex milk spilling from her swollen vagina and running over the man's hand, she massaged her firm breasts though her blouse and pinched her elongated nipples. Gasping, writhing, she knew that she was a common slut as she rode the crest of her climax, the old man sustaining her mind-blowing pleasure.

'Once a slut, always a slut,' she whispered in her sexual delirium.

'You're heaven-sent,' he said, lapping at her pulsating clitoris.

'I'm the Devil's daughter,' she managed to gasp as the peak of her orgasm passed.

Finally drifting down from her sexual heaven, she gazed at the man as he slipped his fingers out of her spasming vaginal sheath and lapped up her orgasmic milk. That was a good start to the day, she thought happily as he sucked and slurped between the hairless lips of her vulva. Wondering what else the day had in store for her, she grinned as he looked up at her with expectation in his glazed eyes.

'It's been a long time since . . .' he began. 'Would you allow me to – I mean . . .'

'What do you want to do?' she cut in. 'Tell me.'

'I want to fuck you,' he breathed.

'So what are you waiting for?'

His face beaming, he unzipped his trousers and pulled out his swollen penis, then took hold of the shaft and pressed his purple knob between the splayed inner lips of her vagina. Sheena moved forward on the seat, gasping as he pushed his hips towards her and drove the entire length of his rock-hard cock deep into her drenched vagina. His face still beaming, his eyes wide, he withdrew slowly and then rammed into her again as the train rocked and lurched. Sheena watched her inner lips rolling back and forth along his veined shaft as he found his thrusting rhythm. She knew she'd made an old man very happy, as he slipped his hands beneath her blouse and toyed with the brown peaks of her erect nipples.

He reached his orgasm quickly, pumping his spunk deep into her spasming vagina and draining his swinging balls after only a few thrusts. He'd never forget this train journey, she thought as she listened to the squelching sounds of crude sex. He probably wouldn't tell his friends as they'd never believe that he'd fucked a teenage girl on the train. He'd think of her when he wanked. He'd never forget her tight little pussy and her firm tits.

'God,' he breathed as his cock slipped out of her sperm-laden vagina. 'You really are a sweet little thing.'

'I assume that you liked it?' she said with a giggle.

'It was amazing, Sheena. Thank you, thank you so much.'

'Thank *you*,' she replied huskily. 'You were great.'

He clambered to his feet and zipped his trousers then sat next to her. 'May I see you again?' he asked her. 'We could arrange to meet or . . .'

'I can't,' she sighed. 'Think of this as a dream.'

'Ships passing in the night?'

'Yes, something like that.'

'I'll never forget the dream. I'll never forget you, Sheena.'

'And I won't forget you, Harry. My station is coming up so . . . Goodbye, Harry.'

'Goodbye, and thanks again.'

Grabbing her wet knickers and stuffing them into her handbag, she flashed him a smile then left the compartment. As the train pulled into the station, she wished that she had arranged to meet him. But, she reminded herself as she stepped on to the platform, she had more than enough men on the go. She saw Harry at the window as the train pulled out of the station. He was waving and grinning, and she knew that she'd made him very happy.

Walking briskly home, she wondered again why Rod hadn't phoned her. Would Raymond call? she mused as she reached her bedsit. Despondency set in as she looked around her poky room, and she began to wonder whether she'd ever move out. After a wonderful night in a plush hotel, she'd come back to the real world with a bump. More determined than ever to get out of her bedsit, she clutched her phone and willed it to ring. By the early afternoon, she was feeling hungry and depressed. But her face beamed when the phone rang.

'It's me,' one of the brothers said.

'Hi,' Sheena replied, unsure who it was. 'I'm pleased you called.'

'Are you at home?'

'Yes.'

'So, are we going to meet up today?'

'I'd love to.'

'Is there someone there with you? You don't seem very chatty.'

'Sorry, it was a friend. She's just left.'

'I really want to get to know you, Sheena. After last night ... Need I say more?'

Sure that it was Raymond, she smiled. 'Let's meet, then,' she trilled. 'I'm free now, if you are?'

'I'm at the office and I can't get away until five. That meeting this morning was as boring as hell. Did you get home all right last night?'

'Yes, it didn't take long. Raymond, I – I want to get to know you, too. We were good together, weren't we?'

'Very good,' he said, chuckling. 'I know that it's early days but ... I haven't stopped thinking about you.'

'Meet me after work.'

'Where?'

'The Castle Club.'

'Are you a member?'

'Of course.'

'OK, I'll meet you there at six.'

'Great, I'll look forward to it.'

'And me, Sheena. Bye for now.'

Dropping her phone into her handbag, Sheena punched the air with her fist. She realised that Rod or Charles might go to the club and see her with Raymond, but she didn't care. Charles only wanted sex, a rough teenage slut on the side, and Rod didn't know what he wanted. But Sheena knew exactly what her goal was – to get her foot firmly in the door of the family home.

Wearing her black dress, she felt a pang of excitement as she left early and headed for the club. Passing the back-street pub, she gazed through the window and saw Nat sitting alone at her usual table. Sheena checked her watch. She had an hour to spare, and decided to update her friend on her latest exploits before meeting Raymond. She walked to the bar, bought a vodka and tonic and joined Nat.

'Hi, stranger,' the girl said. 'How did it go last night?'

'The hotel was amazing,' Sheena began. 'The meal was brilliant and then I . . .'

'Got fucked all night?' Nat cut in with a giggle.

'I got fucked senseless all night. I'm going to the Castle Club at six.'

'I wondered why you were dressed up. So, when is the wedding?'

'I don't know. That's what we're going to talk about this evening,' Sheena lied.

'Will I get an invite to the piss-up?'

'Of course you will, Nat. What did you do last night?'

'I've been finding punters for our new business. I've given your phone number to three men so far.'

'Oh, right. I'd forgotten about that.'

'Fuck me, Sheena, you are hopeless. You could get a call at any time so don't fuck up.'

'No, no, I won't. It's just that I've been so busy. What with London and Rod, I've not even had time to think.'

'You are serious about going into business, aren't you? I don't want you backing out when you get married.'

'I won't back out, Nat, I promise you.'

'What about the lesbian porn pics? When are we doing that?'

'I'd forgotten about that, too. I'll see the photographer, OK?'

'It's about time we had a good licking session, Sheena. We haven't had sex for ages.'

'I know, and I'm sorry. As I said, I've been so busy and . . .' Her words tailed off as her phone rang. Sheena left the table and walked over to a quiet corner. 'Hello,' she said, pressing her phone to her ear.

'Sheena, it's Rod.'

'Oh, er . . . Hi, how are you?'

'Sorry I've not called before. Yes, I'm fine. I'm missing you, though. Are you free this evening?'

'No, sorry.'

'Oh. That's a shame. I have a few hours without Deborah and I thought that we could . . . Never mind.'

'I could see you later this evening.'

'What time?'

'Well – about ten o'clock?'

'OK, where?'

'At my place, if that's all right?'

'I'll be there at ten, Sheena. We need to talk.'

'OK, I'll see you later, Rod.'

Slipping her phone into her handbag, Sheena felt a wave of confusion crash over her. Why was Rod keeping her hanging on? she wondered as she went back to the table. There was no way he was going to dump Deborah, so the only reason he wanted to keep Sheena around was for sex. She had to decide whether to go solely for Raymond, or use her young body to earn money from Charles and Rod. If she wasn't careful, she'd lose all three brothers, she reflected anxiously.

'Are you OK?' Nat asked her. 'You look worried.'

'No, no, I'm fine. That was Rod, he's looking forward to this evening.'

'It must be nice to have a man with money,' Nat sighed. 'Still, we'll both be in the money when our business gets going. By the way, I must tell you about . . .'

As Nat rambled on, Sheena again mulled over her predicament. She could never be faithful to one man but, if she was to choose Raymond, he must never discover the truth about her wanton whoredom with his brothers. If she went to the family home with Raymond, his brothers would tell him that she was a common slut who opened her legs to any man. There'd be a huge row.

'You're not listening to me,' Nat complained, rising to her feet and tapping Sheena's arm.

'Sorry, I was miles away.'

'Come on, we're going round the corner where we can't be seen.'

'Why?' Sheena asked her, grabbing her drink and leaving the table.

'Sit next to me here,' the girl replied, having found a new table out of sight of the bar. 'No one can see us here.'

'Why do we have to move, Nat?'

'Because I can see that you're stressed out and you need relaxing.'

Sheena grinned as her friend slipped her hand between Sheena's naked thighs and massaged the swell of her tight knickers. She was incredibly stressed, she realised as Nat's fingers pulled the moist crotch of her knickers aside and caressed the smooth lips of her hairless pussy. What with three brothers on the go, her life had become overly complicated and she did need to relax. Reaching between Nat's thighs, she discovered that the girl wasn't wearing her knickers, and she began to stroke the smooth lips of her vulva. Slipping her finger into her friend's hot vaginal duct, she started to massage her inner flesh and commented on how wet she was.

'You always make me wet,' Nat whispered. 'The trouble is, I hardly ever see you these days. You're always off out with your new man. It's about time we had a good pussy-licking session.'

'I know,' Sheena agreeed. 'We'll have a night together, maybe tomorrow.'

'Yes, definitely. So, how big was his cock?'

'Which one?'

'I thought you were with your new man last night?'

'I was, but I've had three cocks in total. I had two last night, and one this morning.'

'Fuck me, Sheena.'

'I'd love you to fuck me with your tongue,' Sheena said, giggling. 'Now, stop talking and bring me off.'

Her young body trembling as her lesbian lover massaged the solid nub of her sensitive clitoris, Sheena reciprocated by caressing the other girl's swollen pleasure spot. Sheena had missed having sex with Nat, and she vowed to spend a night with her friend. They knew how to pleasure each other, she reflected, recalling their nights of lesbian passion. Many an evening they'd gone back to Sheena's bedsit after the pub had closed and they'd fingered and licked and sucked between each other's legs until they'd fallen asleep with exhaustion. Those had been good times, she thought as her clitoris pulsated beneath Nat's massaging fingertips.

'I'm coming,' Sheena whispered, her long blonde hair veiling her flushed face as she hung her head. 'God, I'm coming.'

'And me,' Nat added, her teenage body trembling. 'Yes, yes, I'm there.'

The girls writhed and stifled their gasps of lesbian pleasure as their orgasms rocked their young bodies. Their fingers massaging between each other's hairless outer lips, they faced each other and locked their pretty mouths in a passionate kiss as they breathed heavily through their noses. Sheena had missed lesbian sex more than she'd realised as her clitoris pulsated and her hot juices of lesbian lust spilled from her contracting vaginal sheath.

136

'I want to lick your cunt,' Nat declared shakily.

'You can't do that here,' Sheena sighed as her pleasure began to fade.

'Come into the loo with me.'

'Nat, we can't . . .'

'I need your cunt, Sheena. Please . . .'

'All right,' Sheena conceded, leaving the table.

She followed her friend into the toilets, where she leaned against a cubicle wall and pulled her knickers down to her knees. Closing her eyes as her friend knelt before her and ran her tongue up and down her dripping sex crack, she let out a sigh. Nat was the best pussy-licker she'd ever known, she reflected as the girl's tongue delved deep into her cream-drenched vaginal duct. Peeling her swollen sex lips wide apart to give Nat better access to her inner flesh, she threw her head back and whimpered as she neared another orgasm.

'I love your cunt,' Nat said, repeatedly sweeping her tongue over Sheena's hard clitoris. 'I want you, I want to spend the night with you.'

'We will,' Sheena replied shakily.

'When?'

'Tomorrow, Nat. Just shut up and bring me off.'

Her pleasure building, she felt her legs sag beneath her as Nat thrust three fingers deep into her vaginal hole. Her clitoris pulsated wildly, and she cried out as her orgasm erupted and rocked her young body to the core. Clutching tufts of the girl's long black hair, she tried to stifle her gasps of lesbian pleasure as her orgasm peaked. The slurping and sucking sounds of lesbian sex resounding around the small room, she hung her head and begged the girl to stop before she reached yet another mind-blowing climax.

'Don't you want to come again?' Nat asked her, slipping her wet fingers out of her friend's hot vagina. 'Let me make you come one more time.'

'No,' Sheena gasped. 'For fuck's sake, Nat. No more.'

'I could taste spunk,' the girl said, giggling as she stood up. 'You are a naughty little girl.'

'That was the man I fucked this morning. He was really old, but he was good.'

'Lick me now, Sheena. I need to . . .'

'I can't, I have to go soon.'

'Bitch.'

'Don't be like that, Nat. We'll spend the night together at my place tomorrow, OK?'

'You'd better not back out.'

'I won't, I promise.'

When they returned to the table, Sheena sat next to her friend and sipped her drink. Her knickers drenched, her hands still trembling, she wondered whether Raymond would drive her to the woods and fuck her. Maybe he planned to take her out for a meal, she mused as she finished her drink. She brushed her tousled blonde hair away from her flushed face with her fingers, then grabbed her handbag and left her chair.

'I'll see you tomorrow,' she said, smiling at Nat.

'At your place?'

'Yes, come round at six. Bring some booze with you.'

'You'd better be there, Sheena.'

'Of course I'll be there. I want your cunt as much as you want mine.'

'OK, well . . . Have a good evening.'

'See you tomorrow.'

Leaving the pub and heading for the Castle Club, Sheena checked her watch. She was a little early, but she needed some time alone to think. Three brothers, she thought as she reached the club and smiled at the doorman. Walking to the bar and ordering a vodka and tonic, she was pleased to find that none of the brothers were there. The last thing she needed was Rod or Charles walking in, she thought as she sat at a table.

Sipping her drink as she gazed at the people chatting

by the bar, she knew that trouble was inevitable. Raymond would find out about Charles and Rod would discover that she'd been screwing his brothers ... Raymond was the best bet out of the brothers. If her relationship with Raymond became serious and he took her home to meet his family, Rod and Charles would probably tell him that they'd screwed her. But she'd deny it and suggest that they were jealous. She might get away with lying, she thought hopefully.

Noticing Raymond walk into the club, she felt her stomach somersault. He headed for the bar and ordered a drink before turning and noticing her. He looked good in tight trousers and a white shirt and tie, she thought, recalling the time she'd spent with him in the hotel. He smiled at her, and she again hoped that his brothers wouldn't turn up as she nodded in reply to his offer of a drink. Her clitoris swelling as he walked over to her table, she hoped that they'd have sex later that evening. At least he didn't have a wife to worry about.

'Hi,' he said, placing the drinks on the table and sitting opposite her. 'I didn't think you'd turn up.'

'Why?' she asked, frowning at him. 'After last night, of course I'd come back for more.'

'You are a naughty girl, Sheena. You were amazing last night. I haven't stopped thinking about it.'

'Neither have I.'

'I haven't stopped thinking about you all day. I – I know that we've only just met but ...'

'But what?'

'Will you marry me?'

'Marry you?' she gasped, almost spilling her drink.

'OK, forget that I said that. I'm sorry, it's just that ...'

'Yes, I will,' she cut in, her pretty face beaming.

'You will? I can't believe this. You mean ...'

'I mean that I will marry you, Raymond.'

'God, I'm stunned. I don't know what to say.'

'Neither do I.' Sheena grinned at him.

This was amazing, she thought, her stomach fluttering as she gazed into his dark eyes. She wished Raymond had been the first brother she'd met. She could hardly wait to move out of her bedsit. Her stomach churned as she realised that she'd have to meet Raymond's family. She thought it would be best to get the marriage ceremony over with as soon as possible. The more distant the date, the more time Charles and Rod would have to change Raymond's mind.

'When?' she asked excitedly. 'Let's get married tomorrow.'

'Tomorrow?' he echoed. 'It will take time to arrange things. Besides, you haven't met my family yet. My brother, Rod, is getting married soon. We'll have to wait until after his wedding before . . .'

'Why wait?' she cut in.

'Well, because – because these things take time. We'll have a church wedding and the reception will be at the family house. We'll have a marquee in the garden and caterers and . . .'

'So, when do I meet your family?'

'Now, if you want to.'

'Now?' she asked, her stomach churning.

'I thought you were the one who was in a hurry?'

'Yes, yes, of course. Will your brothers be there?'

'Yes, they will. There's Charles and his wife, and Rod will be there with Deborah, his future wife, and my father will be there . . . We'll walk in and I'll introduce you as my future wife. That will surprise them.'

'You're right there,' she breathed anxiously. 'Your brothers will be shocked.'

'They'll be pleased for me. Finish your drink, and we'll go.'

Her hands trembling, she knocked back her drink and waited for Raymond to finish his beer. Following him out of the club, she thought about Charles and Rod. Charles couldn't say too much because he was married, and

Rod's wedding wasn't far off, so he could hardly start blabbing about screwing Sheena. When they reached Raymond's car, she sat beside him and bit her lip as he drove off. Her quest had been to get her foot in the door of the family home but, now that the time had come, she was as nervous as hell.

'This is it,' Raymond said as he turned into a long driveway and parked the car outside a huge house. 'The family home.'

'Oh, right,' Sheena said, noticing Rod's car. 'I'm very nervous.'

'You'll be fine,' he said with a chuckle. 'Just be yourself.'

'That's what worries me,' she murmured under her breath as she climbed out of the car.

Raymond opened the front door and led Sheena into a huge hallway. She glanced at the expensive furniture, but couldn't really take anything in. Her heart banging hard against her chest, she took deep breaths and tried to relax as she heard voices coming from one of the rooms. Charles would have a fit when he saw her, she thought anxiously as she followed Raymond to a large open door. And Rod would probably . . .

'Hi, everyone,' Raymond said, leading Sheena into the huge lounge. 'This is Sheena.'

Charles stared at Sheena with his mouth hanging open and Rod's face turned a deathly white. A blanket of silence smothered the room. Sheena smiled at Deborah and then turned to the other woman who she reckoned was Charles's wife. You could cut the atmosphere with a knife, she thought, gazing at an older man she presumed to be the Boss. What was wrong with everyone?

'Well,' the Boss said, walking towards Sheena with his hand outstretched. 'I'm George, the father of these boys.'

'I'm pleased to meet you,' Sheena said, shaking his hand.

'David, my fourth son, is out at the moment. However, this is Charles and his wife, Helen. Rod and his future wife, Deborah, and . . .' He chuckled. 'You obviously know Raymond. So, Sheena, welcome to our home.'

'Thank you,' Sheena said softly as Charles glared at her.

'Sheena and I plan to marry,' Raymond blurted out.

'What?' Charles gasped.

'You're marrying her?' Rod said, staring hard at Raymond.

'That's right.'

'Congratulations,' Deborah said, looking Sheena up and down.

'A word please, Raymond,' Charles muttered, walking to the door.

'Allow me to get you a drink,' Rod said, taking Sheena's arm and leading her through a door into a large dining room.

Sheena said nothing as Rod marched her across the room to a drinks cabinet and poured himself a large whisky. Pouring Sheena a vodka and tonic in turn, he looked over his shoulder to make sure they were alone. This was lecture number one coming up, Sheena thought, taking the drink and knocking it back as Rod downed his drink in one. Refilling both glasses, he shook his head in disbelief and stared hard at Sheena.

'Right,' he finally said. 'What the hell are you playing at?'

'I'm not playing at anything,' she replied.

'Sheena . . . For Christ's sake, you can't marry Raymond.'

'Why not?'

'Because – because I won't allow it. I'll have a word with him later and tell him . . .'

'I might have a word with Deborah later,' she countered.

'What? Look, if you think you can come here and cause trouble . . .'

'The last thing I want to do is cause trouble, Rod. Me and Raymond are getting married.'

'Me and Raymond,' he echoed with a snigger. 'You won't last five minutes with my family, I can tell you that for nothing.'

'You and Deborah won't last five minutes if you force me to tell her that you've been fucking me.'

'Don't keep Sheena all to yourself,' Rod's father said, chuckling as he walked across the room. 'How long have you known Raymond?' he asked Sheena. 'He's obviously been keeping you under wraps.'

'Not long,' she replied.

'How long, exactly?' Rod asked.

'Don't interrogate the girl, Rod. She must be feeling nervous enough as it is.'

'You look very young,' Rod persisted, frowning at Sheena. 'Aren't you too young to be thinking of marriage?'

'Have you no manners?' Rod's father asked. 'You don't ask a young lady her age. I apologise for my son's behaviour, Sheena.'

'That's all right. I'm eighteen.'

'Eighteen and very lovely, if you don't mind my saying so.'

'Where do you live?' Rod asked her. 'Are you local?'

'Not far,' Sheena replied.

'With your parents, presumably?'

'No, I – I have a flat.'

'Oh, that's nice. Surely you must still be at university? What are you studying?'

'For goodness sake, Rod,' George sighed. 'What is this, twenty questions?'

'If Sheena is to marry into the family, we need to know something about her.'

'I'll show you the garden.' Their heads turned to Raymond standing in the doorway and indicating for Sheena to follow him.

So far so good, Sheena thought, following Raymond through the hall to the back door. Wondering what

143

Charles had said to him, she stepped out on to a huge patio and gazed at a massive swimming pool. This was a dream home, she mused, imagining living there. But she knew that she had a long way to go before she married Raymond and moved into the family home. She also knew that Charles and Rod would do their best to warn Raymond off. One step at a time, she decided, sitting on a patio chair.

'Charles was talking to me,' Raymond said.

'Oh?'

'You already know him, don't you?'

'Know him? What do you mean?'

'He said . . . He's seen you in the club.'

'Well, I have been there a few times. But I don't think I've seen Charles there.'

'He said that you go there with different men.'

'Different men?' She frowned and cocked her head to one side. 'I took my friend and her boyfriend once. Oh, and I took a friend and her father.'

'He said that you've been with several different men.'

'I've only been a member of the club for a while. I don't think I've been there more than three or four times. Is everything all right, Raymond? You look worried.'

'It's Charles. It's as if he's trying to warn me off you, but I don't know why.'

'Maybe he's jealous,' she said, giggling.

'Maybe. Anyway, my father seems to like you.'

'He's a lovely man, and so are you.'

'Rod looked shocked when he saw you. It was as if he'd seen a ghost.'

'Telling your family that you're marrying a girl they don't even know must have been a shock.'

'Yes, yes, you're right. I'll get you another drink.'

Biting her lip as he went back into the house, Sheena knew that Charles would corner her before long. Rod might think twice about blabbing his mouth off now that she'd threatened to talk to Deborah, she reflected. Once she'd hurled the same threat at Charles, she was sure that things would calm down. She knew that George was the one she had to win over. Once she had him eating out of her hand, she'd be all right.

Sure enough, barely a minute passed before Charles appeared at the back door.

'What the hell are you doing?' he whispered through gritted teeth as he joined her on the patio. 'I want you to stop this farce with Raymond, stop it now.'

'Farce?' she breathed, looking up at him from her chair.

'You're a slut, Sheena.'

'Oh, thank you very much.'

'I know what you're up to and I'm going to put a stop to it.'

'I might have a chat to your wife later. I might tell her about the hotel, tell her what a nice time we had.'

'Don't you threaten me.'

'We can still be friends, Charles. You can still deep-throat me, if you want to.'

'You won't get anywhere by . . .' His words tailing off as she squeezed the crotch of his trousers, he frowned at her. 'What we had was good, Sheena. Why have you ruined it?'

'Nothing will change between us, Charles.'

'Of course it will. You'll be my brother's wife, you'll be living here and . . .'

'And we'll have times alone together,' she said huskily. 'Nothing will change between us. Now, I want you to tell Raymond that you're happy for both of us.'

Sheena smiled as he stormed off. She was winning the battle, she thought as she relaxed with the evening sun warming her young body. This was a lovely house, she thought, and she was determined to live here as Raymond's wife. She needed to get in with Deborah, she decided. They could go shopping together, have coffee in town and become good friends. But she was going to have to speak properly and try to conceal her true self.

'Charles is in a strange mood,' Raymond said as he appeared with the drinks. 'He's just said that he's very happy for us. He said that he must have mistaken you for another girl.'

'Yes, he must have done,' she said, smiling at him as he sat opposite her. 'Has Rod said anything to you?'

'No, but he keeps giving me funny looks. I think you were right, they were all rather shocked by my announcement.'

'I was shocked when you asked me to marry you, so I'm not surprised that they were. You should have waited a while before telling them.'

'Yes, I suppose I should have.'

'They'll calm down in time, so don't worry.'

Watching Raymond sip his drink, Sheena wondered whether Charles or Rod would have a quiet word with their father about her. The Boss was obviously the one with the influence, she mused, again thinking that she should get him eating out of her hand. She wondered what Rod was up to as he walked across the patio and ambled along the path to the far side of the swimming pool. He probably wanted to talk to her.

'This is my chance to get in with one of your brothers,' she said, leaving the table. 'You stay there and I'll go and chat to him.'

'Good idea,' Raymond replied. 'Work on them one at a time and things will turn out fine.'

She walked around the pool, smiling at Rod. 'What are you thinking?' she asked him, watching Raymond out of the corner of her eye.

'About you,' he murmured. 'I'm wondering what the hell you're playing at by . . .'

'Rod, you don't want me, you made that perfectly clear.'

'I didn't think that you'd go running to Raymond and asking him to marry you.'

'He asked me to marry him.'

146

'When did you meet him?'

'Yesterday.'

'And he's already asked you to marry him? He must be bloody mad. I was hoping that we could have got back together, Sheena. That's why I was going to phone you.'

'Yes, but you didn't phone me.'

'I was tied up with ... Well, it doesn't matter now. You've got your hands on Raymond so there's no chance for us now.'

'There never was a chance for us, Rod. You said that yourself, remember? Anyway, we can still have some fun when no one's looking.'

'You're going to marry my brother, and you still want sex with me?'

'Yes, why not?'

'Bloody hell, Sheena.'

'Why don't you show me around the garden?'

Following Rod as he walked across the huge lawn, Sheena was sure that things would turn out fine. Charles had enjoyed deep-throating her, and Rod wouldn't deny himself the pleasure of her young body. The two brothers would do well once she was Raymond's wife and she'd moved into the house. A resident teenage slut, she thought happily as she glanced over her shoulder at Raymond.

'This is a lovely garden,' she said, wandering behind some bushes to be out of sight of Raymond. 'I can hardly wait to move into the house.'

'Sheena, you can't be serious,' he sighed, joining her. 'I know that you want to get out of that bedsit and find a better life, but you can't marry someone you've only just met.'

'Why not?'

'Because – because it wouldn't be fair on Raymond.'

'What he don't know won't hurt him. Besides, was it fair on Deborah to fuck me behind her back?'

'That was different, Sheena.'

147

'Perhaps you'd better tell her that. Look, I don't want to argue with you. I like you, Rod. I want to marry Raymond and live here happily with your family.'

'Happily ever after? Yeah, right.'

Kneeling before him, she unzipped his trousers and pulled his flaccid penis out. Retracting his foreskin as he looked down at her, she took his purple plum into her hot mouth and sucked gently. He breathed heavily, clutching her head and rocking his hips. His organ stiffened as she rolled her tongue over the velveteen surface of his swelling knob. This was the way to a man's heart, she mused as she savoured the salty taste of his solid cock. He'd said that Deborah wouldn't dream of sucking his cock, so why not have a more than willing teenage slut move into the house?

'This won't change my mind,' he warned as she hauled his full balls out of his trousers.

'I'm not trying to change your mind,' she said, licking his rock-hard shaft and kneading his rolling balls. 'I'm just giving you what Deborah won't.'

Taking his knob to the back of her throat, she wanked his solid shaft as his legs sagged and he let out a moan of satisfaction. How could he deny himself the pleasure of a teenage slut with a shaved pussy and an accommodating mouth? she thought as she sucked and licked his bulbous knob. His fresh sperm flooding her mouth, she knew that she'd won him over as he held her head tight and rocked his hips faster. His balls draining, he gasped and trembled as she sucked the remnants of his sperm from his throbbing knob. That was one satisfied brother, she reflected as she slipped his cock out of her mouth and stood before him.

'I think we'll all live happily ever after,' she said impishly as he zipped his trousers.

'I suppose you'll work on Charles next. You'll have his cock fucking your mouth and . . .'

'Of course I won't,' she cut in, giggling as she wiped the sperm from her red lips with the back of her hand.

'Won't you? We'd better get back to the house before . . .'

'Before you lick my bald and very wet little cunt?'

'Before someone comes looking for us.'

'This will work out fine, Rod,' she said as they walked across the lawn to the pool. 'If you help me to get in with your family, things will be fine.'

'Hi,' Raymond called as they neared the patio. 'What's this, a bit of brother–sister-in-law bonding?'

'You could say that,' Sheena replied.

'She's a lovely girl, Raymond,' Rod said. 'Congratulations.'

'Oh, well . . . Thanks, Rod.'

'I'd better be going,' Sheena sighed. 'I don't want to stay for too long on my first visit.'

'You can stay as long as you like,' Raymond said. 'It's early so . . .'

'Next time I'll stay longer.'

'OK, I'll get my car keys.'

'No, no, I'll walk. It's a nice evening and it's not far.'

'All right, I'll ring you tomorrow.'

Sheena followed the brothers into the house. She couldn't stop smiling as she said goodbye to the family. She'd done well, she thought as Raymond saw her out. After the initial shock, they all seemed happy enough. The Boss had liked her, she thought as she walked home. Savouring the taste of Rod's spunk, she wondered whether Raymond had tasted it when he'd kissed her on the doorstep. Happiness, money, and a lot of sex with three brothers lay ahead, she thought happily. Perhaps she'd service David, the fourth brother, once she'd moved in.

Eight

Sheena called into the pub on her way home. She wanted to tell Nat that she'd met the family and the wedding was definitely going ahead, but she wasn't sure how to explain that Raymond had taken Rod's place. Rod, Ray . . . The names were similar and easily confused, she thought. Hoping that Nat wouldn't notice the difference, she walked into the busy pub and headed for the bar. Ordering her usual drink, she knew that she still had a long way to go before she was part of Raymond's family. Once the wedding had taken place, she would be able to relax. Looking around the pub and noticing Nat at her usual table, she was pleased to see that she was alone.

'Hi,' she said, joining her friend.

'Fuck me, it's the future wife.' Nat giggled as she grinned at Sheena. 'What have you been up to, screwing old men on a train?'

'I've been to meet Ray's family,' Sheena replied triumphantly.

The girl frowned and cocked her head to one side. 'Ray? I thought it was Rod?'

'No, no, that's his brother. I'm marrying Raymond.'

'You said his name was Rod. All along, you've said . . . Oh well, not to worry. So, what were his family like? I hope you didn't swear like a common slut.'

'Of course I didn't swear. They're nice people, especially his dad.'

'And you fitted in with these toffs, did you?'

'They're not like that,' Sheena sighed. 'Just because they have money . . .'

'Come on, Sheena. You must have let yourself down. I mean, the way you talk and. . . .'

'I didn't let myself down, Nat,' she cut in indignantly. 'I know when not to swear and I know how to speak properly. I may be a slut, but I know how to hide it.'

'Sheena, you can no more hide the fact that you're a slut than you can hide your face.'

'Wow, don't you sound posh?' Sheena said, giggling. 'You can no more hide the fact . . .'

'Actually, one can speak terribly well when one needs to.'

'Blimey, that was amazing,' Sheena gasped. 'I wish I could do that.'

'Anyone can do it. You don't have to go that far and sound like a real toff, but anyone can put on a posh voice if they try.'

'Nat, I want to get in with Raymond's family. I want to speak properly and stuff. Will you help me?'

'I'm not really the one to ask, but I'll try.'

'I don't mean talking posh like a stuck-up toff. I just want to get things right, like me and him, or whatever it is.'

'Why don't you get a book on English grammar? Spend some time reading instead of dropping your knickers and fucking old men on the train.'

'Yes, yes, I think I will. The trouble is, my voice sounds rough, kind of like gravel.'

'I know, but I don't think you can change that. You've been looking nice lately. What with your new clothes and having your hair done, you look really good. It would help if you get your posture right and don't accentuate your tits too much.'

'What does accentuate mean?'

'Wearing low-cut tops and sticking your tits out. Anyway, I'm not here to give you fucking English lessons. Let's get pissed. You can buy the drinks, seeing as you're loaded.'

Sheena downed her vodka and wandered over to the bar. She was determined to impress Raymond and his family. In particular, she wanted to impress Charles and Rod. They knew that she was a common slut, but she wanted to prove that she could also act like a lady. She had a real chance to better herself, she mused as she walked back to the table with the drinks. This was probably the only chance she'd ever have.

'I don't want to fuck up,' she sighed, sitting next to Nat. 'This is the chance of a lifetime.'

'You'll be all right, babes. Just think before you open your pretty little mouth, and you'll be all right.'

'How come you know big words and stuff? We went to the same school, so I would of thought that . . .'

'Would *have* thought,' Nat corrected her.

'What? I've always said would of.'

'Well, it's wrong.'

'Fuck me,' Sheena swore sadly. 'I'll never get it right. Me and him, would have . . . How come you know everything?'

'I suppose it comes naturally to some people.'

'Yeah, I s'pose so. Do you want to stay at my place tonight?'

'Now, that is a good idea,' Nat agreed, grinning at her young friend. 'A night of pussy-licking is just what I need. We'll get pissed first, though.'

'You're really dirty when you're pissed, Nat.'

'And you're really dirty all the time. Did you get fucked this evening? I love sucking fresh spunk out of your cunt.'

'No, I didn't,' Sheena sighed. 'I did suck off . . . I sucked Raymond's cock.'

Nat giggled. 'Not in front of his family, I hope?'

'No, we went down the garden.'

'That's a shame, I love sucking spunk out of your . . .

152

I'll tell you what,' Nat trilled. 'Just for a laugh, I'll bet you can't get fucked in here tonight.'

'Of course I can,' Sheena said, eyeing up the men standing at the bar. 'Any one of that lot would fuck me. That reminds me, was you in here that night when . . .'

'You can't say that,' Nat cut in.

'Say what?'

'Was you in here. You can't say that.'

'What the fuck's wrong with it?' Sheena asked.

'I'm not going to tell you. You buy a book and find out for yourself. And don't go into a shop and ask for a book about an English grandma.'

'But you just told me to buy one.'

'Fuck me, Sheena. I don't know how you're going to fit in with that posh family. You start saying something like, was you in here last night because me and Raymond never saw you, and they'll realise that you're a common slut.'

'I know how to say that properly,' Sheena said proudly. 'Because Raymond and me didn't see you.'

'It's Raymond and *I*,' Nat corrected her.

'But you said it was him and me.'

'It depends on . . . Just shut the fuck up, Sheena. Move closer to me and open your legs. I want to finger your cunt.'

Sheena parted her thighs, trembling as the girl's fingers moved the crotch of her tight knickers to one side. As her finger slipped between the hairless lips of Sheena's pussy and delved deep into the wet heat of her contracting vagina, Sheena felt her young womb swell and her clitoris stiffen. They were going to have a good night together, she thought as Nat grinned at her. She needed a damned good orgasm, a night of lesbian lust and passion.

'I'll miss you when you're married,' Nat whispered in Sheena's ear.

'We'll still see each other,' Sheena replied dreamily as her juices flowed. 'You can come to the house and we'll sit by the swimming pool.'

'There's a pool?'

153

'Yes, it's huge.'

'I don't think the family will want me there, babes.'

'Of course they will. You're my best friend and I'll be living there, so it will be up to me.'

Slipping her finger out of Sheena's tight pussy, Nat sighed. 'There are too many people here,' she said, glancing around the pub. 'I'll give you a good sorting out later. Is that your phone ringing?'

'Yes,' Sheena realised, taking her mobile from her handbag. 'It's probably Raymond.'

Leaving the table and walking to a quiet corner of the pub, she pressed her phone to her ear. Raising her eyes to the ceiling, she sighed when she heard Rod's voice. He asked her where she was, and she reckoned that he wanted to warn her off Raymond again. She didn't want another lecture and was about to hang up, but he again asked her where she was.

'I'm in the pub,' she finally replied.

'I'll be outside in a minute to pick you up.'

'What? But . . . Why?'

'We have to talk, Sheena. Raymond is besotted with you and he's been going on and on about the bloody wedding. We have to talk.'

'Talk about what?'

'About a payoff. I'll see you in a minute.'

As he hung up, Sheena realised that he was serious. How much was he willing to give her? she wondered. Ten thousand? Fifty thousand? Her heart racing, she went back to the table and told Nat that she'd be back in half an hour at the most. Ignoring the girl's protests, she left the pub and looked up and down the street as she again wondered how much Rod was willing to give her. She hadn't expected this. She'd realised that Rod and Charles would try to ruin her plans with Raymond, but she hadn't expected to be offered a payoff.

'Get in,' Rod snapped as he pulled up and pushed the passenger door open.

'Rod –,' she began, sitting beside him.

'OK, here's the deal. I'll give you two grand to disappear from the face of the earth.'

'Two grand?' she echoed, frowning at him. 'If you think you can buy me off with two grand . . .'

'Take it or leave it, Sheena. Either way, you're finished with Raymond.'

'What do you mean? It's not up to you, Rod. It has nothing to do with you, so . . .'

'Charles and I have been having a little chat about you, and we've discovered something.'

'Oh, that.'

'Yes, that. You've been screwing both of us, taking money from both of us.'

'I've been having a chat with the girl who rang Deborah,' she countered. 'The girl who said that she was having your baby.'

'What? Sheena, was it you? It was you, wasn't it?'

'No, of course it wasn't. I did some checking, asking around, and I found out who it was.'

'I don't believe you. The town is full of girls, how come you found the very one who rang Deborah?'

'I've been talking to Deborah's photographer friend. The girl was one of his models.'

'Christ, this gets worse. Who is this girl? Whoever she is, she's bloody lying.'

'Her name is Hannah.'

'That's the name Deborah mentioned.' He frowned and held his hand to his head. 'So, why did she phone Deborah and say that she was pregnant with my baby?'

'She was trying to cause trouble because of some fall-out Deborah had with another girl about porn modelling.'

'That's crazy, I don't believe a word of it. Look, this has nothing to do with you and this farcical marriage,' Rod sighed. 'This girl you've spoken to, whoever she is, doesn't change anything. This is nonsense, and you know it.'

155

'Hannah don't think it's nonsense. She's after Deborah, and she won't stop.'

'After her?'

'I don't know the details, but she found out that Deborah was planning to set up in business with the photographer and she don't like it. Why don't you ask Deborah about it?'

'Don't be ridiculous, Sheena. Deborah has already told me that it's over, she won't be modelling again.'

'Then why was she there yesterday?'

'She was at work yesterday.'

'All day?'

'Well . . . Look, this has nothing to do with you and Raymond.' He took a wad of notes from his jacket pocket. 'I'm offering you two grand, Sheena, in cash.'

Taking the money, she grinned. 'OK,' she said, stuffing the notes into her handbag.

'You'll leave Raymond alone now? You'll tell him that it's off?'

'I might.'

'Sheena . . .'

'Where's Deborah now?'

'I've just taken her home. Why?'

'Come round to my place later, and you can fuck me and my friend.'

'It's my friend and me.'

'Whatever it is, you can fuck both of us.'

'What the hell are you up to now?'

'Nothing. I just thought you might like to fuck two horny teenage sluts.'

'OK, but this doesn't change anything.'

'I know that.'

'All right, I'll see you in an hour or so.'

Sheena left the car and watched Rod drive off. She had no idea what her plan was, but she knew that an idea was stirring somewhere in the depths of her mind. If she could get hold of Deborah, get her to turn up at the bedsit and witness Rod screwing Nat ... No, that wouldn't work, she decided. Hoping that Nat would be up for it, she clutched her bag tightly and walked back into the pub. Deciding not to mention the money as she joined her friend at the table and sipped her drink, she grinned.

'Want to share a cock with me tonight?' she asked her.

'What the fuck are you on about?'

'Rod, Raymond's brother, wants to fuck us at my place later.'

'How much?'

'Don't worry, he's loaded. We'll sort out the money later. Are you up for it?'

'Yeah, why not?'

'Good. It looks like you'll be able to suck spunk out of my pussy after all.'

'It's been a long time since we kissed each other with a tasty knob between our lips and ...' Nat's words tailing off, she frowned at her friend. 'What are you up to?' she asked her.

'Nothing,' Sheena replied, winking.

'Come on, tell me.'

'I was thinking that it would be funny if Rod's girlfriend turned up and caught him fucking you.'

'It would be bloody hilarious, Sheena. I'd end up in a cat-fight and ... Why the hell do you want her to find out?'

'It's a long story. Rod is trying to split up me and Raymond. If I had something on him, something I could threaten him with ...'

'Has your mobile got a camera built in?'

'Yes, why?'

'Think about it, Sheena.'

'I don't understand. How will that help?'

'You could take a photo of Rod fucking me and threaten to send it to his girlfriend.'

Her face beaming, Sheena took her phone from her handbag and gazed at the buttons. The idea was brilliant, she thought happily. To take a photo of Rod screwing Nat with the very phone he'd given to Sheena as a present was a nice touch. Wondering whether she could lure Charles to her bedsit and take a photo of him screwing Nat too, she reckoned that she was now well on the way to ending the brothers' interference. With photographic evidence of their infidelity, the playing field would be level.

'Come on, then,' Sheena said excitedly, knocking back her drink.

'I'm not pissed yet,' Nat complained.

'I've got vodka and stuff at home. How about a photo of you with a bottle stuffed up your cunt?'

'What?'

'The photo would show Rod drinking vodka from the bottle.'

'I'm not sticking a fucking great bottle up my cunt, Sheena. You really are a dirty little bitch.'

'And I get worse,' Sheena said, giggling as she led her friend out of the pub.

Pondering the idea of taking photographs as she walked back to her bedsit with Nat, Sheena was sure that she could pull this off. Once Rod saw the photos, he wouldn't have a leg to stand on. The door to the family home was finally wide open for her, she thought as she led Nat into her bedsit and poured two large vodka and tonics. All she had to do now was wait for her prey to walk into her trap, and she'd be home and dry.

'Leave the money to me,' she said, passing Nat a drink. 'I'll talk to him about paying us.'

'I'm stone broke,' Nat sighed. 'We must get our little business up and running.'

'Rod will be our first punter. I think we should get him to strip us rather than start off naked. If you go first, I'll take the pictures.'

'Don't let him see you taking photos, or he'll go fucking mental.'

'He'll be so busy licking your wet pussy out that he won't notice me. Right, let's down a few vodkas before our victim gets here.'

Sheena paced the floor as Nat grabbed the vodka bottle and sat on the bed. This had to work, she mused anxiously as she gazed at her mobile phone. It was strange to think that Rod had given her the phone, she thought dolefully as she recalled the meal they'd enjoyed at the new restaurant. He'd given her the phone, taken her out, arranged membership of the club ... And now they were fighting. Funny how love can be.

Rod had been the one she'd wanted all along, she thought as Nat refilled the glasses. Had Deborah not been in the way ... It was no good looking back, she decided as she downed her drink. There had never been a place for her on Rod's map. But she had her own map now. And Raymond was in the centre. Downing more vodka, she felt her heart leap as a knock sounded on the door. This was it, she thought, grinning at Nat and taking a deep breath.

'Hi,' she said, opening the door to Rod. 'Come in.'

'Two little girlies,' Rod announced, grinning at Nat as he walked into the room. 'You're a sexy little thing.'

'This is Nat,' Sheena said. 'Why don't you join her on the bed and get to know her?'

'Yes, I think I will.'

Sheena sat on a chair by the window as Rod joined Nat on the bed and lifted her T-shirt over her head. Watching as he squeezed the girl's firm breasts, she thought it odd she'd once believed that she'd been in love with him. She'd wanted him so much, she reflected as he sucked Nat's ripe nipple into his mouth and slipped his hand up her short skirt. Had she been in love? she wondered. Was she in love with him now?

She sipped her vodka as Rod removed Nat's clothes, then watched him dive between her open thighs and run his tongue up and down her wet sex crack. This was the

159

man she'd hoped to marry, she thought as she listened to the slurping sounds of sex. Would she have remained faithful to him? By the way he was carrying on with Nat, it was pretty obvious that he'd never remain faithful to anyone. Deborah was at home making wedding plans while her future husband was with a couple of teenage sluts.

Maybe Raymond was the better bet, she thought as Nat ordered Rod to tongue-fuck her wet cunt. Raymond was free and single with no apparent problems, and he wasn't bad-looking. At least he'd asked Sheena to marry him rather than her having to ask him. The brothers' father seemed to like Sheena and ... Wondering what David, the fourth brother, was like, she hoped that he wouldn't cause problems.

'Aren't you going to join us?' Rod asked, his pussy-wet face grinning.

'In a minute,' Sheena replied. 'You give Nat a good fucking and then I'll join in.'

'You're good,' Nat breathed as Rod sucked on her erect clitoris. 'Give me a good licking and bring me off.'

Sheena took her phone from her handbag, held it up and took a couple of photos of the writhing couple. Rod didn't notice a thing as he licked and sucked Nat's solid clitoris. This was going to work out perfectly, Sheena thought excitedly as Nat cried out in the grip of a powerful orgasm. Sheena felt her own clitoris swell as her juices of arousal seeped into the tight crotch of her knickers. Her arousal riding high, she could hardly wait to join in. But she wanted more evidence of Rod's debauchery first.

Eventually Rod stripped naked and lay on top of Nat with his hard cock hovering above her open vaginal slit, and Sheena got the photos she wanted. She felt sorry for Rod, but he'd dumped her and then tried to pay her off, and that had upset her. They'd had a good time together in the restaurant. Had it not been for Deborah ... Then again, Rod had never had any plans for Sheena, apart from using her for sordid sex. Charles would be the next victim, Sheena thought as she took several more photographs. Once she had proof of his adultery, she'd be laughing.

Sheena hid her phone and slipped out of her clothes before joining the naked couple on the bed. Locking her full lips to Nat's gasping mouth and kissing her passionately as Rod shafted her friend's tight vagina, she felt her young womb contract as his hand slipped between her parted thighs and a finger drove deep into her sexdripping vaginal sheath. Sheena pushed her tongue into Nat's mouth, breathing heavily through her nose as Rod's thrusting finger massaged the hard nub of her clitoris and sent her arousal soaring.

She had two thousand pounds in cash, she thought happily as Rod slipped his finger out of her tight pussy and ordered her to face-fuck Nat. Kneeling astride the girl's face, she lowered her young body and pressed the hairless lips of her vulva over her friend's gasping mouth as Rod shafted Nat's squelching vagina. It had been a long time since she'd enjoyed two tongues, she realised, jutting her rounded buttocks out and offering her bottom-hole to Rod. He parted her firm buttocks and licked the delicate brown tissue of her tight anus as he repeatedly drove his solid cock into Nat's spasming vagina, and Sheena was in sexual heaven. Two thousand, she mused dreamily, wondering what to spend it on.

Rod's tongue entering the tight duct of her rectum as Nat slipped her tongue deep into her contracting vagina, Sheena threw her head back and gasped, her naked body shaking uncontrollably. This was real sex, she thought as Nat licked and slurped between her bald pussy lips and finally sucked her swollen clitoris into her mouth to run her tongue over its sensitive tip. She had two thousand in cash, she was enjoying real sex, and she had marriage to look forward to ... Life was looking good, she thought.

Wondering whether the day would come when Charles made up a foursome, she cried out as her powerful orgasm erupted.

'Yes, yes,' she gasped, her vaginal milk drenching Nat's face. Rod announced that he was coming as he rammed his solid cock into Nat's contracting vagina with a vengeance, and Nat began to tremble and writhe as her own climax neared. This had cost Rod two thousand pounds, Sheena thought in her wickedness as the two tongues attended to her most private holes. Again crying out as her orgasm peaked and rocked her young body, she reckoned she'd soon be having sex with Rod and his brothers in a huge double bed in the family home. Would David succumb to her teenage charms?

Rod's tongue left Sheena's anal hole as he sat upright. 'Bloody hell,' he gasped. 'That was bloody amazing.'

'Keep fucking me,' Nat begged. 'I'm still coming.'

Sheena rocked her hips, sliding her dripping vaginal flesh back and forth over Nat's gasping mouth as Rod repeatedly propelled his solid knob deep into the girl's contracting vaginal duct. Hitting another peak, she felt her young womb rhythmically pulsing as she pumped out her orgasmic milk and flooded her friend's mouth. Nat slurped and gobbled, drinking from Sheena's vagina as her own body convulsed and shook violently.

'We'll swap places in a minute,' Sheena said, her orgasm waning as Rod continued to shaft Nat's swollen vaginal duct. 'I'll take Nat's place and you can fuck me senseless.'

'Give me a lesbian show,' Rod said as Nat writhed and gasped in the grip of her orgasm. 'I'd love to see you two tonguing each other.'

Reclining on the bed beside Nat, Sheena grinned at him. 'Just think, you'll never see us again,' she said impishly as he finally slowed his shafting rhythm.

'Well, I . . .'

'You want me off the face of the earth, remember?'

'What the fuck are you talking about?' Nat gasped, her eyes rolling as she drifted down from her orgasm.

'It's a private joke,' Sheena replied.

Rod frowned. 'It's not a joke. I'd like to see you two again, but this changes nothing.'

'Don't it?' Sheena grinned as Nat yanked Rod's deflating cock out of her sperm-bubbling vagina and clambered off the bed.

'Will you tell me what you're talking about?' Nat asked, swaying on her unsteady legs as she poured herself a large vodka.

'Sheena,' Rod began. 'You've had the money so . . .'

'You've already got the money?' Nat said accusingly, gazing at Sheena. 'You cheating little bitch.'

'Nat, will you shut the fuck up?' Sheena hissed. 'And sit down. You're dripping spunk all over my fucking carpet.'

'The carpet wants chucking out anyway.'

'I know but – shut up and drink your vodka.'

'Sheena –' Rod began again.

'And I want you to shut the fuck up, Rod,' she snapped. 'Honestly, you two are like a couple of fucking old women.'

'Fucking,' Nat said, giggling as the alcohol finally began to affect her. 'Nice choice of words, babe.'

Grabbing Rod's flaccid cock as Nat flopped into the armchair in an alcoholic daze, Sheena smiled. 'We'll be one big happy family,' she whispered.

'Sheena, no.'

'And you can see me and Nat again.'

Rod shook his head and sighed. 'Charles went crazy when he discovered the game you'd been playing with both of us,' he said. 'And I must say that I wasn't too impressed either. Raymond is my brother, and I don't want him marrying a . . .'

'Say it, Rod.'

'With all due respect, I don't want him marrying a slut.'

'But you're about to marry a slut,' she retaliated. 'What's the difference?'

'Deborah is not a slut.'

'You're blind, Rod. I've never met anyone as blind as you. Open your eyes, for fuck's sake.'

'Deborah has a past, as we all have.'

'Deborah also has a present, Rod. That's what you should be worrying about.'

'Look, I didn't come here to talk about Deborah. Are you going to give me a lesbian show or not?'

'Nat, get on to the bed,' she ordered her friend.

'I think I'm pissed,' Nat gurgled.

'That's even better,' Sheena returned. 'You're a filthy little bitch when you're pissed. Now, get on to the bed.'

Rod sat in the armchair as Nat lay on her back on the bed with her spunk-dripping thighs parted wide. Sheena positioned herself between the girl's long legs, peeled her bald sex lips wide apart and gazed at her pink folds, the solid nub of her erect clitoris, her cream-oozing vaginal hole. It had been a long time since she'd enjoyed her young friend's wet pussy, she realised as Rod waited expectantly for the lesbian show to begin. Running her tongue up and down Nat's sperm-drenched vaginal slit, she lapped up the opaque liquid as Nat gasped and writhed, eventually swallowing the creamy offering.

Nat breathed heavily, arching her back as Sheena licked her hard clitoris and tongued her sex-dripping vaginal hole. Sucking out the milky cocktail of sperm and girl-cream, Sheena thought about the photographs she'd taken of Rod. He had a mobile phone too, she realised, but he obviously hadn't thought of photographing her lesbian act and using it as evidence against her. That might be his next move, she thought as she pushed her tongue deep into Nat's spasming vaginal canal. If he showed Raymond photos of her lesbian act, that could ruin everything. She was going to have to be careful.

'I'm coming,' Nat whispered shakily as Sheena again

sucked her erect clitoris into her hot mouth and licked its sensitive tip.

'Bring the slut off,' Rod said, moving his chair closer to the bed. 'Give the filthy slut a good clit-sucking and make her spurt.'

Rod was obviously enjoying the show, Sheena thought as Nat began to whimper and tremble uncontrollably. She wished he'd accept that she was going to marry Raymond. She knew things could work out well in the family home. She could please Rod whenever they were alone together, give him a deep-throat job or open her legs wide, and everyone would be happy. He didn't have a sex life to speak of with Deborah, and nothing would change when he married the woman. Why not accept Sheena and have the best of both worlds?

Nat reached her orgasm and squirmed on the bed as her orgasmic milk spilled from her contracting vagina and splattered Sheena's pretty face. Rod could still enjoy lesbian shows, Sheena thought, driving three fingers into the wailing girl's sex sheath as she sucked and licked her pulsating clitoris. It would be easy enough to find somewhere private, and Rod could do more than just watch – he could enjoy two teenage girls, both hungry for cock. Biting gently on Nat's orgasming clitoris and sustaining her mind-blowing climax, Sheena hoped that Rod would realise he had two choices. He could either give the happy couple his blessing and screw Sheena on the side, or she'd marry Rod anyway and he could forget about having sex with her.

'Do my arse,' Nat begged as her climax began to fade. 'Fist my arse like you used to.'

'Filthy slut,' Rod said with a chuckle as the girl rolled over on to her stomach and jutted out her naked buttocks. 'Go on, Sheena, do as she asked.'

'You'll miss this, Rod,' Sheena said, parting the girl's firm bottom cheeks and pushing a finger deep into her tight anal hole. 'Still, you'll have Deborah to satisfy you.'

'Don't start again,' he sighed, watching closely as Sheena drove a second finger into the girl's anal duct. 'My mind's made up, and Charles is with me.'

'That's not what Charles said to me.'

'What do you mean?'

'Nothing.'

Easing all her fingers into Nat's tight anus, Sheena pushed and twisted until the girl's delicate brown tissue was stretched tautly around her knuckles. Pushing further into her yielding sheath, she finally managed to sink her entire fist into her friend's trembling body. Nat gasped, squirming on the bed as Sheena twisted her fist deep within the dank heat of her bowels. Sheena noticed Rod focussing on the girl's brown anal ring, stretched tautly around her wrist, and she knew that he'd miss the crude sex. But the choice was his, she repeated to herself. All he had to do was give her his blessing, and he could have two dirty teenage girls whenever he wanted them.

When Nat ordered Sheena to fist-fuck her pussy, Rod let out a gasp. He obviously couldn't believe what he was seeing, Sheena thought as she forced her fingers into the girl's neglected vaginal sheath. Nat groaned as her vaginal cavern stretched wide open and her juices of lust streamed over Sheena's hand. Deborah was a waste of space, Sheena mused as Rod begged her to push her fist into the slut's pussy. Would he now realise what he'd be missing?

'She's a filthy slut,' he groaned as Sheena managed to sink her fist deep into the girl's vagina. 'I've never met a nymphomaniac before. I didn't think girls like her existed.'

'You met me,' Sheena said, giggling as she twisted her fist. 'I'm a filthy slut, and a nymphomaniac.'

'Yes, but . . . Is there no limit to what you'll do for sexual gratification?'

'None at all. You name it, and I'll do it.'

'I want to see her piss spurting out,' he said eagerly. 'Tell her to piss over you.'

'You tell her.'

'Piss on her, Nat,' he ordered the girl, kneeling on the floor by the bed for a better view. 'Go on, piss all over the filthy little slut.'

Nat drunkenly squeezed her muscles and forced a jet of golden liquid from her young body. Sheena giggled as the hot liquid sprayed over her lower stomach and streamed down between the swollen lips of her hairless pussy. Her arousal running high, she slipped her fist out of the girl's rectum with a loud sucking sound and pushed her tongue into the gaping anal hole as Rod watched in amazement. Licking deep inside Nat's rectal duct, she fisted her inflamed vaginal cave, ensuring that her wrist massaged the swollen bulb of her clitoris. Noticing Rod's solid cock, she ordered him to deep-throat the girl.

Rod wasted no time, leaping on to the bed and lifting Nat's head up to slip his purple knob into her gasping mouth. As she snaked her wet tongue over its velveteen surface, he let out a low moan of pleasure. Deborah was a prude, Sheena thought as he drove his hard knob to the back of Nat's throat. All Rod had to do was accept that the marriage was going ahead, and he'd have two teenage girls to use and abuse. He moaned again as Nat swallowed his bulbous cockhead, taking the entire length of his rock-hard organ into her pretty mouth. Could he deny himself the satisfaction of two nymphomaniacs? Sheena wondered as she tongued deep inside her lesbian lover's hot anal duct.

Nat moaned through her nose, her naked body trembling wildly, as Rod's hips swayed and he repeatedly propelled his knob deep into her tight throat. Sheena reckoned that the girl should endure an anal fucking, if Rod was up to it once he'd flooded her stomach with his fresh spunk. The more crude sex Rod enjoyed, the more he'd want to hang on to Sheena and her slut friend. He'd never experienced anything like this before, she thought as he gasped and increased his throat-shafting rhythm.

And he never would again, unless he stopped interfering in Sheena's life.

Sheena could hear Nat gulping down Rod's gushing sperm as he threw his head back and breathed heavily in the grip of his climax. Nat was good, she thought, fisting the girl's tightening vagina harder. Not only was she good in bed, but she could put on airs and graces so she'd be welcome as Sheena's guest at the family home. The threat of the photographs would shut Rod up. But she didn't want to go down that road. Maybe the thought of Nat's young body would sway Rod's thinking. Finally dragging her aching fist out of her young friend's vaginal cavern, she sat back on her heels as Rod made his last thrusts and drained his balls.

'Do her arse next,' she said, watching Rod's eyes roll back as he buried his cock deep within Nat's hot throat. 'Fuck her tight arse and spunk . . .'

'You two are insatiable,' he cut in, gasping for breath.

'We are,' Sheena said with a giggle. 'Whatever that means.'

'It means that you can't get enough, you're never satisfied.'

'That's true. Unlike Deborah.'

'Not Deborah again,' he sighed as Nat sprawled out on the bed and fell asleep.

'You'll have to force your fist up Deborah's arse,' she trilled, giggling uncontrollably. 'She'd like that.'

'Like it? Christ, she'd run off.'

'There you are, then. You now know how to get rid of her. You could give her a good throat-fucking.'

'Sheena, I don't want to talk about Deborah,' he announced, leaving the bed and grabbing his clothes. 'I won't see you again if all you're going to do is talk about her.'

'Who says you're going to see me again?'

'You know damn well that you want me.'

'I have Raymond and Charles. Why would I want you, too?'

'Come on, Sheena, let's not play games.' Pulling his trousers on, he grinned. 'You want me as much as I want you.'

'No, Rod. I want you *more* than you want me, that's the trouble.'

'Yes, well . . . I'd better get home.'

'I'll be calling your house my home soon.'

'Sheena . . .'

'I have something up my sleeve,' she cut in. 'Something that Deborah would be very interested in.'

'What are you talking about?'

'You'll see, Rod.'

'If you cause trouble . . .' He finished dressing and he moved to the door. 'I've told you before. If you cause trouble . . .'

'I'll do more than cause trouble unless you back off and leave me and Raymond alone.'

'You listen to me, you little slut,' he hissed. 'I want you to finish with Raymond and never come to the house again. Do you understand?'

'Me and Raymond are getting married, so you can go to hell,' she returned. She wiped the tears from her eyes and poured herself a drink. 'This is a chance for me to get out of this fucking slum and make something of my life. I wanted you to be part of my life but you're so fucking stuck on that slut . . .'

'Don't cry, Sheena,' he cut in, stroking her dishevelled blonde hair and wiping tears from her cheeks. 'There's no future for us, can't you see that?'

'Yes, I can see that. That's why I'm marrying Raymond. All you want is my cunt. Raymond wants me as a person.'

'You're only marrying him to spite me.'

'I'm marrying him to get myself out of this shithole. He asked me to marry him, Rod. That proves that he wants me. All you've ever done is ask me to pull my knickers down.'

'As much as I like you, Sheena, I can't allow you to marry Raymond.'

'And I can't allow you to marry Deborah.'

'You have no say in the matter. The wedding is arranged, my father is all for it and . . .'

'That's where you're wrong. I do have a say in the matter. In fact, I'll be seeing Deborah and . . . Well, you'll see what happens.'

'I'm warning you, Sheena.'

'And I'm warning you, Rod.'

As he left the room and closed the door, Sheena knocked back her drink and flopped into the armchair. Rod wanted war, she reflected sadly. But he had no idea that she had a secret weapon. He had one last chance, she decided. She'd show him the photographs and, if he still wouldn't change his mind, Deborah would see them. It wasn't what Sheena had wanted, but Rod was giving her no other choice.

Nine

Sheena left Nat in bed and took a shower before going into town. She felt good with money in her pocket and, after a decent breakfast in a café, she browsed the shop windows and bought some new clothes. A couple of miniskirts and dresses, blouses and T-shirts, shoes and a handbag. She also bought a book on English grammar. She might have to work on her speech. But the next time she met Raymond's family, at least she was going to look good. Loaded with bags, she was about to head for the bus stop when she had an idea. For the first time in her life, she got a taxi home.

Money made all the difference, she thought as she lugged her shopping into her bedsit. She'd planned to give Nat a couple of hundred pounds, but it was nearing midday and the girl had gone. After making a cup of coffee, she tried on her clothes and felt a pang of excitement course through her veins as she gazed at her refection in the mirror. She grinned as she imagined Rod and Charles looking her up and down, then grabbed her handbag as her phone rang.

'Hi,' she said, hoping it wasn't Rod.

'Hi, Sheena,' Raymond said. 'Are you free this evening?'

'Yes, yes, I am.'

'Would you like to come to dinner?'

'Wow, yes. At your house, you mean?'

'Yes, if that's all right with you. The whole family will be there, including David.'

'That's great. What time?'

'I'll pick you up at . . .'

'No, no, I'll walk. It's not far so it's not a problem.'

'OK, if you're sure. Get here around six – that'll give us time for a couple of drinks first.'

'Right, I'll be there at six. Has – has Rod said anything?'

'I haven't seen Rod today. Why do you ask?'

'I just wondered . . . It don't matter. I'm looking forward to meeting David.'

'Don't worry if he seems rather jittery. He's terrified of his wife, Julia. In fact, everyone's terrified of Julia. Anyway, I have work to do. I'll see you this evening.'

'I'll look forward to it, Raymond.'

'You take care, OK?'

'Yes, yes, I will.'

Dropping her phone into her handbag, she punched the air with her fist. Things were going very well, she thought happily as she grabbed her English grammar book and flicked through the pages. She settled on her bed and spent four hours reading the book. It wasn't easy, she reflected. Raymond and me, Raymond and I . . . Unable to grasp the concept, she finally tossed the book aside and began to get ready for the evening.

The turquoise dress was low-cut but didn't reveal her young breasts, she concluded. The matching handbag and shoes were a nice touch, but she decided not to wear any knickers in case Charles or Rod wanted to kiss the smooth lips of her bald pussy. Her makeup impeccable, she checked her reflection in the mirror and smiled. She knew she looked great as she left her bedsit and walked to the family home, her future home. But her heart was racing and her hands trembling as she rang the doorbell.

'Come in,' Raymond invited her. 'You look amazing. Come in and I'll show you off to the family.'

'Thanks,' she breathed, stepping into the vast hallway. 'I'm feeling a little nervous.'

'Don't worry, you'll be fine. I thought we might have a few days away together.' He kissed her cheek and chuckled. 'We're getting married and we don't really know each other.'

'I'd like that, Raymond. Where shall we go?'

'Oh, I don't know. Paris, Greece . . . You decide.'

'Paris? Wow, that would be lovely.'

'OK, we'll talk about it later. Come through to the lounge.'

Sheena smiled as she walked into the lounge with Raymond by her side. They were a couple, she thought, looking at Rod and Deborah and Charles and Caroline. Raymond introduced her to David and his wife, Julia, and Sheena did her best to speak properly and come across as a young lady. Julia was nice, she thought, wondering why everyone was terrified of her. And David seemed pleasant enough. The minute Raymond went into the dining room to pour the drinks, Rod tried to take Sheena aside.

'I'll show you the games room,' he said, indicating for her to follow him.

'Later,' Sheena promised, smiling at him. 'I'd like to get to know your family first.'

'You look lovely,' Julia said. 'I love that dress.'

'Thanks,' Sheena said. 'I bought it today.'

'You're young and very beautiful,' Julia complimented her. 'I envy you.'

'Yes, well . . . I . . .' Sheena stammered awkwardly. 'That's very nice of you.'

'No, no, I mean it. You'll have to watch the brothers, or they'll all be after you. Apart from my David, of course.' She chuckled and held Sheena's arm. 'I've trained David,' she said. 'And you'll have to train Raymond.'

'Oh, I see,' Sheena replied. 'Does he need training, then?'

'All men need training, dear. Especially Charles and Rod.'

'Don't be silly, Julia,' Charles chided. 'We don't want to end up like David.'

'What do you mean by that?'

'I agree with Julia,' Deborah chipped in. 'I have Rod on a tight rein. It's a shame Caroline doesn't rein you in now and then, Charles.'

'She doesn't need to rein me in. What do you say, David?'

'Well, I – I don't know.'

'David likes a quiet life, Sheena,' Charles said. 'That's why he always agrees with his wife.'

'Oh, I see,' Sheena said softly, not wanting to get involved.

'What sort of life do *you* like? Quiet, exciting, dangerous or . . .'

'I like a quiet life,' she cut in, winking at him.

'Rod likes a quiet life, too. Isn't that right, Rod?'

'If you say so, Charles,' Rod sighed.

'By the way, where did you get to last night?'

'I took Deborah home, you know that.'

'That didn't take you over an hour, surely?'

'Didn't you go straight home after dropping me off?' Deborah asked Rod.

'I went for a drive and . . . Aren't we being rather rude to Sheena? She hasn't come here to listen to us bickering.'

'We're not bickering,' Deborah protested.

'I'll show you the garden, Sheena,' Charles said, taking her arm.

Charles led Sheena through the house to the patio before walking her across the lawn to a summerhouse. He was going to lecture her, she feared as she sat on the bench and gazed at the beautiful garden. She said nothing when he asked her whether she'd bought her new dress with the money Rod had given her. Finally he sat beside her, placed his hand on her knee and smiled.

'You're a devious little cow,' he said, chuckling. 'Rod and I went halves on the payoff, but it obviously didn't work.'

'I like your family,' Sheena said, returning his smile. 'They're nice.'

'I'm glad you think so. You're not going to give up, are you?'

'Give up?'

'You know what I mean, Sheena.'

'No, I'm not going to give up. Why should I? Raymond asked me to marry him, and I accepted. Why do you want me out of the way? Am I really that bad?'

'It's not so much me,' he sighed. 'It's Rod. I must admit that I was annoyed when I discovered that you'd been screwing both of us, but Rod's the one who wants you out.'

'So, are you happy about me and Raymond? I mean Raymond and . . .'

'You look after me, and I'll look after you. If you get my meaning?'

'I know what you mean. So, you won't try to put Raymond off me?'

'To be honest, I don't give a toss. I run the family business, and as long as I'm left alone to get on with it I really don't care.'

'I thought your dad was the boss?'

'He is, but I'm beginning to take the reins. He's old-fashioned, doesn't keep up with the times. I can take the business into the future and we'll all profit. The business is important to me, Sheena. Not silly family squabbles or who's marrying whom.'

'I thought you wanted me out of the way as much as Rod does.'

'It's Raymond's life and, if he wants to marry a – a girl like you, that's fine by me. Was Rod with you last night?'

'Yes, yes, he was.'

'I thought as much.'

'Charles, I know that you think I'm a gold-digger. I know that I'm common and a slut and . . .'

'It doesn't matter what I think, Sheena. My father is the one you'll have to worry about. Caroline, Deborah, Julia – they all suck up to him. Actually, Deborah is his favourite. But the way they all lick his arse is pathetic. You're streetwise, aren't you?'

'I like to think so.'

'If you get in with my father, you'll be home and dry. I'm going to give you a tip. He can't abide sycophants.'

'What are they?'

'People who try to please him and lick his arse. And I don't mean literally.'

'I know what you mean but . . . How do I get in with him, then?'

'I was about to say, be yourself. On second thoughts . . . He likes a strong character. He likes someone with guts. I don't mean be rude to him but stand your ground and, whatever you do, don't try to please him. You'll get nowhere by coming across as a weak sycophant.'

'OK, thanks. Charles, why are you helping me?'

'Why? Because I'm very much like my father. I like you, Sheena. You set your sights on something and you don't give up. You don't crumble under pressure. You have guts, and the most beautiful little pussy I've ever seen.'

'I thought that might come into it.'

'We'd better get back before my wife sends out a search party.'

'Thanks, Charles. You've made me feel . . . Well, you've made me feel welcome.'

'I'm a businessman and I like to have a finger in all the pies,' he said, chuckling as they walked back to the house. 'Especially a hot and juicy pie like yours.'

'You can eat my pie whenever you're hungry.'

'Good girl, that's what I like to hear.'

Sheena felt immensely relieved after her talk with Charles. She still had Rod to deal with, she mused as she followed Charles through the house to the lounge. But with photographic evidence of his infidelity, she didn't think he'd cause any trouble. Recalling Rod's solid cock shafting Nat's hairless pussy, she wondered when he'd next call round to the bedsit for sex. He'd be back for more crude fucking, that was certain. Watching Rod as he left his armchair and walked towards her, she smiled.

'I love the summerhouse,' she said as he took her to one side.

'Sheena, I thought you'd agreed to leave Raymond alone?'

'I don't remember agreeing to anything.'

'I gave you two grand, for God's sake. All right, if that's the way you want it, I'll tell Raymond all about you, your seedy bedsit, your lesbian girlfriend, the way you . . .'

'Look,' she said, taking her mobile phone from her handbag. 'I took some pictures.'

'What the hell . . .' he gasped, staring in horror at a photo of himself screwing Nat. 'Give me that bloody phone.'

Slipping the phone back into her bag, she looked around the room. 'Ah, there's Deborah,' she said. 'I'll go and show her . . .'

'I knew you'd be trouble,' he whispered through gritted teeth.

'Rod, the last thing I want is trouble. Why the hell can't you just leave me alone?'

'You win this round, Sheena, but you're not going to win the next one. What were you doing in the garden with Charles? Giving him a deep-throat job?'

'Sheena, the dinner is ready,' Raymond said as he approached. 'My father likes us to be seated when he comes down.'

Following the family into the dining room, Sheena gazed at a maid hovering by the huge table. This was amazing, she thought as Raymond pulled a chair out for

177

her. There was a large chair at the head of the table where she reckoned the Boss would sit. Once the family were seated, silence fell over the room as they all waited. The Boss finally walked in wearing a black velvet jacket, white shirt and bow tie. The maid waited until he'd sat down before serving the soup.

'It's nice to see you here, Sheena,' the Boss said, smiling at her.

'The family is expanding,' Rod sighed.

'The expansion I want to see is grandchildren,' his father returned. 'Let's hope that Raymond and Sheena can produce some.'

'We are trying, George,' Julia said.

'Very trying,' Charles quipped.

'Do you want children, Sheena?' George asked her.

'Well, yes, I do.' She smiled at Raymond. 'Once we're married . . .'

'You don't agree with sex before marriage?' Rod cut in with a snigger.

'I think it's best to wait . . .'

'You don't agree to sex outside our marriage, do you, Charles?' Caroline asked. 'Not very often, anyway.'

Sheena tried to keep out of it as the maid placed a bowl of vegetable soup before her. She watched the others, following suit by covering her dress with her napkin and noting which spoon they used. She was aware of Rod keeping an eye on her, waiting for her to make a mistake, and she wondered again why he wouldn't accept that she was to become part of the family.

It was jealousy, she concluded. She was young, attractive, fun to be with, a whore in the bedroom . . . Why was Deborah so cold in bed with Rod? she wondered, gazing at the woman's full red lips and imagining the photographer fucking her mouth. Listening to the bickering, she noticed that George wasn't at all amused. He frowned at each comment and shook his head despairingly as the women slagged off their men. Sheena took mental notes.

178

He wanted grandchildren, he didn't like people sucking up to him . . . Why hadn't he taken her aside for a chat? she wondered. Maybe he would after the meal.

Sheena enjoyed the roast duck and was careful not to drink too much wine. She didn't join in with the conversation for fear of letting herself down, and she ignored Rod's various quips. After the meal, the women filed into the lounge and the men began talking business. Sheena was about to follow the women when George invited her to walk in the garden with him. This was it, she thought apprehensively, leaving her chair. She grinned at Rod as he mumbled something about me and him. Following George to the patio, she knew that she didn't dare let herself down.

'Sit down, Sheena,' he said, waving at a patio chair. He walked up and down, rubbing his chin pensively. 'What do you think of my family?' he finally asked her.

'They're nice,' she replied, recalling the advice Charles had given her. 'But I don't like the continual bickering.'

'Neither do I. Do you know why Rod keeps digging at you?'

'No, I – I don't,' she breathed softly. 'Maybe he don't like me.'

'I know why,' he said, locking his dark eyes to hers.

'Do you?' Her stomach churning, she waited fearfully as he continued to pace up and down.

'He's jealous,' he eventually said, much to her relief. 'Deborah is a lovely girl, but . . . She doesn't give a man the things he needs, if you see what I mean?'

'Yes, I understand. Me and Raymond . . .' Her words tailing off, she felt her face flush.

'You were saying?'

'Raymond and me . . . We . . .'

'Charles wants me out of the way so that he can take over the running of the business. David is a wimp. Rod doesn't want to marry Deborah, but he's trying to keep me happy. Raymond has one goal in life, and that is to

get married. As for the ladies ... Caroline doesn't care
what Charles gets up to, as long as he gives her money.
Julia treats David like a child, and Deborah – Deborah
has her own plans for the future, and they don't include
Rod.'

'How do you know that?' Sheena asked him.

'I know more or less everything that goes on.'

'You missed one person out.'

'I was coming to you next.'

'No, I mean – what about you?'

'Me?' He chuckled and then frowned. 'What do you
think of me?'

'I don't know, I haven't known you long enough to
decide.'

'I'm the one with the money and the power, Sheena.
Charles wants the power, and the rest of them want the
money. What do you want?'

'I want money,' she replied honestly. 'And I want to
drag myself out of ... I want to better myself.'

'And you think you'll do that by marrying Raymond?'

'I don't know.'

'You're young, Sheena. Why get married at your age?
You have your whole life ahead of you.'

'I like Raymond. When we was at the club the other
night and he asked me to marry him, I knew that we'd be
happy. I would of thought that he'd want someone older
but ...'

'Do you love him?'

'Yes, I do. I've never known no one like him. He's kind
and I like being with him and I think we'll be happy.'

'Where did you meet each other?'

'We was at ... We met in a bar.'

'I have some papers to go through, so ... We'll talk
again.'

Biting her lip as he went back into the house, Sheena
knew she'd let herself down. It was the wine, she reflected
as Raymond joined her on the patio and passed her a

vodka and tonic. What with letting herself down in front of George and Rod going on at her, she was feeling despondent. Raymond sat opposite her and frowned, and she reckoned that Rod had been talking to him.

'Sheena,' he began. 'Rod said that . . .'

'I'm not interested in Rod,' she cut in. 'We've hardly had any time together, apart from when we was at the hotel.'

'We were together last night.'

'We were here, with everyone else. Now we're here with them all again.'

'We've only just met, Sheena.'

'What about going away, like you said? We could go to Paris or wherever.'

'I don't know anything about you. I don't even know where you live and I've not met your parents.'

'They live miles away and I never see them.'

'So, where do you live?'

'In a flat not far from here. What's all this about, Raymond? You sound like you've changed your mind about me.'

'I don't know. Maybe I was rather hasty with my proposal. I haven't changed my mind but I think we should get to know each other before we start arranging the wedding.'

'You have changed your mind.' She hung her head.

'All I'm saying is that we don't need to rush into anything. We will get married, but let's not rush.'

'Something's changed your mind, hasn't it? What's Rod been saying?'

'He said that . . . This isn't easy for me. He said that everyone's been laughing about the way you speak.'

'So, you don't want me because I don't talk posh?'

'No, it's not that. My family are difficult at the best of times. If we're going to live here together . . . Sheena, did you sleep with Charles when we were at the hotel?'

'No, I didn't. What made you think that?'

181

'It was something Rod said. Look, we'll be fine together. I'll get you another drink, OK?'

'OK.'

That was the end of her plans, she was sure as she gazed at the swimming pool, the evening sun sparkling on the rippling water. Rod was behind this, she mused angrily. Digging at Raymond, dropping hints, putting her down . . . As he joined her on the patio and passed her another drink, she knew that he'd been getting at Raymond again. What had he said this time? she wondered. Raymond had gone to get her a drink, so where was he?

'Sheena, we need to talk,' Rod said.

'No, we don't,' she returned angrily, downing her drink. 'I have nothing to say to you, Rod. And I don't want to hear what you . . .'

'I'll give you more money, another three thousand.'

'I don't want your money.'

'If you show those photographs to Deborah . . .'

'You'll be in the shit.'

'All right, you win,' he said, much to her surprise. 'You go ahead and marry Raymond, and I'll keep out of it.'

'That was a sudden change of mind.'

'Come down to the garden with me, Sheena. Let's go back to how we were.'

'You want sex?'

'Yes, why not? If you're joining us, we might as well keep it in the family.'

Following him past the swimming pool and across the lawn to the summerhouse, Sheena wondered what he was up to. Why change his mind? Was he after her mobile phone? After slipping her phone into a bush, she joined him in the summerhouse. Sure that he was up to something as he pulled her dress up and gazed longingly at her hairless vaginal lips and tightly closed sex crack, she dropped her handbag on to the bench.

'Take your dress off,' he said, smiling at her.

182

'Rod, someone might come looking for us.'

'No, we'll be all right. Come on, Sheena, it'll be like old times.'

'You take your trousers off, then,' she returned.

'No, I . . . Look, just slip your dress over your head. It won't take a minute to put it back on if we hear someone coming.'

Sheena lifted her dress and then hesitated as she had a thought. Had he told Raymond to wait a few minutes and then go to the summerhouse? she wondered. Was Rod trying to prove to his brother that she was a slut? Lowering her dress, she again asked him to take his trousers off. He hesitated, but then unbuckled his belt and dropped his trousers to his knees as she knelt before him. Gazing at his flaccid penis, his heavy balls, she retracted his fleshy foreskin and licked his purple knob.

'I will take my dress off,' she said, rising to her feet and grabbing her handbag. 'I'll go round the back and do it. You wait there.'

'Sheena, why not stay here?'

'If someone comes, I can slip round the back and dress. Wait there.'

Slipping into the bushes, she grinned as she noticed Raymond crossing the lawn. She'd only just made it, she thought as he passed the bushes where she was hiding. That was a dirty trick, she thought angrily as he went into the summerhouse. She could hear Raymond shouting as she grabbed her phone from the bushes then dashed back to the house. He must be wondering what the hell Rod was up to, she thought happily. She made her way through the house to the dining room, where she poured herself a large vodka and tonic and breathed a sigh of relief.

'Are you all right?' Deborah asked her as she sipped at her drink. 'You look quite flushed.'

'I'm hot, that's all,' Sheena replied, wondering whether to show the woman the photographs.

'Sheena, now that we're alone, I want to ask you something.'

'Oh?'

'Has Rod been chasing after you?'

'No, he hasn't.'

'I'll find out if he has, so tell me the truth.'

'I wasn't going to say anything, but . . .'

'If you've been having sex with him, I'll make sure that you never set foot in this house again,' Deborah hissed.

'Are you accusing me of . . .'

'I'm not accusing you of anything. I know your type and . . .'

'You know my type?' Sheena echoed. 'What the hell do you mean by that?'

'You're not exactly a refined young lady, Sheena.'

'Deborah, now that we're alone together, I want to show you something.' She took her phone from her handbag, and showed the other woman a photograph of Rod screwing Nat. 'That's your future husband, and it's not me he's screwing.'

'But . . . Where did you get that from?'

'It was sent to me, but I don't know who it's from.'

Deborah gazed open-mouthed at the photographs for several seconds, Sheena flicking through them one by one, before running out of the room in a flood of tears. Rod deserved to be dropped in the shit, Sheena reflected as she heard the woman wailing in the hall. She hadn't wanted to cause trouble and arguments. But Rod had arranged for Raymond to catch her with her knickers down, and he had to pay for his crime. She heard the front door slam shut, and grinned at Rod as he stopped in the doorway.

'Was that Deborah?' he asked her. 'Where's she gone?'

'I don't know,' Sheena replied. 'Did Raymond catch you with your trousers down?'

'It was lucky you'd gone round the back of the summerhouse,' he whispered. 'Raymond walked in and . . .'

184

'It *was* lucky, wasn't it?' Sheena interrupted him. 'It was very lucky that I realised what you were up to.'

He frowned at her. 'What do you mean?' he asked her. 'Hang on, hang on. Do you think that I planned it?'

'You tell me, Rod.'

Charles appeared in the doorway. 'What's the matter with Deborah?' he asked Rod. 'She's stormed out in a flood of tears.'

'It's all right,' Rod said, glaring at Sheena. 'I think I know what it's about.'

'What the hell is going on?' Raymond asked as he joined his brothers.

Sheena took her drink out to the patio, sat down and gazed at the swimming pool as shouting came from the house. This was a right mess, she thought. She hadn't wanted all this but, hopefully, her trouble-making might finally put an end to Rod and Deborah's relationship. Then what? she wondered. Although Rod was the one she'd wanted all along, she knew that he wasn't interested in her any more. Raymond was her only way into the family, she reflected for the umpteenth time, and she was going to have to settle for second best.

'I apologise for my brothers' behaviour,' David said as he wandered out on to the patio. 'They aren't usually like this. I can't think what's got into them.'

'Even the best of families have problems,' Sheena said as he sat opposite her.

'Deborah left the house in tears, Rod and Raymond are having a go at each other ... You're right, families do have problems and we've had our ups and downs. But it's never been like this.'

'Why don't you all have your own houses?'

'Julia and I want to get our own place but ... It's family tradition.' Smiling, he lowered his eyes to her cleavage. 'You're a pretty little thing, Sheena. I wish I'd married someone like you.'

'You don't even know me,' she returned with a giggle. 'I might be a right bitch.'

185

'My wife's the bitch. No, I suppose I shouldn't say that. The only reason I'm able to sit here and chat with you is because she's gone up to bed. The only time I have any freedom is when she goes to bed early with one of her headaches.'

'Don't you have any fun?'

'Fun? I can't remember what fun is.'

'We could have some fun,' she suggested huskily.

'What do you mean?'

'Don't you have a girl on the side to keep you happy?'

'God, no. I'm not allowed out of the house on my own. Unless it's on business, of course.'

'Well, if you want some fun, I'm game for anything.'

'What sort of fun?'

'Whatever turns you on, David.'

'Are you saying what I think you're saying?'

'Maybe.'

Sheena left her chair and wandered past the swimming pool, heading for the summerhouse. She felt her young womb contract and her clitoris swell as she imagined sucking on David's swollen knob and swallowing his fresh sperm. To screw the fourth brother would be quite an achievement, she mused in her rising wickedness. Then again, what with all the trouble she'd caused already, she wondered whether it was a good idea to seduce him. But her arousal was riding high, and she knew that she couldn't help herself as he joined her in the summerhouse.

'You need some excitement in your life,' she whispered, lifting her dress and exposing her hairless pussy lips to his wide eyes.

'Sheena, you're marrying Raymond and . . . What I mean is, I don't think this is a good idea.'

'It's up to you, David. You can see what's on offer. Take it or leave it.'

'Aren't you afraid that I might tell Raymond?'

'He'd never believe you. Do you want it or not?'

Succumbing to his base desires, he knelt before her and breathed heavily as he kissed the swollen lips of her bald pussy. Another brother had fallen for her feminine charms, she thought happily as his wet tongue ran up and down her opening sex crack. Letting out a rush of breath as he parted her fleshy pussy lips and licked the solid protrusion of her sensitive clitoris, she clung to his head to support her trembling body.

She'd be married to one brother, but she'd have four hard cocks to enjoy, she contemplated dreamily as her juices of lust flowed from her contracting vagina. Once she was married, she'd entertain each brother in turn. Sucking one cock in the summerhouse, taking another into her teenage pussy in the bushes, having another shafting her tight bottom-hole in the bathroom . . . Marriage was going to be both financially rewarding and sexually gratifying.

'Do you like my cunt?' she asked David as he licked the erect bulb of her sensitive clitoris.

'Very much,' he breathed. 'Did you shave for Raymond? Is that how he likes it?'

'I shave because that's the way I like it. Does Julie give you blow-jobs?'

'You must be joking. I'm lucky if she allows me to make love with her, let alone anything else.'

'Well, you have me to look after you now. Bring me off and then you can fuck my mouth.'

Sheena gasped as he sucked her ripe clitoris into his hot mouth and repeatedly swept his tongue over its sensitive tip. Hoping that Raymond or one of his brothers wouldn't come looking for her, she knew that she had to be careful. If Raymond caught her now, the marriage would be off. But the danger and excitement of seducing David was too good to resist. Once a slut, always a slut, she reflected as he thrust two fingers deep into the wet heat of her teenage pussy.

Stifling her whimpers as her orgasm erupted within the pulsating nub of her erect clitoris, she threw her head back and closed her eyes. She was incredibly wet, she realised as her orgasmic milk spilled from her freshly fingered vagina and streamed down the naked flesh of her inner thighs. Wet and horny, and desperate to take David's hard cock into her mouth and swallow his gushing spunk.

David finally slipped his fingers out of her inflamed vaginal duct and pressed his lips forcefully against the pink flesh surrounding her sex hole. Sucking out her pussy milk and massaging her pulsating clitoris with his thumb, he drank from her trembling body as her orgasm peaked. He was more than happy to commit adultery, Sheena thought in her sexual frenzy. Were none of the brothers satisfied with their wives? Raymond would definitely be pleased with Sheena when they were married, as long as he didn't discover her wanton whoredom. Her thoughts turning to Deborah as her orgasm began to fade, she was sure that she'd seen the last of the woman. Rod would need comforting, she decided as David took his pussy-wet mouth from her sex-dripping vagina and stood before her. Rod would be in need of a deep throat-job.

'You're amazing,' David said, wiping his lips on the back of his hand. 'Raymond is one lucky guy.'

'You're lucky, too,' Sheena said. 'You can have me whenever you want.'

'Sheena, are you . . . What I mean is . . . Are you doing this with Charles and Rod?'

She giggled and winked at him. 'Do you think I'd allow them to lick me?'

'Well, I – I don't know. We'd better get back before . . .'

'Fuck me first,' she cut in, kneeling on the ground and lifting her dress high over her back. 'Fill my tight little cunt with your spunk.'

'Sheena, I don't think we have time. I mean, they're bound to wonder where we are and . . .'

'In that case, stop wasting time and fuck me.'

Parting the firm orbs of her naked buttocks as he knelt behind her, David gazed at her bald sex lips nestling between her slender thighs. Sheena knew that he was hooked as he lowered his trousers and grabbed his solid cock. She had him just where she wanted him, she told herself as she felt his hard knob slip between the fleshy lips of her pussy. He rammed his organ fully home, driving his thick cock into her tightening vaginal sheath, and let out a gasp. He was well and truly hooked now that he'd committed adultery, she thought happily.

'You're so tight,' he gasped, withdrawing his pussy-slimed cock and ramming it into her again.

'And you're big,' she groaned, reaching between her parted thighs and massaging her erect clitoris. 'Fuck me hard, David. Fuck me like you've never fucked before.'

Wasting no time, he clutched her firm hips and repeatedly thrust his cock deep into her spasming vaginal sheath. Sheena imagined all four brothers using and abusing her young body as he increased the pace of his shafting rhythm. It had been a long time since she'd enjoyed two cocks, but she didn't think the brothers would be willing to share her. That was something she'd work on once she was married, she decided as her trembling body rocked with the illicit coupling.

David reached his climax quickly and pumped his creamy sperm deep into her hot vagina as she gasped and writhed in the grip of another orgasm. This was real sex, she mused dreamily as her vaginal muscles tightened and gripped his thrusting cock shaft. His knob repeatedly battering her ripe cervix, his swinging balls pummelling her hairless mons, he rammed into her again and again. He wouldn't have had crude sex in years, she thought, trying to imagine him fucking Julie. But now he could enjoy her young body whenever he needed to.

'You're wonderful,' he gasped as his cock deflated.

'You're bloody good,' she returned, her eyes rolling as she drifted down from her amazing orgasm. 'I can feel your spunk running down my thighs. Fuck me again, David. Please, fuck my little cunt again.'

'I can't,' he groaned, sitting back on his heels and gazing at the creamy liquid streaming from her gaping sex hole. 'I'd have to wait at least ten minutes. Besides, we must get back to the house.'

'Kneel in front of me and I'll suck your cock clean,' she persisted.

Taking his position, he sighed. 'We'll get caught,' he said as she licked his creamy-wet shaft.

'Naughty boys and girls,' Charles said as he walked into the summerhouse.

'Oh, Charles,' David began, staring at his brother. 'I was just . . .'

'I can see what you were just doing,' he said, chuckling as he knelt behind Sheena. 'I suppose I'd better screw the little slut, seeing as her pussy is ready for me.'

'Fuck me senseless,' Sheena begged, before sucking David's purple knob into her greedy mouth.

Sheena couldn't believe her luck as Charles pushed his thick cock deep into her sperm-bubbling vagina and David rammed his swelling knob further into her gobbling mouth. Her young body rocking back and forth with the double-ended fucking, she closed her eyes and breathed heavily through her nose. She doubted that Rod would join in, his solid cock shafting her tight rectum, but she was pleased that at least two brothers were into group sex. Maybe Rod would be up for group sex once he'd got over Deborah, she thought hopefully.

'She's good, isn't she?' Charles put in, his massive cock squelching his brother's sperm deep within the girl's inflamed vaginal duct.

'She's amazing,' David gasped as Sheena swallowed his purple plum and sank her teeth gently into the root of his rock-hard cock.

'A resident slut. What more could we ask for?'

'God knows what Julia would say if she . . .'

'Don't worry about her,' Charles cut in with a chuckle. 'Our wives don't fuck, but Raymond's future wife is a dirty little slut who fucks and sucks. We've got it made, David.'

Pleased that the brothers appreciated her, Sheena reckoned Rod was out on his own now. He was the only one who wanted to be rid of her. Three brothers against one? He didn't stand a chance. What was he going to do for sexual gratification? she wondered. He didn't even have Deborah to fuck now. Would he go looking for Nat? Or would he go crawling cock in hand to Sheena?

'Here it comes,' Charles announced as he repeatedly rammed his granite-hard cock deep into Sheena's burning vaginal sheath.

'And me,' David breathed, his throbbing knob sliding back and forth within Sheena's hot throat.

Fresh sperm flooding her vagina and pumping down her throat, Sheena moaned through her nose as her own orgasm erupted again within the pulsating bulb of her solid clitoris. Her young body trembling uncontrollably, rocking back and forth with the double fucking, her long blonde hair veiling her flushed face, she lost herself in her sexual delirium as the brothers drained their huge balls. Once a slut, always a slut, she repeated to herself as the men used her teenage body for their sexual gratification. And nothing would change that, not even marriage.

'Sheena,' Raymond called from the house. 'Sheena, where are you?'

'We're here,' Charles replied, yanking his spent penis out of the girl's sperm-laden vagina and leaping to his feet.

'Bloody hell,' David swore, his cock sliding out of her mouth as he helped her to her feet. 'Quick,' he whispered. 'Sort yourself out and sit on the bench.'

'I like the summerhouse,' Sheena said, sitting beside Charles on the bench and brushing her dishevelled hair away from her glowing face. 'It's a nice place.'

'It's a dangerous place,' David chipped in, leaning against the wall and trying to look innocent.

'Oh, there you are,' Raymond said, hovering outside the summerhouse. 'What's going on?'

'We're talking,' Charles said. 'What's Rod doing about Deborah?'

'God knows. So, what are you all talking about?'

'The wedding,' Sheena replied.

'You look flushed. Are you all right?'

'It's hot in here,' she complained, leaving the bench. 'I think I need a drink.'

Walking back to the house with Raymond, Sheena felt a pang of excitement. She loved the danger, she reflected as she sat on a patio chair by the pool. The taste of David's sperm lingering on her tongue, she asked Raymond to get her a vodka and tonic. Obediently complying, he went into the house as his brothers ambled across the lawn. Sheena grinned at the two men and licked her full red lips provocatively. Life was good, she mused as sperm oozed between the hairless lips of her teenage pussy. And it was only going to get better.

Ten

Sheena sat up in her bed as she heard a knock on her door. She kicked the quilt back, leaped to her feet and grabbed her dressing gown as a loud knock sounded again. Wondering who it was as she donned her dressing gown, she checked the time. Seven o'clock. It wouldn't be Nat, she thought, brushing her long blonde hair away from her face. She reckoned the only person who'd call that early was Rod.

'I thought it was you,' she said, opening the door to him. 'You're up early.'

'Sheena, we have to talk,' he said, walking past her into the room.

'I would of thought that you needed to talk to Deborah, not me.'

'It's would *have* thought,' he corrected her irritably.

'Oh yeah, I forgot.'

'Why the hell did you show Deborah those photographs?'

'You forced me, Rod. I told you that I'd show her unless you . . .'

'I didn't think you'd go that far. I didn't think you'd do it, Sheena. No doubt you'll be pleased to hear that Deborah won't be around any more.'

'Yes, I am pleased. I'm pleased for you, Rod.'

'You did it for yourself, Sheena. From day one, you were determined to split us up.'

'*You* were determined to ruin your relationship with Deborah,' she returned.

'What are you talking about?'

'Screwing me, screwing Nat ... You didn't give a toss about Deborah.'

'The way you don't give a toss about Raymond? You happily fucked me and Charles, and now you've lured David into your den of iniquity.'

'You know about that?'

'Yes, I do. That's all four brothers, Sheena. Who's next, my father?'

She giggled. 'Now there's a thought.'

'You would, wouldn't you? If it suited your needs, you'd fuck my father.'

'Yes, why not?'

'God, you're a filthy little slut.'

'I thought we'd established that the day we met?'

'Yes, but I didn't realise the depth of your depravity.'

'Want some coffee?'

'No ... Yes, I suppose so.'

'So, what are we going to talk about?' she asked him as she filled the kettle.

'You, my brothers, me, this mess ...'

'You made the mess, Rod. Things would of – would have been fine if ...'

'You're going ahead with this farcical marriage?'

'Yes, I am.'

'All right, have it your way. It won't last, you realise that? Once Raymond finds out ...'

'Raymond won't find out anything,' she promised, pouring the coffee. 'Not unless you tell him. Even then, he wouldn't believe you.'

'Sheena, I've always had a place for you in my heart.'

'But not on your map?'

'No, I – I couldn't. But now that Deborah's gone ...'

'What are you trying to say?'

'There could have been a place for you in the centre of my map, but you're marrying Raymond.'

'I can't believe this. Are you saying that you want to marry me?'

'The tables have turned, Sheena. You wanted me, but I was with Deborah. Now I want you, and you're with Raymond.'

'I can change that.'

'You can't just dump him. What the hell would my father say if you swapped brothers?'

'It don't matter what he thinks.'

'That's where you're wrong.'

Passing him his coffee, Sheena sat on her bed and sighed. Rod was right. She'd planned to marry Raymond, and she couldn't swap brothers. Sipping her coffee, she was pleased that Rod had now accepted her. She could now marry Raymond and move into the family home and – and have sex with all four brothers? The resident slut, she mused as Rod sat next to her on the bed.

'You want to marry me, even though I fuck your brothers?' she asked him.

'Yes, even though you fuck my brothers.'

'But why?'

'I don't suppose you've heard of love?'

'Of course I have.'

'I'm in love with you, Sheena.'

His words battered her young mind – she couldn't believe what he'd said. This was the man she'd wanted all along, the man who had done his best to keep her away from his family, the man who had given her two thousand pounds to disappear from the face of the earth . . . Why the hell hadn't he dumped Deborah in the beginning and . . . It was no good looking back, Sheena thought dolefully. But what did the future hold now?

'All you've done is call me a filthy slut,' she finally replied. 'If we were married, you'd be forever wondering who I was screwing behind your back.'

'I wouldn't be wondering, I'd know. Anyway, I reckon you'd change if we were married.' Holding his hand to his head, he sighed. 'Why are we talking about marriage? It can't happen, Sheena. Not now that you're with Raymond.'

'I think I'm in love with you,' she breathed softly. 'I always have been.'

'It's too late,' he murmured. 'Even if Raymond dumped you, I can hardly announce our forthcoming wedding to my family.'

'Fuck me,' she said, slipping her gown off and reclining on the bed. 'Fuck my cunt, Rod.'

'You have a wonderful way with words,' he replied, kneeling on the floor and gazing at her tight crack and the swell of her hairless sex lips.

Sheena breathed heavily as he leaned over her naked body and kissed the smooth plateau of her stomach. Moving down, he pressed his lips to the gentle rise of her mons and breathed in her girl-scent. Why couldn't things have been different? she mused as he licked the bald lips of her teenage pussy. He was the first brother she'd met, he was the one she'd wanted and – and now that he was free, she couldn't have him. She sighed as he ran his wet tongue up and down her opening sex valley. This was the man she'd wanted, she thought dreamily as her clitoris swelled and her lust milk flowed. Life was cruel.

Parting the fleshy swell of her hairless pussy lips, he slipped his tongue into the wet heat of her young vagina and tasted her juices of arousal as she writhed on her bed. This was far removed from cold sex. She'd been licked a thousand times by a hundred men, but this was so different. This was sex, but with love. Trying not to think of the future as Rod drove two fingers into her tightening vagina and sucked her erect clitoris into his hot mouth, she parted her legs wider and closed her eyes.

'I don't feel like a slut when I'm with you,' she said. 'I feel like . . . I don't know what I feel.'

'You told me that you were a slut when we first met. But I don't think you are. You're just looking for a special relationship and, in the process, going through one man after another.'

'I thought I'd found that special relationship with you, Rod. But Deborah was in the way. All I heard was Deborah this, Deborah that ... The very sound of the woman's name made me angry.'

'She's gone now, but we still can't be together.'

Sheena said nothing as he slipped his trousers off. Kneeling between her feet, he pushed his solid knob between the smooth lips of her teenage pussy. She could feel her young womb contracting as she waited expectantly for his cock to impale her. Reaching out and kneading the firm mounds of her petite breasts, he locked his dark eyes to hers and smiled. Sheena returned his smile as his cock entered her. Her vaginal sheath opening, stretching to accommodate his huge organ, she let out a rush of breath as his knob pressed hard against her ripe cervix. This wasn't fucking, she thought happily. This was making love. Although she'd opened her legs and been fucked by a hundred men, she'd never made love before.

Leaning over her naked body, he sucked her ripe nipple into his mouth and snaked his tongue around her sensitive milk teat. Sheena breathed heavily, her body shaking uncontrollably, as he rocked his hips and found his vaginal shafting rhythm. This was so very different from cold sex, she reflected again as he sucked on her other nipple. But she knew that Rod could never be anything more than one of her many lovers. At least they'd be living in the same house, she thought as he rocked his hips faster. At least they could make love regularly.

His knob swelling, his sperm gushing, he let out a low moan of pleasure as Sheena's hot vagina tightened around his thrusting cock and she reached her climax. The squelching sounds of sex resounding around her

197

bedsit, the worn-out bed creaking, she whimpered and squirmed in the grip of one of the most powerful orgasms she'd ever experienced. Her pleasure rolled on and on, reaching every nerve ending and tightening every muscle in her young body. Her solid clitoris was massaged by his wet shaft, pulsating wildly as her orgasm peaked. She knew that she could never live without Rod. No matter what happened, she'd make love with him whenever she could.

'You're the best,' he admitted, slowing his shafting rhythm as she drifted down from her climax.

'You're the best ever,' she whimpered, her head lolling from side to side. 'You're incredible.'

He brushed her blonde hair away from her flushed face. 'Am I better than my brothers?' he asked her.

'You're better than any man, Rod. I've never made love before. I've had sex, but I've never made love.'

'So, where to from here?' he asked, sliding his deflating penis out of her sperm-bubbling sex sheath. 'What happens now?'

'I don't know,' she sighed, propping herself up on her elbows. 'You tell me.'

'I wish I could, Sheena. The truth is, I have no idea where we go from here.'

'When I'm living in the house, we can make love every day.'

'What about Charles and David? I mean, will you be screwing all four of us?'

'Well, I . . . I don't know. I suppose so, yes.'

'At least you're honest,' he said with a chuckle as he rose to his feet and pulled his trousers up.

'I can't be honest with Raymond, can I?'

'No, no, you can't. Look, I'd better get going. I suppose you'll be at the house this evening?'

'Yes, Raymond did invite me round.'

'OK, I'll see you there. It won't be easy, Sheena. Having to watch the girl I love with another man . . . It won't be easy.'

198

'It will work out, Rod. I'll think of something, OK?'

'OK, well . . . I'll see you this evening.'

Flopping back on to her bed as he left the room and closed the door, Sheena decided that looking back was futile. She couldn't change the past but she could dump Raymond for Rod and change the future. Raymond hadn't once said that he loved her or made her feel wanted, and she had no feelings for him. But she'd be risking everything. If she dumped Raymond and Rod changed his mind, she'd be out in the cold, living a life of poverty in her bedsit. Raymond was a means to an end. She'd planned to marry Raymond and live in the family home, and she was going to have to accept that.

Walking to the pub at lunchtime, Sheena hoped to find Nat there. She felt trouble brewing and needed to relax and chat with her friend before meeting Raymond at the house that evening. Would Deborah go back to Rod? she wondered as she sat at her usual table. Her plan had been to use his money to set up in business with the photographer. Would she throw all that away because he'd screwed a teenage slut?

'Hi, babe,' Nat said as she emerged from the loo.

'Nat,' Sheena said, her face beaming. 'I didn't think you were here. I saw the drink on the table and hoped it was yours.'

'I'm always bloody here,' the girl sighed.

'Are you OK? You sound like you're pissed off.'

'I've been trying to find punters for our little business but no one's interested. I think I've lost my touch.'

'You need to try the Castle Club. There are people with money there, businessmen, unlike the scum you get in this dump.'

'Yeah, but how do I get in? Could you get me membership?'

'I could try.'

'Let's go there this evening. I could go as your guest and . . .'

199

'I can't this evening, Nat. I'm seeing Raymond.'

'I'm bored without you, Sheena. I know that we had a good time the other night, but I hardly ever see you any more. We used to spend all our time together, do everything together. Until your delusions of grandeur trip.'

'What does that mean?'

'It means . . . Oh, it doesn't matter. Rod was great the other night. Is he looking for a wife?'

'Er . . . No, no, he's not.'

'It was just a thought. Imagine us both marrying into a rich family. God, we'd have a great time.'

'That's an idea,' Sheena murmured pensively. 'If you went off with Raymond . . .'

'That's the one you're supposed to be marrying.'

'Yes, I know. I'm just thinking aloud. You see, I started off with Rod but he was marrying someone and – Rod is now free, but I'm stuck with Raymond.'

'You can't swap,' Nat said, giggling.

'That's what Rod said. But if Raymond dumped me for you . . . It might work, Nat.'

'What's this Raymond like?'

'It don't matter what he's like, he's loaded.'

'Yes, good point. OK, let's go for it.'

'I'll take you to the house this evening.'

'I've got nothing to wear.'

Sheena opened her handbag. 'There,' she said, passing Nat a wad of notes. 'Go and buy some clothes.'

'Fuck me,' Nat gasped, counting the money. 'Two hundred quid? Where the fuck did you get that?'

'It don't matter where I got it.'

'You can't say that,' Nat corrected the girl.

'Say what?'

'It don't matter – you can't say that.'

'What the fuck are you talking about, Nat? Look, buy something decent to wear, and I'll meet you here at six.'

'Wow, you're on. So, what shall I do? Sort of chat this bloke up or . . .'

'Leave it to me,' Sheena cut in, grinning at her young friend. 'I'll make sure that you two are alone together, and then you can move in for the kill.'

'Cool, I like it. OK, let's get another drink.'

After a few drinks, Nat went into town to buy some clothes and Sheena headed home. This was a crazy plan, she knew. It was also dangerous and she risked losing everything, but she was desperate to marry Rod. She dreaded to think what the Boss would say, but she decided to cross that bridge when she came to it. Things would work out if Raymond dumped her, she thought as she rummaged through her new clothes. The Boss would see that Rod had gone to her rescue and they'd fallen in love and ... One step at a time, she told herself as she dressed.

Walking to the house with Nat, Sheena thought how attractive the girl was. She looked stunning in her red dress and matching shoes. She'd been to the hairdresser and her makeup was beautiful, and Sheena reckoned she could easily get work as a model. What if Rod made a move towards her? she wondered anxiously as they approached the house. More to the point, what if Deborah was there?

'This is Nat,' Sheena said as Raymond opened the door. 'She's my best friend.'

'Oh, right,' Raymond breathed, smiling at Nat. 'Er ... Come in.'

'Gosh, this is a beautiful house,' Nat said in her posh voice, which annoyed Sheena. 'It's Edwardian, isn't it?'

'That's right,' Raymond replied, leading the girls into the dining room. 'We had the garage built on a few years back, but the house is original.'

'Yes, I did notice the garage. But it blends in nicely with the architecture.'

'You never noticed the garage,' Sheena said, frowning at Nat.

'Now that's Victorian,' Nat said, admiring the drinks cabinet.

'It is,' Raymond said, obviously impressed. 'What would you like to drink?'

'Vodka and tonic,' Sheena mumbled.

'And I'll have the same, please,' Nat said.'

Sheena realised that she wasn't going to have to do any matchmaking with Nat and Raymond. They were getting on rather too well, she thought as Nat put on her stuck-up voice and Raymond suggested that he show her round the garden. Fortunately, Rod wandered into the room as Nat and Raymond headed for the garden. He frowned at Sheena and then shook his head as Nat walked past him.

'What the hell is she doing here?' he asked her.

'She's my best friend,' Sheena replied. 'This will be my home, soon. I'm allowed to bring her here, aren't I?'

'Thank God Deborah isn't here. You really do play dangerous games, Sheena.'

'She's getting on very well with Raymond. It would be funny if they ended up together, wouldn't it?'

'So, that's your game. I might have known that you were up to something devious.'

'Rod, I want to marry you.'

'I know, but . . .'

'If Nat and Raymond hit it off, there'll be nothing to stop us.'

'Devious isn't the word,' he said with a chuckle. 'Conniving little devil is more appropriate. Look, if they do hit it off and things turn out well . . .'

'You'll marry me?'

'Yes.'

'Wow,' she said, knocking back her drink and holding her empty glass out. 'I'll be Mrs Robertson.'

'God knows what my father will say,' he sighed as he refilled her glass.

'He'll be fine, don't worry. Where is everyone?'

'They're all out somewhere. My father's upstairs, he'll be down in a minute.'

'I like your dad. I got on really well with him.'

'That's just as well because he wants to talk to you.'

'Oh? What about?'

'You and Raymond and the wedding. He'll be down any minute, so I think I'll disappear.'

'Don't leave me alone with him, Rod.'

'He wants to talk to you alone. He'll take you into his study, more than likely.'

'You've got me worried now.'

'Don't mention us, OK? Just play it by ear and don't mention anything that might annoy him.'

Sheena felt her heart race as she imagined being interrogated by George. She'd got on with him, but he was a formidable man. She'd come such a long way in her quest to marry into the family, but she knew that she was now treading on dangerous ground. Hoping that Nat was in the summerhouse and had taken her knickers off for Raymond, she asked Rod to refill her glass as she heard someone crossing the hallway.

'Good evening, Sheena,' George said as he appeared in the doorway.

'Oh, hi,' Sheena said, taking her drink from Rod.

'Come into my study and we'll have a little chat.'

'I'll see you later,' Rod promised, winking at her.

Sheena followed George into a huge room lined with books, sat opposite him at a leather-topped desk and tried to appear relaxed. He poured himself a glass of neat whisky and smiled at her as she fidgeted in her chair. Recalling the advice Charles had given her, she reckoned that if she followed it she'd be all right.

'You look lovely,' he said.

'Thank you.'

'The thing is ... This business with Deborah. I've spoken to her, so I know all about the problem. Did you take the photograph?'

'No, I . . . It was sent to me.'

'By whom?'

'I have no idea. I thought it was a joke at first but then – then I realised that it was Rod and . . .'

'So why cause trouble by showing Deborah?'

'She's only after his money, George. She plans to set up in business with a photographer friend and . . .'

'How do you know all this?'

'I know the photographer. You probably think I should have kept out of it, but I couldn't stand by and watch Rod . . .'

'Sheena, I know this will come as a blow to you. You can't marry Raymond.'

'What? But why can't I?'

'You're a very attractive young girl and . . . I'm sorry, but you're just not suitable.'

'Why aren't I?'

'Because . . . You'll probably think me a snob, but you've not had the upbringing that I'd like . . .'

'I'm common, is that what you mean?'

'To be blunt, yes. We have business associates here to dinner and . . .'

'And I'd let the family down?'

'Well, yes.'

'I've been trying to speak properly, George,' she sighed, hanging her head. 'I've been trying to be posh and . . .'

'Don't cry, Sheena. There must be plenty of young men who would . . .'

'I only want . . .'

'Who do you want? It's not Raymond, is it?'

'What do you mean?'

'I'm not stupid, Sheena. I know what's been going on. You and Charles at the hotel, you and Rod, you and David . . . And now you've set your sights on Raymond.'

'How do you know?'

'I have my methods. Who's that girl you brought here?'

'Nat, my best friend.'

'And the plan is?'

'There is no . . . She likes Raymond.'

'And you like Rod?'

'Yes. Why ask me if you know everything?'

'I don't know everything. But I do know that you live in a bedsit and you don't work and you have no money.'

'So what happens now? Do you want me to leave?'

'No, not yet. I admire you, Sheena.'

'You admire me? Why?'

'Because I started out like you. I was broke and out of work when I was your age, and I was determined to change my life. I didn't try to marry into money, the way you are, but I . . .'

'I'd make a good wife,' she cut in hopefully. 'I might not talk posh, but I could change that. I've bought a book about English and I'm trying to learn.'

'Sheena, if you married one of my boys, you'd be sneaking off with the others and . . .'

'No, I wouldn't. I've told Rod that I'd be faithful.'

'What if I said that I'm looking for a wife?'

'What do you mean?'

'I'm rich and not unattractive. I own this house and the company. I have cars and holidays abroad several times each year. I even have a villa in Spain. Would you go for me if you had the chance? Would you marry me?'

Sheena bit her lip as he gazed at her. Was this a proposition? she wondered. Or was he testing her? He couldn't be serious, she reflected as he sipped his whisky. His sons would go mad if he married a teenage girl, especially a slut they'd all screwed. She left her chair and paced the floor, trying to appear confident. This was a test, she concluded. But she had no idea how to answer his question.

'Would you want a girl like me?' she finally asked him.

'I'm asking the questions, Sheena.'

'No, you're not having this all your way. Would you want a teenage girl as your wife?'

'Yes, I think I would. It would certainly brighten things up around here.'

'What about your posh business friends? What would they think?'

'They'd think me a very lucky man, I would imagine.'

'They'd think you were mad.'

'Why?'

'Because it would be obvious that you only wanted me for sex.'

'And you'd only want me for my money.'

'I don't just want money, George,' she returned indignantly. 'I want a life.'

'You're a pretty little thing.'

'Yes, but I'm not stupid like Julia and Caroline. They suck up to you, they treat their husbands like shit . . . Sorry, I shouldn't swear.'

'Go on.'

'They're just – just useless women who are only here for the money and the lifestyle. Your sons aren't happy with them. Rod wasn't happy with Deborah. He told me that he was only going to marry her to please you. They're all psychophants, or whatever the word is.'

'Sycophants. Yes, you're right. I must admit that, out of all the females, I like you best.'

'You like me best, but you want me out? That doesn't make sense.'

'You're too young to understand, Sheena. You're right about Julia and Caroline, but they fit in with the family.'

'What if Rod wants to marry me? What can you do about it?'

'There are several things I can do, Sheena. But hopefully you won't force me into a corner. I suggest . . .'

Sheena left the study, heading down the garden to the summerhouse. She hadn't expected the old man to block her plans, she realised as she heard Raymond and Nat talking. She slipped behind the summerhouse and spied through a crack in the wooden planking as her best friend kissed Raymond. The situation was crazy, she thought as Raymond suggested that Nat meet him later that evening. She'd lost Raymond, she wanted Rod, and the old man was trying to ruin everything.

'Sheena's OK,' Raymond said. 'But she's not the type of girl my father would want in the family. You're beautiful, Natalie. You look stunning, you've obviously had a good education . . . I'm sure my father will accept you.'

'I hope so,' Nat sighed. 'I am worried about Sheena, though.'

'I should never have asked her to marry me. I suppose I rushed in without thinking. Looking back, I must have been mad.'

'Will you marry me?'

'Yes, but I want a lengthy engagement first. I can hardly tell my father that I'm marrying a girl I've only just met. After announcing my intention to marry Sheena, I can't really tell my father that . . .'

'When will you tell Sheena?'

'Later, I suppose. I'll let you into a little secret, but don't repeat it to anyone. My father is looking for a wife.'

'Really? Are you and your brothers OK with that?'

'Yes, of course. The thing is, he wants a young girl. He's always had an eye for young girls, and . . . I shouldn't say too much.'

Grinning as she pondered the revelation, Sheena headed back to the house. Deciding on a change of plan, she knew that she had to go straight to the head of the family, straight to the Boss. If the old man wanted to marry a young girl, she was more than happy to oblige. There were too many complications with the brothers. Rod had been with Deborah, but he now wanted Sheena, Raymond seemed to want Nat . . . Knocking on the study door, she knew that this was her only chance of getting into the family.

'Oh, you're back,' George said as she closed the door behind her.

'I've been thinking,' she said, smiling at him. 'You asked me a question earlier.'

'Ah, yes.'

'You asked me if I'd go for you if I had the chance.'

'I'm not saying that you have a chance, Sheena. But answer the question anyway.'

'Yes, I would go for you. I would marry you.'

'You are desperate to marry into my family, aren't you?'

'And you're desperate to be with a young girl.'

'No, I'm . . .'

'You are, George. I've seen the way you look at me, so don't deny it.'

'I will admit that I find you incredibly attractive, but . . .'

'But what? Come on, George. Don't tell me that you get offers of marriage from teenage girls every day.'

'No, no, I don't. Lock the door and we'll get to know each other a little better.'

Sheena turned the key in the door lock and smiled at him. Walking towards his desk as he beckoned her with his finger, she knew she still wanted to be with Rod. But she needed a sure way of getting her foot in the door of the family home, and the only one available now was via the Boss. She stood by his chair, looking down as he lifted her dress up and gazed longingly at the hairless lips of her teenage pussy. This was a sure way to an old man's heart, she thought as he ran his finger up and down her wet sex crack.

He eased a finger between the swollen lips of her pussy, breathing heavily as he massaged the hot flesh surrounding the entrance to her tight vagina. She was sure he was hooked as he pushed his finger deep into her creamy-wet vaginal sheath and caressed her inner flesh. No man could resist a teenage girl, she thought happily as her clitoris swelled and her pussy milk flowed over his hand. Reckoning she was finally in with the family, she reached out to the desk and pushed the papers to one side.

'If you want to get to know me, you'd better take a good look at me,' she offered huskily, grabbing his hand and yanking his finger out of her tight vagina.

'Very nice,' he said, eyeing her open sex valley as she sat on the edge of the desk with her legs to either side of him. 'I think we're going to get on very well together.'

'Now you can get to know me properly.' Reclining, she pulled her dress up over her stomach and parted her thighs wide. 'I'm all yours, George.'

Leaning forward, he kissed her bald pussy lips and ran his tongue up and down the open valley of her vulva. Parting the fleshy swell of her outer labia, he lapped fervently at her open sex hole as she writhed and gasped in the grip of her arousal. He was good, she mused dreamily as he sucked out her teenage juices of desire. Older men knew how to please young girls, she thought as he slipped his hand up her dress and squeezed the firm mounds of her petite breasts.

'It's been so long since I've been with a girl of your age,' he said, examining the pink folds of her inner lips nestling within her sex valley. 'You're so fresh and tight.'

'Just for you, George,' she breathed shakily.

'I dream about young girls with shaved pussies. You're my dream come true, Sheena.'

She should have gone straight to the Boss in the first place. Then again, she'd never have met him if it hadn't been for Rod and his brothers. She was sure things were working out as the old man sucked her erect clitoris into his hot mouth and drove two fingers into the contracting sheath of her teenage pussy. At least George would now invite her to his house, and there was nothing anyone could do about it. He was the Boss, she reflected as he sucked and licked the solid bulb of her sensitive clitoris.

Sheena let out a squeal as he forced a finger deep into her hot rectal duct. This was what she'd wanted, she thought, recalling Rod's love-making as a second finger drove into the heat of her tight rectum. Sex with love was nice, but cold, hard sex was immensely gratifying. Maybe she could have both? she thought as her orgasm erupted within the hard nub of her pulsating clitoris. Her young body shaking uncontrollably, she cried out in the grip of her illicit ecstasy as he repeatedly thrust his fingers deep into her contracting sex holes. Sex with Rod, Charles, David, George . . . Would Raymond stray from Nat and use Sheena's young body to satisfy his lust?

George slipped his fingers out of her inflamed sex ducts. Sheena lifted her head and watched as he unzipped his trousers and hauled out his erect penis. He was huge, she observed as he pressed his purple plum between the puffy lips of her hairless vulva. As his knob entered her tight vagina and his cock shaft stretched her open to capacity, she couldn't believe how far she'd come since first meeting Rod in the back-street pub. She'd had all four brothers and, much to her amazement, she was now screwing their father.

Although she'd done well, she felt that she was really no closer to marrying into the family. It was obvious that George only wanted her for sex, and she couldn't see him marrying her. Why should he marry her when he had her young body to keep him happy? Besides, his sons would be up in arms if he announced his forthcoming wedding to a teenage slut. How was she going to move into the house? she wondered as he pushed his cock deep into her contracting sex duct and impaled her fully on his huge organ. Would George move her into a spare room as the resident whore?

His rock-hard cock repeatedly sliding in and out of her hot sex sheath, squelching her copious juices of arousal, he lifted her feet high in the air and rocked his hips faster. Her lower stomach rose and fell as he rammed his swollen knob into her ripe cervix. He watched her bald outer lips rolling back and fourth along his veined shaft as she again whimpered and writhed on his desk. He could have her young body every day if he wanted to, she mused as he began to gasp. If he moved her into the house, gave her a room and money, he could use and abuse her whenever he needed to. But she couldn't see that happening.

'You're a tight little thing,' he groaned, grinning at her.

'And you're bloody big,' she gasped. 'I've never had such a big cock.'

'I can see your clitoris,' he said with a chuckle. 'It's forced out by my cock and . . . Your body is perfect.'

'It's your body now, George. When we get married and . . .'

'Are you ready for my spunk, my angel?'

'Yes, yes, give it to me. Fuck me senseless and spunk in me.'

Rocking his hips faster, he moaned softly as the squelching sound of her sex juices echoed around the study. Sheena imagined the brothers listening at the door as she whimpered and writhed on their father's desk. What would they say if they discovered that he was fucking a teenage whore over his leather-topped desk? They'd probably be eager to ram their hard cocks into her tight little pussy, she thought excitedly as his balls repeatedly smacked the rounded cheeks of her firm buttocks. Hoping that Nat was taking Raymond's cock into her wet pussy, Sheena gasped as her climax neared. Her eyes rolling, her head lolling from side to side, she finally cried out as her vagina flooded with fresh sperm and her clitoris exploded in orgasm.

'Fuck me,' she whimpered. 'Fuck my little cunt and fill me with your spunk.'

'You're a beautiful little slut,' he panted, throwing his head back and rocking his hips faster. 'A dirty little whore.'

'I'm your dirty little whore, George. I'll always be here for you to fuck and spunk.'

Sheena reckoned he was well and truly hooked now that he'd pumped his sperm deep into her teenage pussy.

Her orgasm rocking her young body, she again cried out as he repeatedly rammed his knob against her spermed cervix. She'd done it, she thought happily as his spunk overflowed and ran down to the tight hole of her anus. She now had her foot firmly in the door, and no one was going to prevent her from moving into the house.

Her climax waning as George slowed his shafting rhythm, she was squirming on his desk when a knock sounded at the door. George made his last thrusts into her sperm-bubbling vagina and called out that he was busy chatting to Sheena. Whoever it was went away, and Sheena grinned. She was with the Boss, she reflected as he slipped his dripping cock out of her inflamed vaginal duct and sat back in his chair. And she'd be moving into the house very soon.

'You were fantastic,' she said, sitting upright on the desk and grinning at him.

'So were you,' he replied, gazing at her hairless sex lips, bulging between her slender thighs. 'We must do this again.'

'Yes, we will. We'll do it every day, George.'

'I'd rather you didn't say anything to the boys, Sheena. I know that you wouldn't tell them but . . . Just don't say anything at all.'

'No, I won't. We're going to be great together. I'm so pleased that we . . . Well, I'm pleased that I've got you. I did want Rod, but it's you I want now.'

'Back to our discussion,' he said as she slipped off the desk and adjusted her dress.

'Yes,' she trilled, her pretty face beaming. 'So, what are our plans?'

Watching as he left his chair and zipped his trousers, she thought he looked concerned. He paced the floor and then poured himself another glass of whisky, and she feared the worst. He turned round several times, and faced her as if he were about to say something, but then just sipped his drink. Was he planning to tell his sons? she

212

wondered hopefully. Or was he about to tell her that there would be no wedding?

'What is it?' she finally asked him.

'We don't have any plans, Sheena,' he admitted. He knocked back his drink and refilled his glass before sitting on the edge of his desk. 'I can't marry you, if that's what you're thinking.'

'But – but I thought . . .'

'I asked you whether you'd go for me if you had the chance. I didn't ask you to marry me.'

'Oh, I see,' she sighed, hanging her head. 'So, we're back to where we started?'

'Yes, I'm afraid so. Look, we've been locked in here for long enough. I don't want the boys getting the wrong idea.'

'So, you want me to leave the house and never come back? You won't allow me to marry Raymond or Rod, and you don't want me . . .'

'You don't have to leave the house just yet. Go and talk to the others and have a few drinks and . . . Maybe we'll talk again some time.'

'Some time?'

'You don't seem to appreciate the position I'm in, Sheena. As it is, that friend of yours is getting her clutches into Raymond. There are too many problems, and I don't like it.'

'No, but you like fucking me,' she murmured, walking to the door. 'That's all I'm good for, isn't it? I'm a young slut who satisfies you and your sons, but I'm not good enough for . . .'

'We'll talk about it another time, Sheena.'

Sheena opened the door, walked through the hall and left the house before she was confronted by one of the brothers. She'd made a mess of everything, she thought as she headed for her bedsit. Wishing that she'd never become involved with the family, she wiped the tears from her cheeks and hurried along the road. The money, the Castle Club, the wealthy family ... She'd tried to infiltrate another world, but she had to accept the fact that she'd failed. As Nat had said, once a slut, always a slut. She'd make money from prostitution, she decided. She'd rent a nice flat and earn money and – and accept the world she lived in.

Eleven

Rod phoned Sheena the following morning. He wanted to know what his father had said, but Sheena didn't want to talk about it. She didn't want to talk to Rod about anything, in fact, so she hung up. The phone rang again as she came out of the bathroom. Dressing in a very short skirt, skimpy top and leather boots, she again ignored it. She was trying to move on, to get away from Rod and his family and plan her life, and the only way to do that was by earning a lot of money and getting out of her seedy bedsit.

Walking into town, she wondered whether to go and see the photographer and try to set something up to bring in some money. But she knew that he'd only pay a pittance for lesbian photos with Nat. She sat outside a café and ordered a cup of coffee to help her with some serious thinking. Forget the photographer, she decided. Although she wouldn't be seeing Rod or his family again, she was still a member of the Castle Club. The punters at the club had money, she mused as a waitress brought a cup of coffee over to her table. They were businessmen, and they'd have wives who were prudes and weren't into deep-throat sex. There was a market waiting to be exploited, she concluded, paying the waitress and sipping her coffee.

The first thing to do was to rent a decent flat, she decided. She had a couple of thousand pounds which would cover the deposit and, if Nat moved in with her . . . Wondering how the girl had got on with Raymond, she imagined her marrying into the wealthy family. That would be ironic. Then again, there was no way that George would allow Nat into the family. But she could put on a posh voice and she came across as educated, Sheena thought anxiously. If she got into the family and . . .

'I want to talk to you,' Deborah said as she stopped on the pavement and frowned at Sheena.

'What about?' Sheena asked her, fearing the worst.

'You know damn well what about. Did you take that photo of Rod and that – that slut?'

'I've already told you, it was sent to my mobile phone.'

'Why would anyone send it to you?'

'I don't bloody know,' Sheena returned angrily.

'Anyway, I'm no longer with Rod and I'm steering well clear of that family. I suggest you do the same.'

'I have done the same,' Sheena sighed. 'Me and Raymond have split up.'

'I reckon Rod sent you that photograph.'

'Rod?' Sheena breathed, staring at the woman. 'Why would he send it to me?'

'He wanted you all along, Sheena.'

'What do you mean?'

'He's been after you for ages.'

'But I only met him twice at the house.'

'And the other times. I'm not stupid, Sheena. I knew he was seeing you from the day you met him at that nasty little pub.'

'You knew? But . . .'

'I was prepared to allow him a little fun with a dirty slut on the side. But when Raymond brought you to the house and said that you were getting married . . . I knew what your game was, Sheena. You wanted to move into the house so that you could be with Rod.'

'Yes, you're right,' Sheena confessed. 'I wanted Rod all along, but . . . Well, it doesn't matter now. George made

216

it clear that he didn't want me in the family, so that's the end of that. Will you be going into business with the photographs?'

'How the hell do you know about that?'

'Like you, Deborah, I'm not stupid.'

'You're not, are you? To answer your question, I won't be going into business with him. I'm going to set up on my own.'

'So am I,' Sheena said proudly.

'Doing what?'

'I have a little business plan. But I can't tell you what it is.'

'I can guess what it is. Oh well, I might see you around some time.'

'Yes, maybe.'

Sighing as the woman walked away, Sheena thought it ironic that everyone seemed to know what everyone else had been up to. To think that Deborah had known about Sheena and Rod from the day they'd met in the pub was incredible. And George had known what Sheena had been up to with Charles in the hotel and . . . Trying not to think of the past, Sheena finished her coffee and walked aimlessly in the direction of the park.

Her phone rang several times as she sat on a bench beneath the summer sun, but she ignored it. Her thoughts turning back to Deborah, she thought about how well the woman spoke. She was a slut, she was into porn pics, but she came across as sophisticated. Even Nat had amazed Sheena with her posh voice. She'd also impressed Raymond, which had annoyed Sheena. When her phone rang again, she turned it off then parted her thighs and displayed the triangular patch of her white knickers as she noticed a middle-aged man approaching. Deciding that she might as well try to earn a little cash, she smiled as he walked past.

'All alone?' he asked her, stopping and gazing at the bulge of her tight knickers nestling between her naked thighs.

'Yes, I am,' she replied.

'My name's Jim. Mind if I sit with you?'

'I'm Sheena. I don't mind.'

'You look sad. Is there anything wrong?'

'I borrowed some money from my friend and I can't pay it back. My dad will go mad if he finds out. I don't know what I'm going to do.'

'How much did you borrow?'

'Fifty pounds. I borrowed it because my boyfriend needed it. Now he's left me and I'm at college so I don't have any money and . . . I just don't know what to do.'

'Perhaps I could help you.'

'How?'

'I've got plenty of money with me.'

'How does that help me? You're not going to give me fifty pounds, are you?'

'I could. But I'd want something in return.'

'Like what? I haven't got anything.'

'I'm sure you have, Sheena.' He gazed at her naked thighs again and grinned. 'You have something that I'd love to look at.'

She looked down at her legs and then frowned at him. 'Do you mean you want to look at my . . . No, I don't think so.'

'Why ever not? It'll be the easiest fifty pounds you've ever earned. Come into the trees with me and take your clothes off, and I'll give you the money.'

'What?' she gasped, holding her hand to her mouth. 'You want me to take all my clothes off?'

'I just want to look at you, Sheena. Let me look at you, and I'll give you the money.'

'No, I – I can't.'

'Don't be so silly. It'll only take a few minutes and then you'll be able to pay your friend back.'

She bit her lips and sighed. 'Well, I – I suppose I could,' she allowed, trying to look anxious. 'You only want to look, don't you?'

'Yes, of course. It'll only take ten minutes and your problem will be solved.'

'All right,' she agreed, leaving the bench and walking towards the trees.

He followed her, eyeing the backs of her shapely legs as she took a narrow path into the woods. This was easy money, she thought happily as she stopped in a small clearing. Turning and facing him, she knew she could earn a small fortune from her young body. She didn't need Rod or his family to better her life. She had all she needed between her legs to earn more than enough money.

She dropped her handbag on the ground and unbuttoned her top as the man watched, then opened the front of the skimpy garment and exposed the firm mounds of her braless breasts to his wide eyes. He licked his lips and adjusted the crotch of his trousers as she slipped her top off her shoulders and dropped it to the ground. Focussing first on her elongated nipples, he lowered his gaze to the smooth plateau of her lower stomach as she tugged her skirt down. Imagining taking fifty men into the woods every day as she stepped out of her skirt and stood with her feet wide apart, she knew that this was the business to be in. It's so easy, she thought proudly, showing off her tight knickers as he knelt before her.

She knew his cock would be as hard as rock as he moved closer and gazed at her sex crack, clearly outlined by the tight material. Finally slipping her knickers down, she concealed a grin as he stared in disbelief at the hairless lips of her young pussy and let out a rush of breath. There were dozens of men who'd pay to see her young body, she thought as she allowed her knickers to crumple around her ankles. If she rented a decent flat and went into business with Nat, she was sure they'd soon build up a huge list of eager clients. It wasn't the lifestyle she'd really wanted, but needs must.

'You're so young and beautiful,' he breathed, his eyes transfixed on her puffy outer labia, rising to either side of her tightly closed sex crack. 'God, it's been years since I've seen a bald pussy. You're an angel.'

'What about the money?' she said softly. Clasping her hands and concealing the most private part of her naked body as if she were embarrassed, she hung her head. 'Can I get dressed now?'

'All in good time,' he replied. 'Tell me, do you masturbate?'

'No,' she gasped as if shocked.

'You've never touched yourself?'

'No, I – I haven't.'

'You said that you had a boyfriend. Didn't he do anything to you?'

'I wouldn't let him touch me. That's why he went off with another girl.'

'So are you saying you're a virgin?'

'Yes, I am. Can I get dressed now?'

'Yes, in a minute. Have you never touched a boy's cock?'

'No, I haven't. My boyfriend wanted me to but . . .'

'Sheena, would you allow me to touch you?'

'No, I . . .'

'Fifty pounds is a lot of money. Surely you'll just let me touch you?'

'Well, all right.'

As he reached out and stroked the bald lips of her teenage pussy, Sheena felt her young womb contract. She knew he'd do more than touch her, and she grinned as he moved forward and kissed the smooth cushions of her succulent outer lips. She was irresistible, she realised as he ran his wet tongue up and down the opening crack of her teenage vulva. Her pussy certainly was – it was worth a fortune. Wondering how many men she could entertain each day, she reached down and parted the smooth lips of her pussy, offering her gaping vaginal entrance to the man's tongue. He breathed heavily through his nose and clutched her naked buttocks as he slipped his tongue into the creamy-wet heat of her young vagina. Sheena reckoned he'd want to drive his solid cock deep into her tight pussy before he left.

'Do you like that?' he asked her as he lapped up the hot milk flowing from her open sex hole.

'Yes, yes, I do,' she gasped. 'No one's ever touched me before and . . . It's amazing.'

'Would you like to have an orgasm?'

'I've never had one, so . . .'

'I'll give you your first-ever orgasm,' he said proudly. 'Once you've had one, you'll want a thousand more.'

Sucking her erect clitoris into his hot mouth, he snaked his tongue over its sensitive tip and managed to drive two fingers deep into the tight shaft of her teenage vagina. Sheena let out a rush of breath, her legs sagging as waves of sexual ecstasy rolled through her trembling body. She must have had a million orgasms since she'd discovered her clitoris. But she liked playing the role of an innocent little virgin girl, and the man was obviously enjoying teaching her the delights of oral sex.

Her orgasm welling from the depths of her contracting womb, she clung to his head as her pleasure exploded and rocked her young body deeply. Rod and his family could go to hell, she thought dreamily as her vaginal juices streamed in torrents down her inner thighs. She didn't need them or their money. She was young and sexy, she had what older men wanted, and she intended to exploit her feminine wares to the full.

Her orgasm peaking as the man massaged her hot inner flesh and sucked on her pulsating clitoris, Sheena parted her feet wider to allow him better access to her yawning sex crack. The slurping and sucking sounds of illicit sex resounding around the trees, he sustained her mind-blowing pleasure as she trembled and whimpered. He knew exactly what to do, she thought as he sucked her clitoris and squeezed the erect protrusion between his lips. Lapping at her slit, he fingered her spasming vaginal

221

sheath until her legs crumpled beneath her trembling body and she collapsed to the ground, writhing in the aftermath of her orgasm.

'You're beautiful,' the man breathed, kneeling beside her and squeezing the firm mounds of her petite breasts. 'I've never known a girl like you. We must meet again, Sheena. Please, tell me that we can meet again.'

'Yes, yes, we will,' she gasped, still reeling after her amazing climax as he pinched and twisted her sensitive milk teats.

'You're so young and innocent. I can teach you things, Sheena. I can teach you about sex and . . . I'll teach you everything if you meet me here regularly.'

'And pay me?' she asked him, her pretty mouth smiling as she recovered from her mind-blowing orgasm.

'Well, I . . . Yes, yes, I'll give you money.' He reached into his trouser pocket. 'Here's the fifty pounds,' he said, passing her the cash.

She stuffed the notes into her handbag and smiled. 'Thank you, now I'll be able to pay my friend back. So, what sort of things will you teach me?'

'We could start now,' he said eagerly. 'I'll teach you how to suck my cock.'

'Suck it?' She propped herself up on her elbows and frowned. 'You mean, put it in my mouth?'

'Yes, that's right.'

'No, I don't think I want to . . .'

'Just try it, Sheena,' he persisted, kneeling beside her and unzipping his trousers. Holding his solid cock by the base, he retracted his fleshy foreskin and smiled. 'Go on, I'm sure you'll like it.'

Sheena concealed a grin as she parted her pretty lips and sucked his purple knob into her wet mouth. Running her tongue over the velveteen surface of his swollen globe, she breathed heavily through her nose and savoured the taste of his salt. He gasped, his eyes rolling as she took his huge knob to the back of her throat and sank her teeth gently into his veined shaft. How many men had fucked and spunked her mouth? she wondered in her wickedness as she grabbed his rock-hard shaft and moved her hand up and down its length. How many more cocks would she take into her mouth? Would Rod's be one of them?

As Sheena sucked and gobbled, the man's spunk came quickly. The creamy liquid bathed her snaking tongue, jetting to the back of her throat, and she repeatedly swallowed hard as he gasped and trembled in his illicit ecstasy. This was easy money, she told herself again as he held her head and rocked his hips. His throbbing knob battered the back of her throat as he fucked her pretty mouth until his balls drained and his cock finally began to deflate.

'You were excellent,' he groaned shakily, his wet penis slipping out of her spermed mouth. 'God, you were perfect.'

'I've never done that before,' she whispered, wiping her spermed mouth with the back of her hand.

'Did you like it.'

'Well, I – I don't know. I suppose it was quite nice.'

'We must meet here again, Sheena. We'll meet every day and . . .'

'Every day?' she echoed, her blue eyes frowning. 'Can you afford it?'

'It won't be fifty pounds each time, will it?'

'Yes it will,' she replied, grabbing her clothes. 'Or don't you think I'm worth it?'

'No, no . . . Of course you're worth it. It's just that fifty pounds is a lot of money.'

'I have to go,' Sheena said as she dressed. 'I must go and pay my friend back.'

'But . . . Tomorrow, can we meet tomorrow at the same time?'

'All right, we'll meet here tomorrow.'

'You're not . . . I mean, you don't charge men for sex, do you?'

'I've never been with anyone. You're the first man, I promise you.'

'That's good. I'll get some cash out of the bank and see you tomorrow. Have you got a phone number?'

'No,' she lied remembering that she'd switched her phone off. 'I must go, OK?'

'Stay and talk to me for a while.'

'I can't, I have things to do.'

Sheena grabbed her handbag and left the woods. She noticed a man sitting on the bench. He was wearing a suit with a white shirt and tie, and she reckoned she could lure him into the woods and take his money. The taste of sperm lingering on her tongue, she again pondered going into business with Nat as she hid behind a bush and watched her client leave the woods. They could earn a small fortune and afford a decent car as well as a flat. She switched her mobile phone on, and was about to approach the man on the bench when she had a call.

'I've been calling you all morning,' Rod complained. 'Where are you?'

'Out and about,' she replied, hovering behind the bush.

'Sheena, we need to . . .'

'There's nothing to say, Rod. Your dad made it clear that I'm not wanted.'

'He wants to talk to you.'

'What about?'

'Come to the house.'

'No, Rod,' she sighed, watching the man leave the bench. 'I've finished with you and your family. Your dad said that I was common and I wouldn't fit in. Anyway, I'm busy at the moment.'

'At least hear what he has to say.'

'Are you at home?'

'Yes, I've taken the day off. Please, Sheena, come over to the house.'

'OK, I'll be there in five minutes,' she conceded as her prospective client walked away.

Slipping her phone into her handbag, she walked briskly across the park and headed for Rod's house. What did the old man want to talk about? she wondered anxiously. She reckoned he probably wanted sex. She thought he'd make a good client. In fact, with the amount of cash he had, he'd make a very good client. Nearing the house, she realised that she was wearing a ridiculously short skirt. Her hair was a mess, her knickers were wet, her top was grubby . . . Just be yourself, she thought as she rang the doorbell. Once a slut, always a slut.

Rod answered the door and invited her in. He looked pleased with himself as he led her through to the huge kitchen and filled the kettle. She was sure he had something planned as he looked her up and down and said how attractive she was. Wondering where the old man was, she felt strange being in the house once more. She hadn't expected to see Rod again, let alone be invited to the house.

'What's going on?' she finally asked him.

'I told you, my father wants to talk to you.'

'If he wants to pay me off, he needn't bother. I've finished with you and your family.'

Passing her a cup of coffee, he smiled. 'He's not going to pay you off,' he said with a chuckle.

'What, then? He said that I was common and he has business people round for dinner and I wouldn't fit in.' She looked around the luxury kitchen and sighed. 'Are you back with Deborah? Will she be moving into the house as your wife?'

'No, no way. Deborah and I are finished.'

'How long did Nat stay last night? I haven't heard from her.'

'She went out with Raymond. They went for a meal at that new restaurant.'

'She's well in with your old man, then? She can put on a posh voice so I suppose she got on well with him.'

'My father didn't meet her, Sheena. She went off with Raymond soon after you'd left the house.'

'Your dad knows everything about me. He knows about my bedsit and . . .'

'He'll be calling you in a minute. Drink your coffee and brace yourself.'

'For what? Rod, I don't want to be here. I don't want to be part of your family and I – I just want to get on with my life.'

Rod said nothing as Sheena sat at the huge table and sipped her coffee. She looked like a right slut, she thought, noticing grubby marks on her white top. Brushing her dishevelled long blonde hair away from her pretty face with her fingers, she wondered whether the old man wanted to hire her as a resident whore. That would be interesting, she thought, and very profitable. No, he wouldn't do that, she concluded. But he might set her up in a flat, she mused hopefully.

'That's what they do in films.'

'What?' Rod said, frowning at her.

'Rich old men set up teenage girls in flats so they can fuck them whenever . . .'

'That's the last thing my father would do,' he cut in with a laugh.

'I suppose Raymond has dumped me for Nat. Still, that was our plan.'

'Yes, I know all about your plan.'

'Rod, you seem to know everything so at least tell me what I'm doing here.'

'Wait there and I'll find out whether my father is ready to see you.'

'Aren't you going to tell me what this is all about?'

'Wait there, I'll be back in a minute.'

As he left the room, Sheena looked around the kitchen and let out another sigh. This wasn't just money – it was millions. She had to get out of her bedsit, she thought for the umpteenth time as she finished her coffee. She walked to the window and gazed at the swimming pool, imagining the old man asking her to marry him. Would she accept? With the amount of cash floating around, how could she turn him down? But she'd made her plans. She'd decided she wanted nothing to do with the family, and there was no turning back.

Sheena felt her stomach churn and her hands tremble as Rod wandered into the kitchen and said that his father was waiting for her in his study. This was it, she thought, following him through the hall. In a way, she hoped that he was going to offer her money to disappear. Ten thousand? Twenty thousand? No, he wouldn't do that. She walked into the study and gazed at George. Rod closed the door behind her and left her to her fate. What the hell did the Boss want with her?

'Good morning, Sheena,' he said, looking up from his desk and indicating for her to sit opposite him. 'I'm glad you could make it.'

'So, what's this all about?' she asked, standing before him.

'After our little chat last night, I did some thinking.'

'Oh?'

He looked her up and down and frowned. 'What on earth have you been up to?' he asked her. 'Your clothes are . . .'

'I've been to the woods,' she cut in, brushing her blouse. 'I like the woods.'

'Oh, I see. As I was saying, I did some thinking and I came to the conclusion that . . .'

'You want to hire me as a slut?'

'No, no. I came to the conclusion that I could help you.'

'Help me take my knickers off, you mean?'

'You wanted Rod all along, didn't you?'

'Well, I did. But if you . . .'

Sheena walked to a door leading out to a balcony as he answered his phone and started talking to someone about business. This was a waste of time, she thought, wondering what the hell she was doing in the house when

227

she could have been earning money from men in the park. She opened the door and stepped on to the balcony, then gazed across the lawn at the summerhouse. The garden was like a park, she thought, sure they must have a gardener. It would be lovely to live there, but what with Rod and Charles and David and Raymond and George . . . She'd never fit in, she was convinced. George joined her on the balcony.

'Do you like it here?' he asked her. 'The gardens are lovely.'

'Yes, of course I do,' she returned. 'I've always lived in flats, I've never had a garden. You should try living in a poxy bedsit with no bloody money.'

'As I said last night, I've been in your position. Talking of last night, I had a long chat with Rod after you'd gone.'

'Just get to the point.'

'All right, come with me.'

Following him out of the study and up a huge flight of stairs, Sheena couldn't begin to think what he had in mind. Apart from sex, of course. Walking along the landing past half a dozen oak doors, she was sure that he wanted to screw her. That was fine, she thought, as long as he paid well. He led her into a huge bedroom, closed and locked the door behind her and sat on the edge of the double bed. She was about to unbutton her top when he pointed to a fitted wardrobe and asked her to open the sliding doors.

She did as he asked and gazed longingly at dozens of expensive dresses hanging on the rail. There must have been twenty pairs of shoes on the floor of the wardrobe along with fitted drawers full of silk knickers and stockings. Was he going to ask her to marry him? she wondered as he stood behind her and stroked her long blonde hair. She couldn't see a wedding dress. He turned her to face him, unbuttoned her top and slipped the garment off her shoulders. She smiled as he squeezed the firm mounds of her teenage breasts and toyed with her elongated nipples. It was sex that he wanted, she concluded, wondering how much to charge him.

'You're a pretty little thing,' he said, tugging her skirt down. 'But you're also very naughty. You've destroyed Rod's relationship with Deborah and Julia is threatening to leave David. And Caroline isn't at all happy with Charles because of . . .'

'What are you going to do about it?' she cut in as he tugged her wet knickers down and gazed at the hairless pads of her full sex lips. 'I'm a naughty little girl, so what are you going to do about it?'

'Give you a good spanking, for starters.'

'Really?'

'You've caused a lot of trouble, Sheena. Now bend over the back of that chair.'

She took her position over the back of the chair with her rounded buttocks jutting out, and grinned as the palm of his hand landed squarely across her bum cheeks with a loud slap. She still had no idea what his long-term plan was, but she was more than happy to have crude sex with him. He knew how to treat a dirty little teenage girl, she mused as he repeatedly slapped the rounded cheeks of her reddening buttocks. Again and again, his hand landed across her tense flesh, the stinging pain permeating her young bottom as she squirmed and gasped. This was more like it, she reflected, hoping that his cock was hard and ready for her tight vaginal sheath – and that he had his wallet with him.

'You're a bad girl,' he groaned, slapping the backs of her thighs. 'A very bad little girl.'

'More,' she gasped. 'Spank me harder.'

'I'll spank your little bottom until you beg for mercy, you naughty little girl.'

The gruelling spanking drove Sheena into a sexual frenzy. She parted her feet wide as she felt her pussy milk streaming from her hot sex hole to course down her inner thighs. She lifted her head as he stopped spanking her, hoping her punishment wasn't over. He unbuckled his leather belt and held it high above his head, then brought it down across her firm bottom with a loud crack. Sheena let out a cry of pleasure as the belt lashed her stinging buttocks again. Had he lost control? she wondered as the leather repeatedly bit into the taut flesh of her glowing buttocks.

'Naughty little girl,' he bellowed as he thrashed her. 'I've a good mind to fuck your little bottom-hole for the way you've behaved.'

'Yes, please,' she whimpered as the belt lashed her rounded bottom. 'Fuck my arse hard. Fuck my arse and spunk me.'

He dropped the belt to the floor, lowered his trousers and pressed his solid knob between the fire-red cheeks of her twitching buttocks. She gasped and quivered uncontrollably as his purple globe forced its way past her defeated anal sphincter muscles and sank deep into her rectal duct. If this was the sort of husband he'd turn out to be, she'd be the happiest slut in the world, she thought dreamily as he impaled her completely on his huge cock. She again cried out as he grabbed her shapely hips and began his long, slow fucking motions. Mumbling crude words as he repeatedly drove his huge knob deep into the dank heat of her bowels, he again slapped her glowing buttocks as she squirmed and whimpered in the grip of her illicit ecstasy.

His cock was thick and long, she thought happily as he buried his bulbous knob deep in the very core of her teenage body. It was far bigger than any of his sons' – he'd make an ideal husband and lover. Did Rod know of his father's plans? she wondered as her anal ring rolled back and forth along his veined shaft. Had the old man told him that he'd be marrying Sheena? Rod had seemed happy enough, she reflected. Although they were an odd family, she knew she'd be happy living in the huge house as Mrs Robertson. She'd also be happy to fuck all five men.

Her inflamed rectal duct finally lubricated with creamy sperm, Sheena listened to the old man's gasps and moans as he drained his swinging balls. She'd make him a very happy man, she promised to herself as he repeatedly spanked her rounded bum cheeks. She'd also make his sons happy, if that's what they wanted. Five men, she thought again. Five men, five hard cocks, money ... What more could a young girl want?

'I needed that,' George gasped as he slowed his anal shafting rhythm. 'I've been thinking about fucking your tight little bumhole since last night.'

'As long as I make you happy, that's all that matters,' Sheena breathed as his cock slipped out of her rectal tube with a loud sucking sound. 'I'll always be here for you, George.'

'That's good to know,' he allowed shakily. Sitting on the edge of the bed and recovering from his orgasm, he grinned at her. 'So, do you like your bedroom?'

'My bedroom?' she said, frowning as she hauled her young body upright. 'You mean, this is my bedroom?'

'Yes, of course. And the clothes and shoes are yours. I had them delivered this morning.'

'Wow, I can't believe it,' she trilled. 'So, when will I become Mrs Robertson?'

'Sooner than you think. By the way, I've opened a bank account for you.'

'That was quick.'

'I arranged it on the phone earlier. Your cheque book and papers are in the bedside drawer.'

'I've never been happier,' she whimpered, sitting in the chair and wiping a tear from her glowing cheek. 'I can hardly believe this.'

'I realise that you'll screw around, but ...'

'No, no, I won't.'

'There's no need to lie to me, Sheena. There'll be other men like the one you met in the park this morning.'

'You – you know about that?'

231

'I know everything. All I ask is that you be careful.'

'Yes, yes, I will. George, I – I don't know what to say. I'll be Mrs Robertson and you're giving me money and my freedom . . .'

'There's no need to say anything. All I ask in return is a little naughty fun now and then.'

'Yes, of course. There's nothing I'd like more than . . . What about the boys? Have you told them?'

'Rod knows, obviously. But the others are at the office. I'll talk to them this evening.'

'Wow, this is amazing. Oh, er . . . How did Nat get on with Raymond?'

'He's fallen for her big time. Mind you, Raymond falls in love every five minutes so I don't think it will last. Are you worried about her?'

'Yes, I am. We've been friends since we were kids. I suppose I don't like the idea of leaving her behind.'

'Well, let's see what happens. I suppose, at the very least, she could be a live-in housekeeper or something.'

'Really? Wow, that would be great.'

'I'll leave you to dress. The clothes and shoes should all fit you.'

'Thanks, George. You've made my life.'

'Thank *you*,' he said, chuckling as he pulled his trousers up and left the room.

Trying on several dresses, Sheena couldn't believe that she was going to marry George. She looked around her room and discovered an en-suite luxury bathroom, as well as a television and hi-fi equipment neatly concealed in a cabinet opposite the bed. She opened the bedside drawer and gazed at the cheque book, then punched the air with her fist. She'd made it, she thought excitedly. After a long and hard quest, she'd finally reached her goal. But what if the boys tried to put a stop to the wedding? she wondered fearfully. Charles might be angry, or Raymond or David might . . .

'Hi,' she said as Rod walked into the room.

'Wow, you look great in that dress.'

'Yes, it's really nice. Have you heard the news?'

'I knew all along,' he replied, grinning at her.

'And? I mean, you don't mind?'

'Mind? Why the hell should I mind?'

'I don't know,' she sighed, sitting on the edge of the bed. 'I suppose I thought we would of . . .'

'You are lovely, Sheena. I thought we would of . . . You're wonderful. So, are you a happy girl now?'

'Yes, very.'

'My father has gone to the office for a while. When he gets back, we'll arrange a party for this evening.'

'Wow, yes. Can my friend, Nat, come?'

'Of course she can.'

He sat next to Sheena on the bed, pushed her back gently and slipped his hand up her dress to massage the swell of her vulval lips through her silk knickers. Sheena breathed heavily as he pulled her knickers to one side and slid two fingers into the wet sheath of her young vagina. This was amazing, she thought as her juices of arousal flowed and her clitoris swelled. She'd be married to George and have Rod to please her and . . . Did George know that Rod would be fucking her? she wondered. Would he mind sharing his wife with his four sons?

As Rod parted her legs wide and drove his solid cock deep into the wet heat of her young vagina, she let out a rush of breath and locked her full lips to his in a passionate kiss. The old man's spunk oozing from the inflamed eye of her anus, Rod's purple knob about to flood her tightening vagina with sperm . . . She'd found her sexual heaven, she thought happily. Money, luxury, and all the sex she wanted.

As Rod's sperm jetted from his throbbing knob, lubricating their mind-blowing coupling, he thrust his rock-hard cock into her contracting sex sheath again and again. Sheena reached her own climax, her clitoris pulsating wildly as she clung to Rod's trembling body

233

and pushed her tongue deep into his mouth. As they wrapped themselves around each other, Sheena knew she was in love with Rod. But even if she had become his wife, she could never have been faithful to him. Once a slut, she thought as her orgasm finally began to fade.

'You're from heaven,' he breathed, finally resting his deflating cock deep within the wet sheath of her inflamed vagina. 'An angel from heaven.'

'A slut from hell,' she returned with a giggle. 'I hope you realise that I won't be able to do this when I'm married.'

He chuckled as he slipped his flaccid penis out of her young vagina and lay on his back beside her. 'I'll fuck you every day when you're Mrs Robertson,' he said.

'You are a naughty boy. What will your father say if he finds out? I would of thought . . .'

'He'll be very happy to think that I have a lovely wife who . . .'

'What?' she exclaimed, sitting upright. 'What the fuck do you mean?'

'I mean, my father will be happy that we're married and . . .'

'But I thought . . .'

'Thought what?'

'I . . .'

'By the way, I've booked our honeymoon. I'm taking you to Los Angeles. After the wedding, we'll have the reception here and then we'll fly out to . . .'

'Rod.'

'Yes?'

'I love you.'

'And I love you, my soon-to-be Mrs Robertson. You'll like Los Angeles. What we'll do is . . .'

'Rod.'

What?'

'Just shut up and fuck me again. Fuck me senseless.'

nexus

The leading publisher of fetish and adult fiction

TELL US WHAT YOU THINK!

Readers' ideas and opinions matter to us so please take a few minutes to fill in the questionnaire below.

1. Sex: Are you male ☐ female ☐ a couple ☐?

2. Age: Under 21 ☐ 21–30 ☐ 31–40 ☐ 41–50 ☐ 51–60 ☐ over 60 ☐

3. Where do you buy your Nexus books from?

☐ A chain book shop. If so, which one(s)?

_____

☐ An independent book shop. If so, which one(s)?

_____

☐ A used book shop/charity shop
☐ Online book store. If so, which one(s)?

_____

4. How did you find out about Nexus books?

☐ Browsing in a book shop
☐ A review in a magazine
☐ Online
☐ Recommendation
☐ Other _____

5. In terms of settings, which do you prefer? (Tick as many as you like.)

☐ Down to earth and as realistic as possible
☐ Historical settings. If so, which period do you prefer?

_____

☐ Fantasy settings – barbarian worlds
☐ Completely escapist/surreal fantasy
☐ Institutional or secret academy

- ☐ Futuristic/sci fi
- ☐ Escapist but still believable
- ☐ Any settings you dislike?

_____

- ☐ Where would you like to see an adult novel set?

_____

6. In terms of storylines, would you prefer:

- ☐ Simple stories that concentrate on adult interests?
- ☐ More plot and character-driven stories with less explicit adult activity?
- ☐ We value your ideas, so give us your opinion of this book:

_____

_____

_____

7. In terms of your adult interests, what do you like to read about? (Tick as many as you like.)

- ☐ Traditional corporal punishment (CP)
- ☐ Modern corporal punishment
- ☐ Spanking
- ☐ Restraint/bondage
- ☐ Rope bondage
- ☐ Latex/rubber
- ☐ Leather
- ☐ Female domination and male submission
- ☐ Female domination and female submission
- ☐ Male domination and female submission
- ☐ Willing captivity
- ☐ Uniforms
- ☐ Lingerie/underwear/hosiery/footwear (boots and high heels)
- ☐ Sex rituals
- ☐ Vanilla sex
- ☐ Swinging
- ☐ Cross-dressing/TV
- ☐ Enforced feminisation

☐ Others – tell us what you don't see enough of in adult fiction:

_____

_____

_____

8. Would you prefer books with a more specialised approach to your interests, i.e. a novel specifically about uniforms? If so, which subject(s) would you like to read a Nexus novel about?

_____

_____

_____

9. Would you like to read true stories in Nexus books? For instance, the true story of a submissive woman, or a male slave? Tell us which true revelations you would most like to read about:

_____

_____

_____

10. What do you like best about Nexus books?

_____

_____

11. What do you like least about Nexus books?

_____

_____

12. Which are your favourite titles?

_____

_____

13. Who are your favourite authors?

_____

_____

14. Which covers do you prefer? Those featuring:
(Tick as many as you like.)

- [ ] Fetish outfits
- [ ] More nudity
- [ ] Two models
- [ ] Unusual models or settings
- [ ] Classic erotic photography
- [ ] More contemporary images and poses
- [ ] A blank/non-erotic cover
- [ ] What would your ideal cover look like?

_____

15. **Describe your ideal Nexus novel in the space provided:**

_____

_____

_____

_____

16. **Which celebrity would feature in one of your Nexus-style fantasies? We'll post the best suggestions on our website – anonymously!**

_____

THANKS FOR YOUR TIME

Now simply write the title of this book in the space below and cut out the questionnaire pages. Post to: Nexus, Marketing Dept., Thames Wharf Studios, Rainville Rd, London W6 9HA

Book title: _____

NEXUS NEW BOOKS

To be published in September 2008

THE INDULGENCES OF ISABELLE
Penny Birch

In her third year at Oxford, Isabelle Colraine is still indulging her private obsession with dominating girls. Unfortunately for her, others are aware of her predilection and are determined to spoil her fun. There's Portia, an upper-class brat who refuses to accept Isabelle's dominance, and Sarah, a mature women who believes the right to dominate has to be earned with age and experience. But worst of all is Stan Tierney, an older man who wants to take advantage of her and won't take no for an answer.

£7.99   ISBN 978 0 352 34198 3

To be published in October 2008

THE PERSIAN GIRL
Felix Baron

Sir Richard Francis Burton was a soldier, spy, explorer, linguist, diplomat, master of disguise and the greatest swordsman of his time. He was also a notorious rake, and during the period of his life recounted in *The Persian Girl*, he carouses and womanises his way around the world. From the depraved 'governess' Abigail and her debauched young wards, to the Ethiopian Amazon who takes him prisoner, Burton's journey leads him to his greatest challenge of all – schooling a dozen lusty young wenches in the more arcane arts of the bed chamber.

£7.99   ISBN 978 0 352 34501 1

NEXUS CONFESSIONS: VOLUME 5
Various

Swinging, dogging, group sex, cross-dressing, spanking, female domination, corporal punishment, and extreme fetishes . . . *Nexus Confessions 5* explores the length and breadth of erotic obsession, real experience and sexual fantasy. This is an encyclopaedic collection of the bizarre, the extreme, the utterly inappropriate, the daring and the shocking experiences of ordinary men and women driven by their extraordinary desires. Collected by the world's leading publisher of fetish fiction, these are true stories and shameful confessions, never-before-told or published.

£7.99   ISBN 978 0 352 34144 0

If you would like more information about Nexus titles, please visit our website at www.nexus-books.co.uk, or send a large stamped addressed envelope to:
  Nexus, Thames Wharf Studios,
  Rainville Road, London W6 9HA

NEXUS BOOKLIST

Information is correct at time of printing. To avoid disappointment, check availability before ordering. Go to www.nexus-books.co.uk.

All books are priced at £6.99 unless another price is given.

NEXUS

☐ ABANDONED ALICE	Adriana Arden	ISBN 978 0 352 33969 0
☐ ALICE IN CHAINS	Adriana Arden	ISBN 978 0 352 33908 9
☐ AMERICAN BLUE	Penny Birch	ISBN 978 0 352 34169 3
☐ AQUA DOMINATION	William Doughty	ISBN 978 0 352 34020 7
☐ THE ART OF CORRECTION	Tara Black	ISBN 978 0 352 33895 2
☐ THE ART OF SURRENDER	Madeline Bastinado	ISBN 978 0 352 34013 9
☐ BEASTLY BEHAVIOUR	Aishling Morgan	ISBN 978 0 352 34095 5
☐ BEING A GIRL	Chloë Thurlow	ISBN 978 0 352 34139 6
☐ BELINDA BARES UP	Yolanda Celbridge	ISBN 978 0 352 33926 3
☐ BIDDING TO SIN	Rosita Varón	ISBN 978 0 352 34063 4
☐ BLUSHING AT BOTH ENDS	Philip Kemp	ISBN 978 0 352 34107 5
☐ THE BOOK OF PUNISHMENT	Cat Scarlett	ISBN 978 0 352 33975 1
☐ BRUSH STROKES	Penny Birch	ISBN 978 0 352 34072 6
☐ CALLED TO THE WILD	Angel Blake	ISBN 978 0 352 34067 2
☐ CAPTIVES OF CHEYNER CLOSE	Adriana Arden	ISBN 978 0 352 34028 3
☐ CARNAL POSSESSION	Yvonne Strickland	ISBN 978 0 352 34062 7
☐ CITY MAID	Amelia Evangeline	ISBN 978 0 352 34096 2
☐ COLLEGE GIRLS	Cat Scarlett	ISBN 978 0 352 33942 3
☐ COMPANY OF SLAVES	Christina Shelly	ISBN 978 0 352 33887 7
☐ CONCEIT AND CONSEQUENCE	Aishling Morgan	ISBN 978 0 352 33965 2
☐ CORRECTIVE THERAPY	Jacqueline Masterson	ISBN 978 0 352 33917 1
☐ CORRUPTION	Virginia Crowley	ISBN 978 0 352 34073 3

NEXUS CLASSIC

NEXUS CONFESSIONS

NEXUS ENTHUSIAST

NEXUS NON FICTION

- - - - - - ✂ -

Please send me the books I have ticked above.

Name ....

Address ....

....

....

.... Post code ....

Send to: Virgin Books Cash Sales, Thames Wharf Studios, Rainville Road, London W6 9HA

US customers: for prices and details of how to order books for delivery by mail, call 888-330-8477.

Please enclose a cheque or postal order, made payable to **Nexus Books Ltd**, to the value of the books you have ordered plus postage and packing costs as follows:

UK and BFPO – £1.00 for the first book, 50p for each subsequent book.

Overseas (including Republic of Ireland) – £2.00 for the first book, £1.00 for each subsequent book.

If you would prefer to pay by VISA, ACCESS/MASTERCARD, AMEX, DINERS CLUB or SWITCH, please write your card number and expiry date here:

....

Please allow up to 28 days for delivery.

Signature ....

Our privacy policy

We will not disclose information you supply us to any other parties. We will not disclose any information which identifies you personally to any person without your express consent.

From time to time we may send out information about Nexus books and special offers. Please tick here if you do *not* wish to receive Nexus information. ☐

- - - - - - ✂ -